FIND HIM!

FIND HIM!

A NOVEL

ELAINE KRAF

Introduction by Violet Kupersmith

THE MODERN LIBRARY
NEW YORK

2025 Modern Library Edition

Published in the United States by The Modern Library, an imprint of Random House, a division of Penguin Random House LLC, 1745 Broadway, New York, NY, 10019.

THE MODERN LIBRARY and the TORCHBEARER colophon are registered trademarks of Penguin Random House LLC.

Originally published in 1977 by Fiction Collective

Excerpts of this novel first appeared in *Fiction Magazine* and *New Directions Anthology* No. 31, edited by James Laughlin.

ISBN 978-0-593-73191-8
Ebook ISBN 978-0-593-73190-1

Printed in the United States of America on acid-free paper

modernlibrary.com
randomhousebooks.com

1st Printing

BOOK TEAM: Production editor: Jennifer Rodriguez • Managing editor: Rebecca Berlant • Production manager: Chanler Harris • Proofreader: Tricia Wygal

The authorized representative in the EU for product safety and compliance is Penguin Random House Ireland, Morrison Chambers, 32 Nassau Street, Dublin D02 YH68, Ireland, https://eu-contact.penguin.ie.

To You

INTRODUCTION

BY VIOLET KUPERSMITH

Find Him!, Elaine Kraf's third novel, was first published in 1977 by the experimental author-run Fiction Collective. The book is dedicated to you. And throughout it, you, the reader, will be addressed directly, questioned, sometimes taunted by the novel's unnamed narrator. The title itself is a desperate plea from her to you.

The book is wildly innovative, almost giddily constructed; in addition to its periodic breaking of the fourth wall, it incorporates musical notation (compositions by Kraf herself), fragments of poetry, streams of different consciousnesses, a questionnaire, and a drawing of a giraffe. The writing style is linguistically unbound, with descriptions of taste and texture and sound and color all dripping into one another. This playfulness of form and syntax counters the novel's nightmarish plot, the story of an adult woman who awakens one day with the mind and faculties of a child and no memory of her past, and her "education" in isolation at the hands of Oliver, a man who raises her, teaches her, molds her, and abuses her. It is a tale of patriarchal oppression and feminist liberation, but a discomfiting one. For how can a woman ever truly be free from patriarchy, it asks us, when patriarchal systems have shaped every aspect of her existence—her language, her history, the way she interfaces with the world? One of the most disturbing aspects of *Find Him!* is the narrator's steadfast devotion to Oliver despite his subjugation of her. Because she believes she owes her entire personhood to this man, she is either unable or unwilling to ever speak ill of him, even as she describes her horrific treatment at his hands. What Kraf seems to suggest is that freedom, or the closest thing to it, can be found in the subversive power of art. For our narrator, it is through writing this book to you, and even by deceiving you—in a sense, creating her own work of fiction—that she is able to find some autonomy within her story.

The novel begins with our narrator recounting her first moment of consciousness. She is sitting on Oliver's lap while he spoon-feeds her and orders her to chew. When she spits out her mouthful of meat, he uses his hands to open and shut her jaws for her, manually forcing her to masticate. She instinctively bites his finger, and the act of sinking her teeth into his flesh causes her to match the word "chew" to its meaning. It is her first lesson, and her first word. And for the reader, it is a canny and symbolic introduction to our two central characters and their relationship: Oliver holding the narrator like a ventriloquist's dummy as he moves her mouth for her; the narrator interpreting the proverb about biting the hand that feeds *quite* literally; the acquisition of language tied intrinsically to the assertion of agency.

While the narrator is in Oliver's custody, she is a kind of living doll to him. In her early development, when she is learning to feed and wash herself and use the toilet, he dresses her up "in the costume of a child," a schoolgirl's plaid skirt and ruffled blouse. Later on, when his lessons grow more complex—how to read in both English and French, how to cook, how to count—and his methods more cruel—her mistakes or disobedience are punished by food deprivation or being locked in a room—he gives her a purple rayon dress to wear instead.

Though Oliver does not begin having intercourse with the narrator until she graduates to wearing the purple dress, she is a sexual object to him from the very start, even in her mental infancy. The narrator is aware that he gropes her breasts and masturbates in front of her during the schoolgirl skirt era, before she is able to even comprehend it, let alone consent to it. When she reflects on this time, she compares herself to a child or pet and calls herself Oliver's "hollow instrument," but still can never fully condemn him, insisting instead that she was lucky to have had him as a sexual instructor, that "had he ignored my woman's body, my development would have been slowed and possibly impaired."

The event that prompts the switch from skirt to dress and marks the transition from being fondled to being fucked also comes with another type of sartorial symbolism. The narrator tries on a pair of his trousers, and Oliver is so threatened by this display of independence, by the implications of her *wearing the pants*, that he beats her, puts her into the new, overtly feminine outfit, and takes full sexual control over her body.

Kraf's Oliver is a particularly repellant version of Pygmalion, the most repulsive Henry Higgins imaginable. He is described as a gigantic, ogre-like man who reeks of urine and is usually dribbling saliva from his overhanging bottom lip. The narrator describes (with both tenderness and more than a touch of fiendish glee) his gigantic ears full of impacted wax, and his brown, claw-like toenails that are so thick, he must trim them with a saw. When he isn't conducting his lessons, Oliver is writing an encyclopedia of great men in history where, among other insanities, he praises Hitler for his commitment to his ideals and claims to have had a personal relationship with Vincent Van Gogh.

"Well, what do you think so far?" the narrator asks you at the end of Part I. "Is he a pervert who kidnapped me and took unfair advantage of me, or is he delusional—paranoid, schizophrenic or some other category?... Or do you think that I am crazy as well as being a pest?... Do you think I am trying to seduce you and manipulate you like some other writers do? Should I have left you out of it and just told the story?"

—

There is one person who might know how the narrator ended up as Oliver's ward, and her absence hangs over the entire book: Edith, Oliver's missing wife. The narrator tells us from the beginning that the house she lived in with Oliver was Edith's. She sneaks in and out of Edith's old room, trying to piece together who she was from the objects within it, surreptitiously reading letters from Edith to Oliver that he has kept, but ripped the dates off of—there is no reliable method of tracking time in his realm. The purple rayon dress she is given to wear once belonged to Edith.

But why does the dress fit the narrator perfectly? Why do the rooms in the house seem not wholly unfamiliar to her, and why do several of Edith's belongings—a pair of red gloves, an engraved bracelet, a coffee mug—cause a tug of distant recognition? Why does the narrator casually bring up her research about lobotomies and remark that the postoperative condition might closely resemble her own? Why does Oliver never give his charge a name?

Kraf does not hide her clues so much as make them recurring patterns in the kaleidoscope of *Find Him!*. Edith is or was an artist herself, a creator of stained-glass objects and huge, collage-like tapestries quilted from fabric scraps that drape the hallways of her former home. Her work is an exercise in fragmentation and a mirror of the novel itself, in all its chaotic, pieced-together glory.

Find Him! is a story that exists beyond the confines of the page. It asks you, the final character, to sift through its parts and determine what you deem true. It provides a space for you to draw a picture, if you would like. It encourages you to play the music in the book yourself, or (as I did) find someone else with a piano who can, and experience the narrative through sound: Oliver's theme, an off-kilter tune with unpleasant interval jumps that never really resolves; "The Mad Giraffe," a carnival song that grows progressively more demented as it changes keys; and the nameless eight note motif that shifts slightly over the course of the book, like a haunted music box that plays something a little different each time you open it. It is an uncannily brilliant way of making you feel like you are inside the damaged mind of the narrator; the slippery motif never quite allows you to grasp it, remaining, like her memories, somewhere just out of reach.

"I am inviting YOU to enter and eat the feast that OLIVER and I created," our narrator declares early on. "In order to do this, you must abandon your world, at least temporarily." Though be warned: partaking in Kraf's bizarre feast is like tasting the pomegranate seeds of the underworld—a part of you will never leave this strange book once you enter. There is a bit of sad irony in the fact that *Find Him!* is a book that was essentially lost for decades, that Kraf's tale of a woman with no memory was largely forgotten after being published. But I hope that if Kraf were here she might see it as darkly funny, now that we have finally found each other.

—

VIOLET KUPERSMITH is the author of the short story collection *The Frangipani Hotel* and the novel *Build Your House Around My Body*, which won the Bard Fiction Prize, was a finalist for the Center for Fiction First Novel Prize, and was longlisted for the Women's Prize for Fiction. She has been the recipient of fellowships from the National Endowment for the Arts, the University of East Anglia, the Fulbright Program, and MacDowell.

MODERN LIBRARY
TORCH
BEARERS

I

The first word I remember is the word "chew." Fat fist clutching the handle of a large spoon, up in into my mouth, covered with black hairs, gray ones and random brown dots is what my eyes remember of their first consciousness. Obediently my mouth opened with eyes to a collection of hot colors. Out came something unpleasant to my tongue—it was hard, lined down and wouldn't slide. "Chew." Persistently he replaced the brown thing on the spoon. Loudly, "Chew." I spit it out again. Realizing at last that I did not understand, he gave a demonstration. Not with his own teeth; he knew that *looking* at things and understanding them was beyond my abilities. Neither gently nor roughly he opened and closed my mouth. Using two hands he knocked my teeth together—"rach rach"—my eyes shut also. I didn't like it. He continued—"rach rach"—threw it into my mouth between crashes—that brown stringy thing, cold and hard. "Chew." He moved my jaws together manually while juggling the meat into the proper position. I gave him a deep bite on his thumb and forefinger. "Chew." His pain was well worth it because at the instant my teeth bit into his flesh, I understood the lesson. Smiling, not knowing or noticing his pain, I proceeded to pick out other pieces of the brown stringy meat from the pot of colors. And I chewed deliberately with satisfaction. He smiled. At that time, prior to my becoming a person, my achievements were his own—he patting my head and laughing. I smiled as he held me on his lap singing "Chew chew chew," while bouncing his knee in rhythm. We were happy in those early months when I was learning the rudiments of ingestion, control of excretion and simple commands—days when I flickered awake for a second seeing a fingernail or an ear. Music in those early recognitions. I cry for *then* when I had no existence and did not even realize that my body belonged to me. Few adults are so privileged to begin in this manner. OLIVER. Few adults have begun their existence with only Oliver's assistance. And in spite of what came later, I would not change places with anyone on the entire earth. None!

It is important to me, *the beginning*. I remember it in detail with my eyes, with my tongue *then then*—fat fist clutching the handle of a large spoon, up in into my mouth hot colors—soft pale green leafwings, round orange flowers wet with yellow in the center, and those hard pieces of brown composed of thick threads lined down that had to be chewed. Chewing and swallowing are my own now, done alone or in the company of others. Nothing tastes as good. It is my own business like so many other things. But *then* I was Oliver and my eating was *our* business—one of the things that we later lost, slipping away as everything.

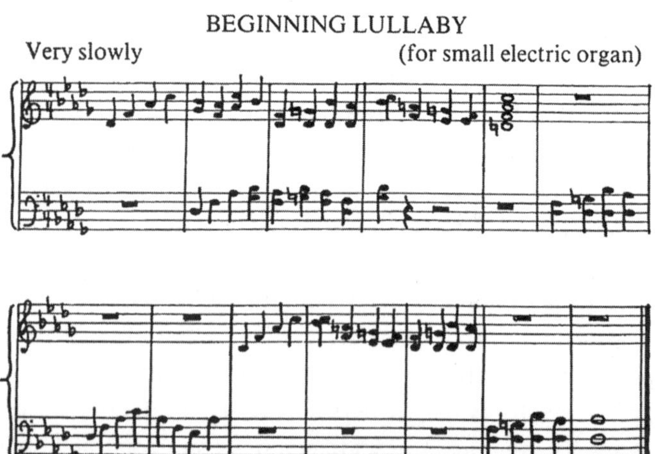

Understand my beginning with Oliver. You will see that my love for him is not a romantic fantasy. Every bit of this love was formed from the reality of primary needs—ingestion, excretion, simple pleasure and pain.

I am inviting YOU to enter and eat the feast that OLIVER and I created. In order to do this, you must abandon your world, at least temporarily. I hope that you will be able to understand what I am talking about. It will not be easy for you. I appreciate this because I have tried and failed to understand *your* world: *your* vocations, customs, social divisions, politics and wrist-watches. Oliver taught me something about the society outside our walls but he never prepared me for its complexity. I am a woman from another star. Someone returning from another century would not have been as alienated. I read a lot. Not about way back when it was all being made by someone or falling together like a big accident, but about after that, century to century, B.C. to A.D. The differences between people from one century to another are not as great as the differences between any people of any time and myself. There were always groups not just two except for Adam and Eve and that might even be a poem. Except for Adam and Eve there were always groups, special ceremonies, looking for food, fighting for land, worshipping, paying for things, laws and burials for everyone, the right clothing, horses or ships, and fairy tales. But I came into existence with one man and had no contact with any society—knew only what I learned from him. He, Oliver, was *my* culture and *my* society. We had no horses.

—

The exact date or hour of my appearance is forever out of my reach. I have no knowledge of how I arrived or why. Even the physical manner of my entrance is a mystery since there were no doors in Edith's house. There was no *Edith* there either. Yet that is not entirely true. (Things can be both true and false, you know, despite logicians.) But I will try not to confuse you. I never made her acquaintance, in the way that I might meet you in the grocery store and introduce myself, although I lived in her house for three years and gradually discovered her importance to Oliver.

Here it is dark and light dark and light
Crosshatched patterns on the floor move
Then disappear or a light flashed over or
Turned on by shuffling feet not the same
Away a yellow balloon half-deflated with
A shadow on its left lies on a windowsill
Right in the center every morning wings of
Real silver birds flap up and down forever
Not there

Since I had no identity, no ability to think or speak, how can I believe in any existence prior to the one into which I first opened my eyes? But I was already an adult at the time of my appearance. Logically it would seem I had a past. Of what significance is a logically assumed past when I can experience nothing of it, can remember nothing before my three years with Oliver. How I arrived, how Oliver reacted to my arrival—these are things that will never be clear to me, although I have some theories about the latter question. If there was any name or identification on my body when I appeared, Oliver never disclosed this to me. No name. Perhaps he did not consider a name important—my Oliver ignores many things. He has his reasons. If he destroyed my identification, I trust that it was after careful consideration and for the best.

My early memories are diffuse; I have already told you of the hand with the spoon. That is my first clear memory. It is important and remains with me more vividly than later things—the taste of the hot vegetables, some fibrous and bitter, others fragrantly pliant, the tough brown meat I chewed, and ever always the taste to my teeth and tongue of Oliver's metallic, saltysweet fingers.

There are so many things I must guess. The first memory of the hand and spoon occurred some months after my arrival. My mind lapsed often—slipped backward into soft-wet non-differentiation. Everything, nothing, secret. Again a kind of awareness, my eyes focused, saw Oliver walking slowly toward his room, always *away*—my wide stare without comprehension hurt. Then I ran softly down the long hallway pulling at his shirt from behind. (Perhaps I feared his disappearance even then.) Slowly, so slowly Oliver became aware of my tugging and of the low sounds I made—"Oomah . . . geeeh, geeeh, geeeeeeh . . ." He turned toward me—always at the last instant before going into his room—patted my head, looked. Then the door closed. Away. Until I slept or until he came out again, I lay near his door. "Geeeeeeh." Even then, before I could understand or think, I felt some kind of anguish or discomfort when Oliver was not near me. I feel this now, although I know what it means and how to interpret it. It is the exact feeling now, only changed by words inside. It was a feeling that I was to know in hundreds of variations before his final disappearance.

—

The garden is something which never existed. Not until Oliver disappeared. After that, the garden came into my brain like a fever hallucination.

> It is through a garden that I am walking with my eyes closed. The air is sweet and full of water. This wetness I feel on my bare feet as they sink into soft tufts. My toes experiment and

pull up pieces. I am happy swimming in floral scents, knowing no names. Oliver comes. He holds something near my nose and a sweet gush makes me dizzy. It tickles. He rubs it against my cheek and it feels like Oliver's whisper. Frightened when Oliver's fingers try to open my eyes, I squint tightly. But finally when he has stroked my eyelids and kissed them with the petals or with his lips, they open up. Then I fall into the soft grass and cry with delight seeing each piece green, each insect. Up above is blue. "It is a garden," Oliver says, smiling. I am smiling also, wanting to find the heavy smell that made me giddy. It is in Oliver's hand—a bunch of purple that I tear apart in my joy and smell and try to eat. Oliver lifts me up high and we twirl around in the blue. Round and round. "Show me everything," I plead as Oliver turns to leave. "In time," he answers. We leave to come back again.

I can keep this garden—Oliver's and mine—as long as I want to, as long as I live. This is because it never existed. Would he understand if he knew, if I could tell him? The wonderful thing about this garden is that it becomes more real, more precise each time we visit it. It is not a dream. I do not dream. It is a creation I make up in the daytime right now.

—

Edith's proprietorship was vague. Did Oliver know the truth? Was it something spinning down in his belly, too deep to catch? That we were suspended, simply waiting for her to appear did not matter at first; it was a deep bottom theme, too constant to hear until it receded entirely or came into sharp upside-down focus, distorting everything. Slowly—as my awareness grew, *her* presence was intensified, particularly for Oliver. She jumped up outside him taking different forms. The hazards were invisible at the beginning. Edith was to me (in the latter part of the first year, after I had mastered the essentials of physical independence and rudimentary perception) the same mystery as she has become, now, to you. But *I* accepted and lived with her subtle radiance without your sophisticated sense of speculation.

"Flush the toilet," directed Oliver, placing my hand under his and pulling a long braided rusty chain. Deep dark whirling in all directions with sounds of sucking me inside. I held my hands over my ears, eyes shut. Oliver laughed gently, absently—the old Oliver. "We won't fall into it—it's too small. Look." I think he said "we" rather than "you." I prefer "we." Too much like something surrounded by everything trying to reach out blindly, the word "you." Busy in a carnival of "we" *then*—whirling toilet, twirling potato skins knifed off in a slow deliberate turn, blue purple yellow flames up and down under yellow eggs, guggle gugle hsssss pah pah. Ch ch ch ts ts ts of salt and pepper falling on flat gold circles. All this a circular laughing dance of water, flamestove sounds as surprising and new as your early rains on springgreen leaves spun from sleeping yellow buds. Innocent.

Edith took the form within me of an uneasiness or a presentiment of something unpleasant. *Fear.* I know now that it was *fear* I felt so far in. Always remember that in telling of my life with Oliver I use words for emotions, words that are more or less appropriate according to my present knowledge. How else could I progress? Oliver was remiss in explaining emotional states, even as I learned words. The part of me that combines the words with feelings remained underdeveloped. It is too late, perhaps; I am still childlike. Remember also that my mind, if not disordered, was at the very least unreliable. I am now referring to my exaggerated reactions when I "awoke" and recognized my surroundings.

Had the rooms been totally unfamiliar, I wouldn't have had that dizzy feeling in my stomach. It was the occasional object half hidden in a dusty corner assaulting me with a prior fragrance that upset my boundaries. Upon a wooden table whose surface I examined with my fingertips sat my own ashtray, a brown fish carcass mounted on an iridescent seashell. How did I know this ashtray was mine? I cannot answer; do not—please—demand too much of me. I can tell only what I experienced then. Barbaric tapestries hung from the walls, patched together from wildly disconnected fragments of cloth. These webs of disintegrating fiber absorbed the sudden shocks of recognition. Again I found something of my own—a bracelet with an engraved letter, a mustard-colored coffee mug with a slanted crack, an earring with its small amethyst embedded in silver, green velvet bows, a tarnished chain from which hung a cross screaming with patterned blue glass, and a ring. The objects that seemed to belong to me numbered twenty. Everything else was hers—the wooden table, the kerosene lamp, breakfront with protruding keys, and of course the tapestries which echoed *my* moods despite the years *she* must have spent cutting, sewing and covering the corridor walls with them.

No doors, no windows, no beginning or end to this quilt-covered hall. Thick triangular pieces with diagonal stripes, thinner flowered squares, purple and green oblongs, remnants of old silk, yellow satin, gauze—all sewn together with black thread—covered the long rectangle, our world. Through this incoherent pattern, sewn neatly and then hastily or carelessly, Oliver had roamed a long time before I came. Half-conscious himself, he imagined Edith, lived in the time when she had been real, when her fingers had put together those patchwork walls. What right had I to be there at all? Initially my intrusion was welcomed, I think. A balance was created for Oliver—something to care for and to instruct but without an existence of its own—tangible enough to keep his fantasies from straining him, yet no more disrupting to his life than the yelp of a housepet. "Oomah, geeeh, geeeh, geeeeeeh."

Here it is dark and light dark and light
Shapes on the floor dance wings pass near
Away a balloon with no shadow lies on a

Windowsill hit right in the center by sun
Not there

He did not notice when the mustard-colored cup disappeared, when the bracelet no longer sat on the spice shelf. The cross vanished, and so did those other objects I don't want to remember anymore.

The tapestried hall and the four rooms that broke off from it exploding into strange nests formed our world. No stairs or view of trees, no birdsong or cricketfeet, no buzz or honk honk—no sounds other than our own voices or the things we made move—and her silent whisper—that was and is my universe. The garden I invent to be inventive and to take Oliver and myself somewhere outside; it is like a translation of old things into a new language but with different accents, no language being absolutely translatable. This subject brings us quickly to my greatest difficulty. Although our world became made up of words, strewn all over with them, as soon as Oliver's lessons began, our world was not one of *useful* language—of verbal communication and conversation. This is more complicated than it may appear. To me language is still a skill or a game. Sometimes I can almost make the connections between words and the feelings of the body or in the head, but it is with some effort. My head aches. You must imagine me constantly translating movements, sights, sounds, body changes, heartbeats which I felt *then* and didn't know. I am doing my translation into word-feelings. It is like translating a colorful abstract painting into sounds for a blind man. (I know blind men.) That describes my condition. Not to translate would be to remain silent and I cannot do that. I need your assistance with things. Perhaps a style will develop as I go along.

—

He was patient, picking up the pieces of the plate I broke, bending down heavily, slowly, his lip dripping saliva. Slowly his fingers fat, brown-stained with black under square nails touched broken china. Up, up at me, his eyes. "Your hands have too much soap on them." Flat—not angry then. That was all he said. I understood the words. I remembered about the soap. Just breathing from me. Just looking and breathing, watching.

—

I have studied many contemporary authors trying to find a proper style. Those I like best make one word follow another like colors sparking together, ringing flying mounting slowly and clang-clang-clang singing in my ear. When I do it you will know that I am having fun with the sounds. Others twist lazily along in proper order with everything connecting calmly and ending in an ice-cold stop. I cannot. Things were not like that with us. It was toneless on the surface, Oliver and I walking the corridor—Oliver always moving so slowly, looking distracted, peeling potatoes in endless swirls, turning the page of an out-of-date calendar, concentrating so hard. Myself trailing after him or sitting in some corner waiting staring a long time at small things like the grains of wood up and down crooked and smooth, not knowing what was happening until later. Sometimes I have to use that kind of language—child language of touching feeling smelling parts. Other times I must invent language for precision. How angry all of this would make Oliver if you knew him. And I will mention his name in every sentence if I want to because I love to spell out his name and to say it. When I get tired I will leave and go into my garden. The purpose is not a literary work. The purpose is for you to understand about Oliver's disappearance so you can tell me why it happened. At least I think that is my purpose. I will do my part the best I can, and don't make fun of me because I am not like you and can't understand your world. I come from a prettier star.

Perhaps you have seen me in my gray suit and light blue

blouse. I try to look inconspicuous but I stare and stare or else I walk with my head down, a habit I picked up from Oliver. My posture is something he didn't pay much attention to except when he tried to get me to hold my legs closer together and to take smaller steps. But my shoulders slope. Sometimes I am with a man who is wearing dark glasses and tapping a cane; he is not Oliver. Oh yes, I wear many rings—the cheap glass kind you can get at the five-and-dime jewelry department. Each one is a different color. And the sun shines through them. They remind me of Edith's glass studio. There are small scars on my fingers from cuts I got on her glass-cutting machine. I usually carry a yellow umbrella because you never know when it's going to rain.

—

I made my entrance, or rather my "appearance" in the costume of a child. My blouse was a long-sleeved blue cotton with a ruffle encircling the neck. Underneath was a shapeless slip or camisole which was tight at the armpits since my breasts are quite large. A brassiere was something I learned about later when Oliver saw fit to explain. However, I never had one in all my days with Oliver. Even when he grudgingly presented me with the lovely violet dress, my breasts hung free. That was much later. My breasts, I might mention, are flattened forever from that tight camisole day after day. My skirt was a familiar plaid—that green tartan with the usual thin reddish and yellow stripes running through which has been seen for years around the waists of schoolgirls. Mine was just such a pleated skirt with a button and a zipper on the left side. I mention this outfit, particularly the skirt, to explain that I was dressed in a decidedly girlish manner and that my appearance was by no means neuter. It was rather that of an arrested femininity, since I was far too old for that outfit. Nor were my legs shaved. They were long and hairy and bare except for blue ankle socks and a pair of cheap moccasins decorated with small yellow beads. But what I am getting to, what I wanted to say and should have said at once was that I had no idea of my sex. Nor of the sex of Oliver. At least not on what you call the cognitive level. But I knew in the same way that very little children know, the way animals and even flowers know. Oliver and I were different. That was as far as it went for a long time.

Reading in recent months about everything, I happened to read about prefontal lobotomies. And although that was not the case with me, as was proved by my later development, by my fantastic evolution, I was then in exactly that postoperative condition. Had a psychiatrist been present, he would have searched through my tangled hair for the mark of an incision—unless it is done inside the nose or behind the ear—I must check the facts at the medical library lest you think that I am still stupid. My behavior was at a level where new associations have to be made. That is how the doctors would have proceeded after my lobotomy. I would have been taught in a systematic impersonal way—*trained* is the word I am seeking. They would have trained me to go to the toilet myself, to dress, to eat and so forth. Fortunately this was not the environment that I found myself in. In sexual matters, for example, I was very lucky. From almost the beginning, Oliver was fascinated by my breasts, which I made no effort to hide. At any moment, when the camisole became too restricting, I might remove my clothes without self-consciousness. He held them and touched them quite often while he was helping me to eat or at other times. His manipulations were tentative and not specifically sexual. Don't forget that Oliver was not so conscious either. Don't you forget this. He was, however, more knowledgeable and at a higher level of development than I. Nor were my reactions sexual in the adult sense of the word. I liked Oliver to touch my breasts. It was the perfect thing to do, considering my age and state. Had he seized me and raped me suddenly or had he ignored my woman's body, my development would have been slowed and possibly impaired. Even now, now when I know that my breasts are like pancakes and hardly what nice breasts would look like, I remember that Oliver didn't mind. Had he ignored them, I would surely have some shame or complex and would avoid getting undressed in front of anyone. I don't. Only at the beginning, when my consciousness came and went without warning, was I sometimes startled by his touch. And he also seemed to draw away as though he had not known what he was doing. Oliver was also going back and forth between his fantasies and the reality that my presence was beginning to impose upon him. That is part of the tragedy of my relationship with Oliver. If I had realized it, I would have left. I swear it. But how could I have known that I was an imposition, a swelling parasite taking all that Oliver had left. It was his fault as well. I could have remained as I was, little more than a housepet. But my Oliver is a creative man. (Sometimes I refuse to speak of him in the past tense. It is not ignorance of tenses.) My Oliver is a creative man and he could not let me remain as I was. In addition, he developed a sense of responsibility which he could not help any more than I could help being there.

When my consciousness became stable and there were no more recessions deep black, I *always* liked when he played with my breasts. I liked it best when he was feeding me or putting me to bed. Those days were the best in our relationship. And I am sorry for you. I am sorry that you never experienced such contentment. Words were not involved. Nor were there great desires, passions, or intricate interactions. Mutual distrust, which I now know is always inevitable, had not yet arisen; and what is called "the battle of the sexes" could not exist, neither of us having a clear idea of our sexuality. Don't misunderstand this. Oliver knew everything about anatomy and all about our different sexual functions. But time (how much time I cannot possibly know or calculate) alone waiting for Edith had caused his instincts and his specific male identity to recede. There were two Olivers, you might say—the Oliver who dreamed and the Oliver who attended to me. His dreams were sexual. I know this now and I knew it even earlier. He masturbated sometimes, while eating or walking around. It had nothing to do with me or with my breasts. My early presence (I will stress this again and again) did not seriously affect his inner life. It was not a deliberate masturbation. The way he did it was perfunctory and usually while he was doing something else such as eating or writing. Sometimes, distracted by something, he stopped in the middle getting small not seeming to notice. Other times he ejaculated with a small quantity of semen coming forth but hardly any orgasm. "Aah aah, unh unh" soft sound and then catching his breath. I was not frightened by his erect penis as a small child might have been, nor was I yet excited by it. I simply watched without comprehension. Oliver's penis had nothing to do with me for a long time. We were so well suited—he had his dreams and someone real to take care of, and there was no conflict or connection between them. And I—I had a sane simple environment in which to develop. There has been nothing better in my life since. And although I have invited you, I resent, deeply resent your intrusion.

—

Slowly, unbroken, the brown twirling skin is coming to an end. I begin to chew it. "Raach raach." Oliver rinsing the potato which is softwhite, perfect, without a blemish—Oliver, lost rinsing, somewhere far away, does not notice my gagging. "Aaach aaaaach." His head which is big and heavy on his short thick neck turns toward my sounds, but not quickly. Hands reach out salty, open my mouth and remove potato skin. "No." His head shakes heavily around and around. His eyes are half-closed. It is enough; I understand. "Aaach," spitting the last chewed pieces out, listening to the knife falling sweetly into porous potato flesh, the juicy glistening sounds of each slice are in my body. Pleasure. Dazed, I see the wet surface shining on my eyes. Oliver's hands. I stand close breathing him. "Ooom, ooom."

—

Against the quilted wall in the middle of the corridor was a tall breakfront with three bottom drawers. Tarnished keys jutted mysteriously from the center holes. Oliver's "Don't touch," was sufficient to keep my hands off these keys during the early stages of my growth. I wonder now about his carelessness; he could have locked the drawers and hidden the keys. (Later on many things were forbidden me.) Perhaps he forgot. Perhaps he couldn't imagine those drawers ever being opened again. It was a terrible mistake on his part, not hiding the keys and locking the drawers. I confess that I opened every one of these forbidden drawers during the time that I was learning to deceive Oliver, during the time when I could read much better than I dared to let him know. It was when he was asleep. Oliver slept soundly, and although we had no working clocks, I always had enough time. Remember, that was later.

I am afraid that *you* will go away just like Oliver did if I don't show you something interesting; that is why I will show you some of the letters right now. Don't even attempt to assign a chronology to these messages from Edith. She or Oliver deliberately tore off the upper right hand corner where the date is usually written. The envelopes also vanished. It was probably Oliver. He does not like hours or dates except in history or for lessons, and he became very angry when I accidentally fixed one of the broken clocks. Maybe it was the ticking that disturbed him. If he had been asleep, he would never have heard the ticking or even the screaming. You can do anything you want to when Oliver is asleep. Oliver never slept halfway like I sleep. Oliver's sleep was deep and heavy and still, with soft snoring and a wet open mouth. That is how I was able to open all the drawers and turn all the keys week after week until I knew every word in her letters by memory. But if you see Oliver, you must promise not to tell him that I read the letters. By the time I am finished, you will know him so well that you will recognize him from either the back or front. That is another reason why I am writing this. If you find Oliver, I want you to get in touch with me immediately. I know that this is not proper but I am asking you to do it. Oliver's ears are very large and they cup forward. The earlobes are longer than those on any man I have ever seen. Long black, red and gray hairs come out of his ears and they are full of hard brownish orange wax—not yellow wax. Remember that. Even if he cleans his ears you will still know him. When he walks, he tugs at his left earlobe, and he is missing the third finger (not counting the thumb) on his right hand. Except the third phalange which comes out from the palm. It moves. (Don't count the thumb!) It took me a long time to notice that something was missing from Oliver's finger. My fingers are scarred from the cuts I got on Edith's glass-cutting machine but I have all the parts of all my fingers. Don't tell him that you read Edith's letters, please. Don't mention Edith!

These letters and notes were all written on pale blue paper in a looped floral style of writing. The ink is always real bottled blue ink. I think she used a penholder with a small crow-quill penpoint which accounts for certain blots and uneven coloration seldom seen in today's letters, which are either typed or written with synthetic pens that have blunt points, felt tips or electric motors.

Dear, Dearest Oliver,

We have a film club here and we decide upon the films ourselves. Last night's film was about preying birds who attack little children. We had been warned but voted for it anyhow. Many people were upset by it. I like birds. You know that Oliver. But the film was in black and white which spoiled it. I like green blue and purple birds best. I wasn't afraid. Today I made a bird from bent plastic. I am not allowed anything glass. My bird is gold. The wings are gold and it has a black beak. But I am not finished yet. I hope it sticks together. There is a hypodermic filled with liquid that is injected into the seams to make the pieces fuse. The gold wings are very large. I wish I could fly. I made it for you. I prefer that you don't write to me. I still feel that way, but I will be home soon. Don't forget to dust my glass things carefully. I would be very upset if anything broke.

Your Own Edith

Most Darling Darling Oliver,

I don't understand why people want to travel. The blue skies of Florence disturb me as does the clarity of the strange reddish tile. I can't look up. It isn't real. I won't stay long. The nights are much better.

Yours Forever, Edith

Oliver, I've gone for a walk and may not be here when you return. Don't worry about me. The snow is warm, Edith

Beloved Oliver,

Don't throw anything away. I worry about that more than anything. Your letter will be returned unopened. Dearest, you know better than that. I am told that I have an ethereal beauty but I refuse to have my picture taken. A photograph is so definite even when it makes mistakes. Will you please keep my shoes polished. I worry about my shoes and all my pretty dresses. Dust gets into things like velvet. You will keep everything ready for me, I trust. I trust you Oliver. Please test the glass-cutter and keep it oiled. I miss it.

Your Only Love, Edith

My Most Beloved Oliver,

You must never forget me no matter where I am, no matter what I do, or what happens. This sounds silly but often I think of my life as being in your keeping and that it is safe there. Even when I am doing other things this is true. Don't hurt your beloved by forgetting a single detail. Forgetting is a sin, of this I am certain. I would cry day and night if I thought you would ever forget me or not welcome me when I return. It doesn't matter how long we are apart. I bought a lilac hat which is almost the same color as my violet dress. The shops are very exclusive and original here. I tore up your letter without reading it. I can't bear it. I cannot bear it. Do you hear me once and for all??? Do not ever write again. After I tore up your letter I stole a match and burned it. Then I was very upset and couldn't stop crying and screaming. Don't do that to me, Oliver. In my room is Botticelli's "Venus Coming Out Of A Half-shell." It looks like me. I like Botticelli. I also have a reproduction of some flowers by Rédon. I walk every morning, but I don't like trees at all. I can't explain that to you. They oppress me and make me want to do violent things. They are so black when it rains. Dust my studio every day so it will be ready for me when I arrive. I am allowed to go shopping alone on Saturdays. Can you love me in any state I am in? I must believe that you can.

Your Devoted Edith

Dear Oliver,

Do not belittle my religious transformation. I must keep growing. Abstinence can increase spirituality. Although you cannot understand, I am now of the spirit and my virginity has been restored. I used to believe that flesh and spirit could be one. It was a mere self-deception. Although I fast I feel strong. My body feels pure and new. I feel light and blessed and sometimes I laugh for no reason at all like a child. You, Oliver are of the flesh. When I return you will have to accept my days of abstinence. I will be in prayer and meditation much of the time. I hope you will learn to be proud of my change. This transformation is not as abrupt as it may appear to you, and I beg you not to view it clinically. I never respected the flesh although I yielded to it. I know that it may be difficult for you at first but that in time you will come to learn and to know what I am thankful to know. If you love me you will want to be with me in the light of God and you will be truly joined to me as One. I wear plain clothes now and never look at my reflection in mirrors. It is a temporal illusion.

May God Keep You and Love You Well.

Faithfully, Edith

Oliver My Darling,

We can meet in two weeks, the Thursday after next. I am so happy. I can think of nothing else. I will be wearing a lovely blue dress trimmed with lace. I should have let that be a surprise but I would like to think that you are imagining how I look. I have beige shoes with tiny green bows and I will wear my hair straight down but with the fluffy knot at the crown just the way you like it. Oh I would die if anything happened and we couldn't meet. You must think of me every day until then. I will feel your thoughts.

Love, Edith

Oliver, Oliver,

I am upset. I was going to name my bird after you. I wanted to because I love you. But I named it after myself. I couldn't help it. It is such a pretty bird and some day you will see it. Don't say you don't like birds because that hurts me very much.

Your Edith

My Beloved Oliver,

I pray for you each night. You must not worship my flesh anymore since it is only a temporal illusion and will return to the dust from whence it sprang. Try to prepare yourself for our new life and its reward. Do not ever say that I am wrong about this, the greatest thing in my life, or that you prefer your old Edith. If you do not love what is purest and best in me then what do you love? I am praying for you so that you will no longer be blind to True Beauty. I have not reached perfection yet and I will not expect it from you, only a great effort. I will forgive you and be as patient as He is.

With Love Too Great To Express, Edith

My toilet training proceeded rapidly since my muscles were well developed. I would skip over it entirely except that it gives me an opportunity to show off the unique, creative mind that was Oliver's.

Hidden in Oliver's huge closet were many rolls of paper. Many varieties of colors and textures were piled as high as a mountain. Perhaps he used to wrap gifts for Edith, choosing a pattern and degree of softness appropriate to her current mood. Or else (and this thought has come to me only recently) the paper was related to a previous occupation from which Oliver once earned money. I know about earning money in your world. But what is important to me is that this was the beautiful paper that inspired Oliver's idea for my toilet training.

For some reason I always defecated and urinated in the corridor and never in my room. I don't know why this is so, any more than I can explain the instinct I had for getting my skirt out of the way. (I owned no underpants.) These facts simplified his task to some extent and that is why I have mentioned them.

He led me into his room—I remember it so well because that was the only time Oliver willingly opened his door to me. Usually I was left outside when his door closed. *Away.* (Imagine what all this must have cost him.) Opening his closet, he displayed the shining colors. In an instant the bright red roll was in my hands. Oliver had some difficulty retrieving it, but he had done his research. Red is still my favorite color, although I don't like to admit it.

Soon the floor of the entire corridor was covered with the red paper. I was drawn to it, fascinated, and naturally I defecated and urinated upon it. Day after day his scissors snipped around the used area and disposed of my work. Somehow I never soiled the bare floor; it was always on the red paper that I disposed of my waste products, even when only the smallest amount of red remained. It was at that moment that Oliver held his breath. He removed the few remaining scraps of red covering. My reaction was to run up and down the hall in dismay. I was not a very active being; do not imagine me tearing things up or running about wildly with screeching sounds. I was not like that. And Oliver knew. Otherwise he would have feared that I might simply tear the red paper to bits before my training had begun. He would have found a different method.

Before an accident occurred, before it was too late, Oliver led me to the toilet which he knew I feared because of its cavity and roaring noise sucking me in. It was covered inside and outside with red paper. In the past I had refused to sit on it and my Oliver was too kind to force me. In love with the red paper, the inevitable occurred. I connected defecation and urination with shiny red and then with the lovely red toilet. The lesson was learned. I did not need the paper for very long, but my Oliver who was so good and kind to me at that time, painted the toilet my favorite color inside and outside. It remained that way almost forever. Red. Who else, may I ask, has been toilet-trained so pleasantly and with such imagination? I cry when I think of the work and consideration he put into this project—my huge Oliver who preferred to live in dreams. But he enjoyed it as much as I did. I know. He was proud when I mastered something with his help. But even then Oliver made some mistakes. I am not trying to pretend he was perfect.

Here it is dark and light dark and light
Crosshatched patterns spill on the floor
Change then disappear or the sun turns
Over upside down by fingers not the same
Away a yellow balloon lies deflated with
Shadows everywhere on a windowsill center
Of real gray nightwinged birds up and down
Not there

He should have made an effort to speak more often. But he had been without speech for so long. It was late, even too late, when he began our conversations. There was no dialogue between us. It was my own fault; I never even attempted to speak. There was no excuse for it; I heard his commands and understood: "Eat," "chew," "go away," "wash," "sleep," "come here," "sit here," "take the spoon in your hand." That was how Oliver communicated verbally for a long time. And I never uttered a word. Why? I grunted and whined and made various sounds. These sounds were soft. Unfocused, undeveloped, I was eager to obey. No screaming, stamping, or tantrums in the early months or rather in what I have designated as the first year. Never truthfully can I say that anything happened one day or that it happened on another day. Since there were no windows we had no idea of day or night. He made morning and night. When Oliver awoke we began our morning tasks, and if he had a brief nap later on, it was morning again. Morning meant eggs, toast, simple tasks, and later in my life, lessons. Night meant lamb or pork, peeling potatoes, coffee and undressing. Sometimes there were many rapid mornings and many nights. The eggs disappeared quickly. Other times they remained forever and morning never came.

—

He comes barefoot down the corridor pulling his left earlobe; his toenails, brownish, curve downward like claws. I have touched them and they are hard as stone. I am sitting near my door which is at the other end of the corridor farthest from Oliver, having no thoughts, broken-winged, still. My ear sees Oliver's footsteps and I awake alive laugh and run and pull at him. Sleepy and confused. Not sure he likes it this Oliver pats my head. Barefooted he is buttering the pan and I hear eggs, guggle gugle hsssss pah pah hsssss. "Wash," he says without looking at me. I understand and run into the bathroom. Red. I take everything off as he has taught me. Fun. Splashing water and soap over my body, I forget to come out. Oliver comes in. Frowns and then something makes him laugh. Magic early laughing orangesweet. It disappeared. He dries me with a towel. "Breakfast is ready," flatly to no one—a distance I know in my hands or feet. He says that every "morning." I dress (I can) and sit at the table. "Pick up your spoon," even though I know it already. We eat, making eating sounds. No words and not looking at each other. Not yet at the time when I stare always at Oliver. Eating with a spoon takes all my concentration. I would prefer it if he would feed me but he doesn't anymore unless I am very tired or can't cut the meat. Then he does it with his fingers. Obediently I get up and wash the dishes. Oliver has just taught me and I break them, but he doesn't yell; Oliver does not lose his temper yet because I am not so important. He goes slowly back into his room far away while I am playing with the soap and dishes. Then he comes with his big shoes and his khaki pants and a navy blue shirt which is heavy and smells good like Oliver. He doesn't like to wash as much as I like to or to splash. I follow but he says, "No," and locks the door from inside. Outside I am pulling at my hair, hearing a buzzing and a sweeping sound. Happy when he comes out again, I take the broom like Oliver has shown me. I sweep. He sits at the table with his big head in his hands, rubbing his eyes. Again he goes toward his room, enters, closes the door. I whine. "Geeeh, geeeh, geeeeeh." I play with two spoons knocking them together slow fast slow fast. Music—tin clunks water plops—pah pah, egg yellow stabbed shining on top of my eyes. I don't know if he is inside a long time or a short time. It is silent except when I move something or my feet tap or I clap my hands. But if I sit still there is nothing. Finally I lie down outside Oliver's door and look at the ceiling. Blank.

—

Each night I do something very cruel; you would have to know Oliver to realize the viciousness of my act. Otherwise you would laugh. So much time since *then*—months or years, maybe. It doesn't make any difference at all, you would think. But I know. Oliver was selfish with words; it was his knowledge of words that kept him ahead of me when we were secretly struggling for power. He gave me words—that was Oliver's gift—carefully apportioned. I blasphemed by finding intricate ways to use his measured vocabulary. I began to realize that he kept the best for himself. I hate him for it. Not because I am curious anymore—at least not about words. They answer nothing. Only because I want to spite Oliver do I learn a new word every evening. Once, looking into the mirror during this activity, I saw a flushed face with a maniacal glint in the eye. Me. Angry, I know more words than Oliver, and when I think about it a cruel laugh comes out; it is not fair to him. I am sick of words and wish no one had taught them to me. Are you an *omaphagist,* Oliver? Surely you know what I am talking about. That is my word for tonight, *omaphagic*—I am certainly not omaphagic although there are worse things and in times of necessity it is understandable, even forgiveable. That is my word and I will use it over and over again as though I am putting a knife into your throat where words come out. No other reason. Of what use is such a word to me, or any word? Only to taunt you, Oliver. You cannot choose words for me anymore, deliberately keeping the longest and best for yourself. And when we meet again I will speak to you with my own vocabulary and you will blush, not knowing some of *my* words. You, Oliver, taught me to be selfish and spiteful. No, I don't go in order; I choose words that were not in your writings, words that sound like words even you don't know. This is my secret revenge. But perhaps you know all the words in the dictionary, Oliver. That would be just like you—to have stolen every one. Then I will learn the medical dictionary, a Chaucerian dictionary, a dictionary of rare fossils or insects. Somehow I will triumph. I am no longer an example of the *integer vitae.* Do you hear me? I am an omaphagist after all. Your rules are not irrefrangible. If you will not share your words, then I will take all of them, every single one. No guilt. But what is the difference now? I will drink *lixivium,* Oliver. What is the difference?

I am sitting in the garden waiting for Oliver, fingering the smooth coral bench, following red veins beneath. They wander carelessly carefully cracking up blood to the surface. Yellow leaves are falling. Others, tissue-brown lie curling. The lilac bush to the left of the bench used to bloom. He walks toward me tapping a white-tipped cane. Eyes closed he takes my hand. His face is as white as plaster. I kiss him and pull his beard until he smiles and opens his eyes with plaster flakes shattering. "You are supposed to be happy here," I say. Oliver looks at me with his eyes that are not one color but a mixture like some of the leaves. I notice a velvet box, black, held in his right hand which is missing the third finger except for the last section. He gives it to me and I open it with excitement, thinking it is a jewel or a flower. Asleep on cotton is a cold dead bird. "Edith," he says stroking the blue and green feathers with his broken finger. I am angry. Laughing I pick up his cane which is lying on the leaves; laughing I beat the dead bird until it dissolves into the ash of dead leaves.

"Never do that again," loud, stamping his boot and tearing off my clothes with rough rips, red-faced, gasping, lower lip way down inside-out dripping long sticky saliva. Next a purple beating, "Aaooow, aaooow," belt-strap wump wump wump. The big hand is over his eyes and dazed he turns away dragging his boots, not turning back, disappearing. Pain. I lie waiting outside his door a long time.

He is not a faultless man. Understand this. All his weaknesses are now my own. Perhaps they were hidden deep inside me all the time just waiting. I am not sure. Must I tell you everything. Even that—even why he ripped off my clothes? He didn't like it. Eyes open, I began to imitate him. If he had been a woodpecker, I would have banged my nose sore against the wooden table. There was no one else! He wore old khaki trousers tucked into high boots or shoes. And he either went bare-chested or wore a heavy blue shirt over his belt—never tucked inside. Hair on his chest like dried curling grass, even sweeter. His shirt was warm, smelling of Oliver, but he had taken it away when I tried to sleep with it. That day, "Aooow," I am ashamed to tell you, he found me dressed in his trousers, enormous as they were. I devised fantastic methods to keep them up, wound coarse string from top to bottom, rolled up the legs as far as they would go. My manual dexterity had improved greatly; I cut holes on either side of the zipper and stuck my arms through. The fly came up to my neck. (My Oliver is very tall though stooped, and very fat.) Quite pleased with myself, I was walking legs apart down the corridor smiling Oliver's smile, tugging at my left earlobe. He didn't laugh when he saw me. It was the first time his kindness failed, I think. Yelling, he tore his clothes off me—it was one of his weaknesses, one I can understand now when it is too late. He did not like his private things to be handled; this was basic to my Oliver, so make a note of it. Later when we were having sexual intercourse or coitus, he objected to my touching his genitalia, unless he gave me special permission. I am referring to his penis and scrotum sac in case you are not sure. There were some privacies about his person that not even the fiercest passion on my part could overcome. Was it different with Edith? I won't think about that. His anger about my possession and mutilation of his clothing was understandable. Not that I understood then. Nothing. I know he would have controlled himself if he had been able to, or if he had been warned. Oliver hates surprises. After a year of seeing me in my torn plaid skirt, having no idea of my discontent and of my desire to dress as he did, his shock was justifiable. I have given the matter much thought. The beating frightened him more than it frightened me. "Never touch my clothes, you are a girl and must not wear a man's clothing." For all his eccentricities, he was a conventional person and remained true to basic principles of your society. He always stayed on top which is most proper and never from behind or inside the other place like some people.

I refused when he tried to make me put on the plaid skirt. How can I explain? Perhaps I needed to go on and wanted some proof that I was not as I had been when I first arrived. Or I needed him to tell me in clear words about my sex. There are a million possible reasons. And I will no longer pretend that I did not want to annoy him, that the beginning of a mounting rebellion had not started. Puzzled by my refusal, particularly since I was usually so obedient, he withdrew from me for some time (measured differently then). Sometimes I wonder if he did not consider sending me away at once, did not even consider disposing of me in some way. But when he reappeared days or hours later, he took my hand and led me into a room that had been previously forbidden me. This was difficult for him and must have caused him great pain. This room had a large bed with a white ruffled spread, satin on the top and climbing down to the floor with frills, and a dressing table with a mirrored surface where different-sized atomizers stood in groups or far apart. The table was skirted blue, and had small blue and white bulbs along the sides of a vertical mirror. (You read her letters due to my indiscretion.) Oliver trembled, turned pale opening her closet. There was no need for such generosity—I would have put on the plaid skirt. I would have gone naked. Robes, gowns, pale colors. Orchid, wing-yellow, silvery turquoise, lace-trimmed, green velvet. Edith. I had no right. But Oliver had decided. Breaking his brain, clawing his heart, everything, he chose a violet dress made of silk rayon. My arms went through long sleeves and a zipper crawled slowly up my back. No pattern, no ornament. Only a small gold belt fastened around my waist. He seemed satisfied, but inside torn mutilated where the belly is like his khaki trousers. The closet was locked and we went out of the room pretending we had never entered.

It fit well. Perfectly. He even got used to seeing me wearing it. No. He didn't. The year of the violet dress. That is what I call it. If a new year began, it began on the day he beat me and gave me the violet dress to punish himself. (You read her letters due to my indiscretion.) Should I have left then? There was no door. I could not go. Had it gone too far already? But I know he had given it long thought. Not an impulse like the beating or tearing off the clothes earlier. Not simple like the spoon coming up in into my mouth. Something different in giving me the dress to wear—something torn in separate parts like the trousers.

I hardly knew what I was doing then, but I doubt myself. Sometimes I think it was all planned, done deliberately to start trouble. How can I trust myself, particularly with all the things now going on inside my head: silver horses galloping with speckled woodpeckers on their backs, chipping away the veneer wings folded but ready to open leaving nothing alone until the bleeding horsey falls down spilling his brain, liver, ovaries or spermtanks. Endless, the winding brain. Sometimes I remember nothing clearly. When I seemed to have no thoughts, were they actually all there already acting anyhow? To the best of my knowledge Oliver was mean about sharing words, his clothes and his penis. I may have misunderstood, being only a child at the time. I don't think so. If I hacked at Oliver like a speckled woodpecker, it was not intentional—I knew nothing.

Here it is dark and light dark and light
Shadows of silver horses move on the wall
Of my head real is the morning light cuts
My eyes white through clouds white white
Someone stabs a black balloon in the beak
Not there

It was suggested to me that I change Oliver's name. The name has been used before in books, films and on the stage which might confuse people or detract from the originality. I will never do that. His name is Oliver and there is no more to be said about it. Naturally I did not take this advice calmly—not at all. I stamped my foot, pulled my left earlobe and screamed. (When I am upset my early imitations of Oliver return.) My anger did not stop them—and hardly anything makes me feel angry. They thought I did not understand. Soft voices tried to reason with me. Here. As if any voice or tone or reason could make me change his name. I may go into my garden with Oliver and never come out and never tell anyone about it. That is what I will do if they should say it again. I don't mind the changes in punctuation. It was suggested that I make up a name. Someone thought *Simeon* fit his description. Another preferred Hilbert—what horrible sounds! Otherwise they let me do more or less what I want. And what would *you* think if I lied and called Oliver, Simeon? Next I will be told to put his second and first phalanges back on his third finger or to clip his toenails. They cannot be clipped. Oliver's toenails are like claws and hard as stone. They have to be sawed. He did it once before one of the visits. A nail file would not work and soaking his feet in hot water did not soften the nails but only made his skin red and sore. Inside the glass studio, he found a sharp-toothed saw and worked for hours getting himself into a sweat. But in the end there was no improvement—particularly since the nails grow downward and are close to the skin. Only blood. I am glad. I like Oliver's toenails exactly as they are. So don't tell me to clip them or change his name. I would have every right to do that since he never gave *me* a name; I can't forgive him for that. But that is between Oliver and me—that is between Oliver and me and is none of your business!

During the first part of the second year when I was inside the violet dress, Oliver taught me that everything has a name: bed, man, Oliver, boy, girl, Oliver, bread, stone, glass, pear, bed, man, Oliver. Everything has a name or even two or three variations of a name like sink, washstand and basin—everything except me. I didn't let him know that I realized this nor do I remember at what precise instant such a complex idea occurred to me. Why didn't you give *me* a name? It could have been anything at all. How happy I would have been to hear you call me something: Hefa, Leaf, Vid, Omate, Emit, Mite, Mate, Mote, Mox—I used to make hundreds of names by putting letters together in different ways. They weren't all used up—many names were left over. What was your reason, Oliver? I am angry—I am angry at this omission. Everyone in the world has at least one name. It could have been just a letter or two if you preferred. But maybe you would have given me a name sometime if you hadn't disappeared, or maybe there was a name for me in your head and you just forgot to say it out loud. That is why I will not do that to you—take your name away just because I am angry.

And you fed me and taught me how to dress and wash and write and paste and how to spell and how to hold a spoon and you gave me a violet dress. What right do I have to a name? I have a name now, Oliver, but I don't care about it. It was *your* responsibility to name me. What letter was engraved on the bracelet that disappeared—the one that I thought was mine? I think I hid it myself because it frightened me. Perhaps I am wrong and you hid it.

—

Foamworld of Oliver—porous sponge slowly squeezing green; liquid, life swimming below beyond time in circles of secret words to Edith a shadow visible in the tangled folds of aging palpitating cerebrum. "Anything for you, my sweet bird—go if you must, dance, chirp your pretty painsong in the world. I will wait." The roar of a wave smiling into mudhole gurgles. "You say that, but you hold me here with the desire of your look hooked into me," she whispers through the silver nets inside beyond his eyes. Shuddering he holds Edith carefully, his fingers smoothing her hair, her brow. "I want to protect you, my fragile child, not to take joy from you—you don't understand." A submissive sigh, as her long fingers fold behind his neck, cold stems. Carrying her limp like a sacred shadow, limp on the white white spread. He mounts, rides feeling his thick body turn light stretching blue above her hopeless trembling. "Fragile, fragile love," he whispers rocking in her, trying to shield her as she fades breaks into the orange seagrowths multiplying in his brain. "Wait." A large blood-filled penis moves in his hand slippery rocking the pain of the endless now. He is sitting at the wooden table chewing something warm.

OLIVER'S FOAMWORLD THEME
(for small electric organ)

—

Everything changed with my encasement in her violet dress. His eyes opened and his precious dreams receded leaving me in sharp focus. And the lessons began—lessons of words, painful exercises that I performed only for his love. Oliver's affection was no longer unconditional; it depended upon my accomplishments. Consequently, I became alert. We watched each other.

It was too abrupt a transformation into now. I was not ready although everything depended upon me. Even today I am not certain. Was my error in my easy submission or in my eventual rebellion? In the beginning I followed—a hollow instrument for Oliver: a horn, a formless balloon for him to blow into or choke at the neck, a freshly laid egg for his fat buttocks to sit upon. Shallow filmy eggshell existence was all I had. Did this shadowy echo of his will enrage him? Did I disappoint him? An important time for Oliver and me, this beginning end. Perhaps he needed a will almost equal to his own in order to keep the edge of his new consciousness distinct. I was only a mirror. He had nothing to vibrate against. (Why, Oliver, did you so quickly abandon your life with Edith?) Beginning year of the violet dress, I was less than those silent images he had lived with before. However illusory, those visions had been adequate for the preservation of Oliver's internal order. Between himself and those visions I had become. The images were jealous, confused, could not reach him. How could I have known this? I was not ready to replace anything. *What a terrible thing I did to Oliver!* He didn't know what he wanted of me—how could he have known after everything? (You read those letters due to my indiscretion.) End of the carnival of "we." Warmth of one split into two.

His way of relating to me at this time was by dictation of rules. "Up and down, five times, one two three four five," Oliver turning his head looking up and down the corridor. Then at me. My eyes were open on him, watching his head, not understanding. Breathing loudly, "huhh huhh huhh," he ran back and forth. His face was red, his mouth open. "Up and down five times, one two three four five," he said. Insistent, scary, ice-cold. "Now." This insistence made the birth of my own will more difficult. Still-born, I blame him for not creating a freer environment; he had no right to be angry and bored by my indecision. Nor did he indicate that he wanted me to disagree, to refuse, to speak. Heartless unthinking beast, how could you help yourself? I am not always honest—had I tried I could have disobeyed more frequently and thus gained his respect, even in *my* condition. But I had no previous experience and had to learn everything through his teaching. Still, there is no excuse. I realize this and I am forever sorry. Yet in many ways he seemed to enjoy his domination.

Cruel Oliver, selfishly groping for order—how else can I explain the strange rules and routines that he devised and which I obeyed? Mornings he insisted that I run up and down the corridor five times. It became easier when I finally understood what "five times" meant. Since I could not yet count, I ran sometimes two, sometimes twenty times. Oliver was adamant. "Five times." When I failed I was sent to my room, unable to come outside until he called. Motionless, staring at the ceiling, my ears waiting in my room for "Come out." Whether or not I found my running task agreeable is one of the things that I cannot know. I was in the habit of obeying Oliver and I had no sense of what assignments were fair or appropriate. Only to please him, begging "geeeh geeeh geeeeh," to sit on his lap, to have my breasts stroked as a reward. Only to please Oliver I did everything. Perhaps he was teaching me how to count. I must always try to be fair to him. The benefit of every doubt belongs to Oliver. Four eggs had to be cracked without mutilation of the yellow form as it fell into the pan. Kuk shwaaah, kuk shwaaaah, kuk shwaaaah, kuk shwaaaah. If I failed at this task (and it was repeated each "morning"), my breakfast was divided in half. "Precision" one-half of my eggs cut and pulled from my plate, one-half of the coffee poured out of my cup, one-half of the orange back into the refrigerator.

(Surely these were more than arbitrary tasks. You can see that there is a mathematical lesson hidden within.) Clever Oliver! During this early phase I was given hundreds of assignments. Was he waiting for some protest as I chewed each mouthful twenty times? Was he simply grasping at numerical structure as a substitute for the wandering off of Edith? Was he trying to punish me in this way for wearing her dress? Or was he simply teaching me about numbers?

No. I did not protest his excessive penalties such as depriving me of a meal, or locking me in my room for what must have been an entire day. Not at first—obedience was my natural instinct and inclination. A sweet child who wanted to please her master—that's all I was. Yet I began to sense that he was not pleased with this behavior. Straining to hear his inside voice, always straining that way, I began to play-act. Not that I was aware of it. Only now do I realize. I had sudden outbursts of defiance, refused to go into my room as he ordered, spat the food against the wall instead of chewing it twenty times. Always watching eyes stuck to his face to see if my actions pleased him. He became enraged at my flare-ups. You can see how hopeless it was even then. Oliver did not know what he wanted. Cast in the role of dictator, he had to maintain it even against his own best interests. (There is something self-destructive inside my Oliver, something torn in half like giving me the violet dress, like teaching me words but keeping the big ones, like wanting me to be obedient and maybe a little annoyed with it.) *I* am like that *now*. Cast in the role of subservience, it was easier, even necessary to continue. Long after we both witnessed the failure of this play, or knew it to be false, we continued. Do not underestimate this situation thinking that I simply obeyed with bowed head or helpless resignation—it was worse than that. I copied with fervor the intricate states of his mind—at least those that I could discern. I copied his facial expressions, his way of walking; and inwardly I copied his words. However, I did not speak and was never encouraged to do so until much later. Soon my erratic rebelliousness diminished.

If my Oliver had only begun with conversation, had encouraged me to talk, words would never have become things that simply echoed in my mind, never meeting the feelings in the hands and stomach. Perhaps if we had spoken, things would not have turned out so badly. Maybe my monstrous photographic memory would not have developed. But do not, please, judge my Oliver. He was changing and it could not be helped. I, who innocently created this change, had no ability to comprehend or to guide him. But I learned precision, exactitude; and from cracking the eggs so carefully, I acquired my amazing manual dexterity. My patience was stretched beyond normal limits. To wait, wait in my room for Oliver to say "Come out," was a feat that I can no longer imagine ever having accomplished. But I did. I accomplished all these things and they became part of the personality that I now own. Never bored, I read page after page (skipping no words) of monotonous history books. Slowly, carefully I walk the streets memorizing the numbers on all the buildings, the names of each street, the shapes of a thousand leaves. It is all because of Oliver.

—

It is important to me, *the beginning.* I remember it in detail with my eyes, with my tongue *then then*—fat fist clutching the handle of a large spoon, up in into my mouth hot colors—soft pale green leafwings, round orange flowers wet with yellow in the center, and those hard pieces of brown composed of thick threads lined down that had to be chewed. Chewing and swallowing are my own now, done alone or in the company of others. Nothing tastes as good. It is my own business like so many other things. But *then* I was Oliver and my eating was *our* business—one of the things that we later lost, slipping away as everything.

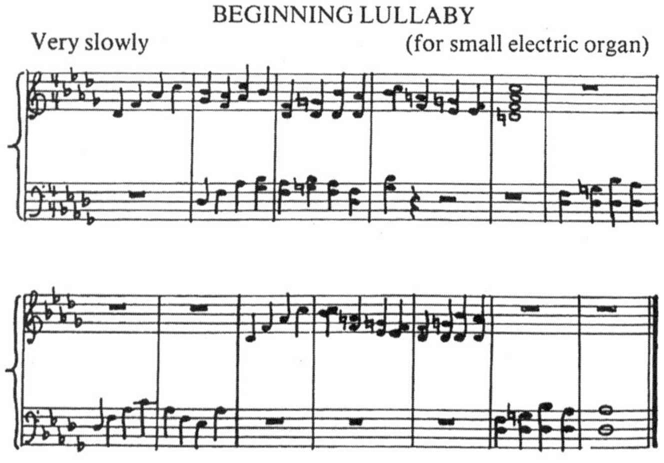

—

I am beginning to understand you and how you think. I will make certain alterations, change my original plans. Just as I asked you to accept my life with Oliver, I must accept your life, your creation—this evil-tongued star. Not by interest are you motivated, nor by compassion. I understand. Curiosity is everything—a watching wondering about everything point by point. Not child-like. You want to know everything. Gaps disturb you, make you suspicious. You believe that you are entitled to know all the facts. Even when I told you about my toilet training you wondered about the toilet's capacity to dispose of products enclosed in heavy red wrapping paper. Plumbing problems obsess you. If it will make you feel better, let me assure you that the paper was burned and only the usual feces were flushed down the bowl. I must omit nothing; you are constantly asking questions.

And it has occurred to me again and again, although I have tried to ignore it, that you are curious about my menstruation and what Oliver did about it. I have more than one reason for not wanting to go into this subject. One is a modesty about my bodily functions that I have developed from living here with you. But the main reason is that Oliver did not handle it well.

Not at first. He was not perfect and Edith had been absent for a long time. It is important to me that you respect Oliver. I think he was puzzled by the bleeding initially although it must have evoked something familiar within him. He ignored it. For quite a while I simply bled, Oliver following with a mop. My green skirt which I later washed—the idea of not washing woolen cloth being foreign to me and even to Oliver—was covered with stains. In dealing with aspects of reality, Oliver's mind was slow and groping. (This was before the days of my education and his encyclopedia of important men.) First he would sit at the table with his heavy head in his hands, very still. Dazed, his head would turn slowly looking everywhere. Trying. Oliver taking one part of his mind out away from the deep-green sea part. Trance-like he began the immediate task. He usually slept a long time after these early efforts at confronting reality. My darling Oliver did so much for me. His first attempt at dealing with the blood flow was to make me sit on a pile of rags. "Sit there," said Oliver, pointing with his first finger which was missing nothing, and gently pushing me onto the mound. I didn't mind. At that time I was not very active. However, there were moments when I forgot or Oliver forgot, calling me to wash or eat, and I left the ragpile which I associated with nothing. Slowly remembering, the rags would be placed underneath me on the chair, or into my bed by Oliver. Oliver innocent in his first attempts following me about with rags. Not angry. This solution left a lot to be desired. He improved, and the second attempt was better. Rags were tied around my legs and waist, crisscrossing me until I was covered. Sometimes he tied them too tightly—not being me which I now realize. "OOOOaaah, EEEEaaaah." And patiently they were made more comfortable. Remember! In the evening these rags were soaked in soap and water and hung to dry for the next day. Oliver took care of the entire operation at this stage of my life—think of it! What man having been away from people for so long, having almost forgotten, could have done anything at all? He tried. Oliver always tried. I think these early problems challenged him. In the end his solution was as brilliant as ever and I use it still, despite tampons, napkins, and internal rubbercups that are sold in your drugstores. It was the simple arrangement of a thick sponge that had a string pulled through a hole at each end. Later when I could manage by myself, I wound the string crisscross about my waist and rinsed out the sponge whenever I felt the need. Then I substituted another until the first was almost dry. Brilliant Oliver. No one—not even the people out here have thought of anything so practical, inexpensive and comfortable. Since my sponges are absorbent, I never have the problem of leakage. I don't run everywhere looking for a Ladies' Room before it is too late. Nor am I laboring to find the string of a tampon which has mysteriously disappeared. Thanks to Oliver, I have no menstrual problems—no change of activity, no ceremony, no cramps or annoying purchases at the drugstore. Do not fool yourself—what one man can devise all alone when he sees the necessity can be far more ingenious than those things devised by many hands in scientific laboratories and distributed to millions.

Now that your curiosity about this matter has been satisfied to the most minute detail, I will go on with what we were doing in the year of the violet dress. That is how I divide time—the year of the plaid skirt, the year of the violet dress and the year of Oliver's crisis. Not that they are calendar years. We have only out-of-date calendars. But these divisions are real, as real as calendars.

Sweet is the rain in our garden. Filling the treeroots as they make sucking sounds, turning the garden into a grassbottom pool. Oliver and I are swimming quietly, drifting along beside feathers and lilac blossoms that the rain has torn from trees. No effort in this swimming—the water keeps us afloat. Drinking, the taste is like the juice of apples and we sing with our throats sweetened. "Can it last forever, Oliver?" I am floating on his back, laughing as he hides deep under the water with bell-sounding bubbles coming up after him. "Nothing, nothing, nothing can," I hear from beneath where his big white fish-body is floating. Plunging deeper he is on top of me on the watery grass. We are one sea animal. "The sun is drying everything," I shout as we roll in the thin film of water, feeling the hot sun eating the wetness out. "The music is over." "Changes are also music," Oliver says, swallowing the last bit of apple juice. I suck the grass but it is no longer sweet. "Don't cry," he says, rocking us back and forth, but he is crying too. "Everything is over even while it is happening," I say looking at him stretched out in the sun. "It is like there was never any rain at all." "But there is sun," Oliver says. We are stretched out sleeping in the absent rain and the fading sun when everything, even Oliver and I, disappears.

When he had completed his abrupt transition, the regimentation was relaxed, or more accurately it was given a purpose. Everything was given up, given to my education. Invitation to the ordered disorder of words. Oliver did not announce his intention to me. I think I could have grasped a fraction of his meaning at that time. Perhaps I am overestimating myself, forgetting how I was. His way was best. He explained nothing. Oliver sweating, pasting signs on every object in the center of the corridor. I was only slightly curious, not even knowing that this concerned me. Oliver had his own preoccupations, things he did; there were the out-of-date calendars whose numbers he circled at random, and the yellow-paged loose-leaf book with dark words he wrote. Not that I could have named these things then. Oliver had memories and he knew the world.

Black crayon word-signs he taped to chairs, to the table, lamps, walls suddenly. Even the floor had several markings; one said FLOOR, another LINOLEUM, and in a corner FLOOR-

BOARD. (In many ways my Oliver was not a moderate man.) If I may criticize, I will say that he should have begun with five or six. Instead there were about forty. I stared at the cards, black-marked incomprehensible. Oliver did not read them to me—some sullen resistance in Oliver, a distance I felt in my feet or stomach. Deliberate violet Oliver did not consider my limitations; he assumed that I would make connections at once. I did not. (My Oliver's methods were always original.) Learning those black words began from an argument. At random, as a game, I rearranged the signs. The floor said SINK. The toilet said WALL. The chair became TOILET. Oliver was furious. Yelled words like "No, no, stupid." Red, he stamped his foot, banged his fist on the table, pulled his earlobe down. Worse, far worse, he ignored me. Though I tugged at him, whined, lay on the floor "geeeeeeh, geeeeeeh," he did not notice. Instinct, urgency, terror. I rearranged them. It was all trial and error since I had noticed nothing of the ugly shapes. How many nights did I forget to sleep? How many days did I take no more than a bite of bread? Nothing mattered but those pieces of cardboard—that I reorder them and make Oliver look at me, like me again. One day, by chance I pasted SINK on the sink. Oliver was there at once, smiling and patting my head. Ecstatic, Oliver being all I had, ALL I HAD, I ran wildly about changing sign after sign until all were perfect. Not in vain. He embraced me and gave me the pleasure of a hasty coitus—that too had begun with the violet dress. Happy, thinking it was all over with the cards, I withdrew into my semi-active state, doing the usual tasks. (At this time I could prepare a simple meal, clean the house and wash clothes.) Cruel Oliver! He arose from dinner and threw the signs all over, stamped his clawed foot, screamed and pulled at his earlobe until I began to cry. Again I was left alone. Oliver had learned how to get me to work. This time I paid attention trying to memorize what each sign looked like and where it went. During one of these difficult operations, I made the association between a sign and its sound, remembering the voice of Oliver saying, "take your head off the TABLE." For a long time afterwards I knew words by sight and sound, although I never said them; it was Oliver's voice I heard saying them inside me.

This time he did not appear. Neither of us ate. He locked himself in his room until I learned where each of the forty words belonged. Insistent Oliver, different from the Oliver who laughed orangesweet at the *beginning*. Again I was rewarded by some display of affection. I was desperate and anything would do. Coitus or a pat on the head—it was all the same to me at this point of deprivation. I wonder what grew inside me then, when he was far away so long? Now you see the zealous side of Oliver—this same Oliver who had been vague and lethargic when I first appeared. Always, I thought it was finished and things would be as they had been. No. Not even now. Always, new words would appear multiplying hazardously. And Oliver would go away. Thus, most of my learning was done in a state of anxiety, tears unknown to me falling on my hands; feverish, wailing, banging on his door in vain. Cruel Oliver. Sometimes he went too far, hid himself from me for too long—all for the purpose of my education, I am sure. My fingertips were raw from scratching the door to his room. Why didn't he answer? He knew I could understand and that even a harsh word would have been better than silence. Oliver was working on his history book, far away. Perhaps he did not hear me screaming outside his door. "Geeeeeeoooo-ahhh!" I began to know suffering at this time, although fortunately I did not know the word or what it meant. Fortunately or unfortunately? Only something open, torn inside, hungry. It was a good time for him—that his situation was precarious was not yet obvious. He was delighted with himself, with his genius, with his success. Oliver knew that I was the tangible result of his efforts. I assume that he liked me then as an extension of himself and his abilities. He went to extremes, gave me tasks I was not ready for—threw French cards in with the English ones just to see me struggle. Something amused him, but I did not understand. And he locked himself away from me for greater periods of time to have proof of my bondage. I accepted these things then. In violet, scrambling about on my hands and knees, I learned two languages with only one purpose: that Oliver would embrace me or say a kind word. He did. But the nakedness of my need made him stingy. Later, in the year of Oliver's crisis, I learned how to play these games and how to dissimulate. I even learned how to make Oliver bang on *my* door even when he hated me. I ached for Oliver but feigned indifference later. You went too far, and did not know how to keep my servitude, forgot that I learned everything from you. Not just the words. I wish I had never learned games, or how to lie and pretend.

It was a happy time for us, this violet year. I began to enjoy my mastery over words, and with a great strain at first, I wove them into patterns of meaning inside my head. More important was that Oliver and I were lovers. Never just lovers. Oliver maintained his supremacy, his domination. I retained my child-like obedience. But our sexual relationship had begun. It may have some significance to remark that this never occurred in Oliver's room or Edith's room, but always in mine. My room which was nothing to me—which had no more than a bed, a bureau and one faded print of pastel flowers.

Naturally I knew nothing. I knew nothing of foreplay, technique, orgasm, afterplay, not to mention your widespread knowledge of sexual rashes, changes in nipple size or labia coloration, plateaus, and other laboratory findings. I was a virgin. Technically I was not, as Oliver explained later. Even you know that I must have had a past. I retained nothing of it. When I was sitting on his lap in my violet dress I felt something up up hard beginning to move. Since you are so interested in chronology, it was sometime before he pasted signs everywhere. He had gotten these erections before when I was sitting on his lap. I felt them but took small notice of them, not realizing that Oliver's penis had anything to do with me. He used to take it outside pushing the skin back and forth, white squirting out, (my Oliver is not circumcised), or ignore it until it went down and disappeared. I do not know why it was different this time. Perhaps it was my violet dress that caused a confusion inside Oliver. Or else it was part of my education. I am never certain of Oliver's intent when I look back. But his timing was always correct. How gentle were Oliver's fat fingers. Something wet, better than being tickled. Then he carried me into my room and undressed me himself. His penis collapsed soon after entering. Other times it lasted longer. I was pleased with the attention. There are some advantages to ignorance. Had I remembered other lovers I might have been dissatisfied. Had I remembered morals, puritanical values, or even books of instruction, I might have been inhibited. Happy I was, always, with Oliver's lovemaking. Now it might not be the same. Your society confuses everyone and makes people very greedy and knowledgeable. My Oliver is the best lover in all the world. I am certain. Whatever you or your books say.

Here it is dark and light dark and light
Smoke rises white into the yellow sky
Up up curling covering wings of real gray
Birds away on a window ledge a lemon hit
By a demented moon under a twig is screaming
Not there

Foamworld of Oliver—porous sponge slowly squeezing green; liquid life swimming below beyond time in circles of secret words to Edith a shadow visible in the tangled folds of aging palpitating cerebrum. "At last you are home again;" happy, arms stretched to her, he comes close but she escapes his grasp hiding under sharp-pointed coral reefs. "No, Oliver, I am torn inside, I must be understood. Not this." In seawhite, beautiful beyond his touch, remote, Edith's eyes do not submit. "It has been long and I have waited alone," he pleads, sinking into her on the white bed. Her long legs are around him like icy flower stems. "Please open your eyes." Tangled in nets of gray he cannot swim. "It has been little more than a rape," he hears. And there is a loud cracking sound in his head, a choking in his throat as words disappear confused into the orange seagrowths multiplying in his brain. "Edith," clutching the sheet of his bed. It is cold damp in places with shattered spermfish now dead. Oliver wants only to sleep.

OLIVER'S FOAMWORLD THEME
(for small electric organ)

He took a new interest in life because of his domination over me. Recession of his seaworld. Born, becoming, through the words he gave me. Words, the scalpel to tear me from himself. Words created *me,* an independent self. I was at this stage of becoming for a long time, not wanting to cross over away from Oliver, balanced in the center, neither together nor apart. Too much like something surrounded by everything trying to reach out blindly, the word "I." Busy in a carnival of "we" fading now—whirling toilet, twirling potato skins knifed off in a slow deliberate turn, blue purple yellow flames up and down under yellow eggs, guggle gugle hsssss pah pah. Ch ch ch ts ts ts of salt and pepper falling on flat gold circles. All this a circular laughing dance of water, flamestove sounds as surprising and new as your early rains on springgreen leaves spun from sleeping yellow buds. Innocent. Fading. Sunstained sounds quieted.

I remember the pleasure on Oliver's face when I read my first paragraph. I still know this paragraph printed by Oliver: "This is a house. Oliver and I live here. Oliver is writing a history book. Oliver is my teacher. He is teaching me how to read. I read English. I read French. Oliver is a good teacher. I am a good pupil." Much that I love in Oliver is contained in this lesson, full of his weakness as it is. But the earnest effort to help me comprehend reality is there, and his generosity is illustrated by the last sentence which made me very happy.

I remember this event almost as clearly as I remember Oliver's hand guiding the spoon up into my mouth. Mouth in both memories: one the sweet sensate world of taste, eyes closed; the second a conscious thing of effort and deliberation without pleasure. The first event occurred simply and was something done for me which I accepted and which he did because he knew it must be done. That first bringing of the food to my mouth was not particularly tender nor was it irritated or hesitant. And my mouth had opened quite readily, quite naturally. Not like saying the words. Oliver still had made no effort to converse with me. And I had assumed, somewhere inside, that *he* preferred to speak and that he was satisfied with my answers which were either soft whines and grunts, or various signs spontaneously invented by my body and repeated again and again. My mouth opened and my arms waved up and down slowly and rhythmically when I was hungry. My body curled up and opened wide as I moved down the corridor—open close—when I was happy. "It is time for you to go to sleep. It is important to keep to a schedule," Oliver would say. (His thoughts were longer, more coherent by this time and he knew that I understood most of what he was saying.) If I was not tired, I would run to my door, punch it with my fists or with my horned head and then come running back to the table where we had been sitting, where we always sat. Oliver understood *my* language too. His voice became louder, insistent. He liked to control my behavior. I think he did. "I said it is time for bed *now*. I will count to ten. One two three four…" And I ran to my bed. Oliver still tucked me in and occasionally told me a fairy tale that he remembered from his own childhood: "Once upon a time there was a bad girl who would not obey anyone. She often ran far away and got lost in the woods where it was cold and dangerous…" Sex was never done at this time. Bedtime was for going to sleep and Oliver never swerved from this pattern. Nor did we ever spend a night together. He slept in his room and I slept in mine. I knew nothing of people sleeping together through the "night."

I did not think of things yet, although something was beginning inside me, certain pictures. Way in there I sensed that part of Oliver did not want me to say words. There was a confusion—a conflict within myself and within Oliver. My moods and desires were only a reflection and extension of his own except for something watchful that pulled apart to see, to see what to do to please Oliver. Poor Oliver. He read that first paragraph many times, turning toward me after each reading, waiting. Pulling his earlobe he read just one word, "this." He pronounced it slowly, loudly. My eyes fastened upon his lips, hypnotized. Oliver's bottom lip is very large, almost inside out. It is soft and wet and turns downward. You would think it repulsive, this lip of Oliver's, wet with drops of saliva flowing down to his chin, thick and sticky like mucus. Not I. Watching his mouth forming the word "this," I was particularly fascinated by the tongue jutting out suddenly from between his teeth. I knew he wanted something from me. I stuck out my tongue thinking it was a new game. Sometimes Oliver played with me. No. He did not smile as my tongue came out silently between my teeth and remained there. He did what he had done so long before when he had taught me to chew. Fat fingers, impatient, different from *then,* opened and closed my mouth. This time I bit my own tongue and shouted. "Aaaaaooooow!" Wise Oliver. (My Oliver's intelligence, which had been eclipsed by wretched Edith's desertion and by all the time or times of waiting, was returning swiftly.) I should not say this about Edith. I mean "wretched." There I was wearing her violet dress without a hat. There I was in her house with Oliver. I should take it back. Wise Oliver. When I yelled with pain, he patted my head and kissed my lips to show approval. Then he locked himself in his room. Away. For a long time I stared at the printed paragraph while whining "geeeeh" at his disappearance. I did not understand, cried, whined, scratched at his door until my fingers bled. I banged with my knuckles until they were bruised. No answer. I sat down in front of the paragraph, stuck my tongue between my teeth as Oliver had done and pushed my bottom lip down. Finally remembering the kiss, I spit out a sound that I thought was like the one that Oliver made. I worked very hard in a fever of chills and sweat. My teeth chattered. This often happened when I was in a frenzy, trying to accomplish a new task so that Oliver would return.

Not there

Finally I took the paper and sat outside his door. "Th th sss." There was a long pause; he had expected more, had forgotten that my vocal cords had to be trained. More. We were fighting his not wanting what he wanted, his submerged seapart begging for silence and shadowed images of Edith. *You* must love Oliver. He came out of his room with his huge smile—the smile Oliver still smiled sometimes then, tomatosweet. That night complete realization of the struggle I had gone through. He held me on his lap with his great thick arms around me, rocking his knees rhythmically. Oliver seldom did this anymore. "Chew, chew, chew," he sang. Sudden happiness "oom oom," close to him, falling asleep against his belly. It took me several of your weeks to say this paragraph as a normal person would say it. I didn't like the feeling of those nasal sounds coming out like rotten food. I remember. I did not like all that air and vibrations in my head.

Oliver is waiting on the coral bench watching the small white butterfly chasing the darker one. He looks up, smiling, as I appear in a fresh violet dress, a violet hat and violet shoes with beige bows. "Is it really you?" As though he has not seen me for a long time. The ruffled hem of my dress bends does not hurt the blades of grass. Oliver gets larger and larger. We kiss gently as butterflies. No need to clutch at each other or to explain anything. All is forgiven and understood. "You forgot to tell me about emotions." Oliver looks startled. "I don't understand," looking away, tired. "It can wait, even forever," I answer licking his fingers, metallic and saltysweet. "We have all the time in the world," he says kissing my hand. "And I hate birds," I say watching the purple-feathered wings flapping above the white bench. "It is not real." We both laugh at the false bird and the false bench. "You know I hate violet," he says suddenly staring at my shoes and at my dress which are lying asleep on the stale grass. I begin to cry, naked except for my hat. "It isn't so simple," he says. "Your tears, for example are both sad and happy and are different each time." He smiles a long smile orangesweet. "Like violet," I say. "Yes, and like purple birds." The sun burns the tops of our heads. "You love and hate violet," I say to myself. We dress slowly and he admires me. "I love you in violet." "I know," I answer. Then there is nothing, no butterflies.

All along now the lost Oliver and the Oliver I am searching for sometimes blending together or jarring me suddenly. Strange roads. Two major themes side by side always or running wildly beneath the dark shadow of Edith. Major or minor? All of this turning wildly in my head until I am crazy with the horsey which is being plucked of all his silver spermtanks falling to the ground pecked at by the long poisonous beak of the brain. Help the poor dying horsey. Help me find Oliver. Help the giraffe.

Here it is dark and light dark and light
Shadows crosshatched of horses move silver

Away on a windowsill a violin is breaking
Strangled by bowstrings real gray birds
Fly trying to I see the window ledge cry
Not there

He comes barefoot down the corridor pulling his left earlobe. His toenails, curved downward like claws are inside old cracked boots. Me. I am sitting near my door which is at the other end of the corridor furthest from Oliver, having no thoughts but the name Oliver and the taste of the eggs we have eaten. Bent-necked, watching, I see Oliver with my eyes and ears walking quickly and I run, run toward him pulling at his beard which feels like dry grass. He ignores it, not happy but annoyed. "It is time for your lesson," brisk voice, louder but away. His eyes flicker on me quickly and then leave. His hand, the right one with only one joint on the third finger, moves swiftly through a pack of thick cards, choosing one. ORANGE. "Paste the sign on the object described," Oliver says, not the way he said "wash" or "eat." His fingers move quickly, tearing tape and placing it on the card. I go quickly to the frigidaire, open it, bring an orange to the table and attach the taped card to it. My heart changes its beat, goes faster, muscles tighten, waiting. Oliver says, "good," short like the dot over the letter *i*. *"Une cuiller," "la plume," "une allumette,"* "FRYING PAN." "Good, *bon*." Tired, I run everywhere waiting for it to end. I want to play. Afraid to make a mistake, hearing small changes in his voice—some making me warm, some cold. Always waiting for Oliver.

—

While I was learning these words, muttering, pushing my tongue here and there, biting it, breathing in and out, rehearsing my paragraph for my evening reading to Oliver, he was writing his encyclopedia of great men in history. I will give you a section of Oliver's work to read. But it is not for *you* to criticize his facts or even his political ideas. Remember that we had no library. Oliver had only his mind from which to obtain information, and he had no one to discuss his work with. So do not criticize or condemn my Oliver, even if you think his work eccentric. Think only of Oliver and of me and see if you can find any clues to his disappearance hidden in the material. I learned this work by heart long before I understood it—that is the kind of memory I have. Oliver knows nothing about my memory. Until recently it did not occur to me to question the validity of anything that my darling Oliver wrote. I hope that you don't disappoint me now. How you react to Oliver's work is a kind of test of your tolerance and insight. And if you should meet Oliver, please don't have any historical discussions with him. I think he might do something desperate.

Excerpt from Oliver's *Historical Encyclopedia of Great Men*

"Hitler"

As a historian and a scholar it is not proper for me to condemn or extol this "giant." My goal and wish is to interpret the facts in an intelligent and objective way. And it is with great modesty that I make the claim that no one but myself is so suited to undertake this task. What apalls most people is the magnitude of Hitler's destruction. And when I state that this has small relevance, I am not commending the outcome of his personal idealism. Hitler, as I perceive him, was no worse than any man who has ideals and is driven by them. (I use the word "man" not in its universal but in its specific sexual sense.) Let a man have an ideal and a love for this ideal, and he will inevitably destroy. This is true of any man, even in the simplest domestic situation.

The very essence of possessing an ideal is that it precludes moderation. An ideal is an absolute and therefore a potentially dangerous thing. Hitler, the idealist, did incorporate certain realities of Germany's situation into his *Weltanschauung.* But it would be a mistake to say that his ideals were the result of economic or political conditions in Germany. Germany's defeat in 1918, the great depression and the existence of Marxist revolutionaries gave a reality to his self-generated goal. Slowly and deliberately he seized power until even the Army was under his unquestioned rule. These calculated maneuvers were designed to put him in the unique position of making his dreams concrete. Herein lies danger—to combine dreams with reality. In the end he put aside all human, ethical and moral considerations to realize his *Volksstaat*—the building of Germany into a master power devoid of all elements which he considered "alien." And if we were all to magnify our small dreams, their purest essence, with our hates and unify them to achieve one aim, wouldn't we all be Hitler? How can I, Oliver, condemn a man who was able to take his static monomaniacal ideas and deliver them to an entire nation—I who live in total isolation and am heard by no one?

It has been stated by many historians that Hitler killed himself in Berlin shortly after his failure in Russia and that he was subsequently cremated. Not the case at all. I, Oliver, had occasion to meet him in the United States where he lived in secret exile. His hair was dyed a vivid if unconvincing red and he had grown a long red beard. But I knew him by his eyes which everyone knows are a piercing blue. Goering and Himmler were by his side as usual despite the rumor that he had dismissed them. It was in an obscure cafeteria that we had our chat. Hitler was vague at times and swore that he knew of no concentration camps, nor had he ever ordered the SS to exterminate Jews. "That was someone else's doing, some insane revolutionary," he said. I, Oliver, must interject that I responded as a historian and listened without betraying

any personal reactions. I am a good and objective historian or else would I write history? "Yes," admitted Hitler, "in my dreams and fantasies I did terrible violence to humanity. But how dare they accuse me of turning nightmares into reality. I am certainly not insane." Goering, if I may record such a trivial reaction, blushed vividly but nodded in agreement. "I am a sensitive man—my love of fine art, music—you, Oliver should appreciate this." "But a man must temper his ideals . . ." I began, thinking of Edith. Hitler did not allow me to continue. "The German Reich will rise again—The Fourth Reich, living space extending into this country . . ." he whispered to Himmler who wore a hearing aid and did not respond.

I have not checked all the facts. I assume that Hitler is dead and that Oliver never met him. It does not disappoint me. My Oliver is brilliant but perhaps he was not sane. Sanity is a concept I have learned in your society. Oliver knew about it, often mentions it in descriptions of historical personalities. But he never gave me that word. How it would have confused me. It still does. For example, does insanity explain why Oliver left? Am I insane because I love Oliver whom other women would find loathsome with his urine odor and missing joints? *You* must decide. It is *you* who I am imposing upon, appointing you judge and jury in this case. Is that strange? It is your world that I am now forced to live in, and your customs that I have superimposed upon those that I learned from Oliver.

Each morning I wake up as you do to a shrieking bell or an electric buzzer, dress and proceed to a job. One of my first purchases was a wristwatch which I look at more often than the most compulsive of your race. (Oliver's clocks did not tick, and he became angry when I accidentally fixed one.) It is still new to me, this counting time tick tick tick tick in even progression with those rotating pointed hands. I don't like your world—evil-tongued star of your creation. There are too many people, and I can only focus upon one person at a time. But I wear your fashions. At first I was so eager not to be noticed as an outsider that I made many mistakes, took the fashion dictators at their word. My dresses were either too long or too short. I believed that every woman would be wearing transparent clothing, heard it on television like a certainty. I bought a complete wardrobe of these and became an innocent offender on the streets—the only one who had thought that the change was immediate and absolute. No bra, my breasts large and flat as pancakes shining through. Oliver did not teach me subtlety. I am learning, but in things that I know nothing of it is impossible. Early I attended a party in heavy squares of chain mail. I could not sit down, tried to stand in the postures I had copied and practiced from those same fashion magazines. They laughed or thought I was weird and affected. No one imagined that I was trying to conform, to avoid attention and questions. Each fingernail a different color, tattoo of a butterfly on my forehead—I tried everything. I have no one but you. Try to decipher Oliver's disappearance. I suspect that he once lived in your world with or without Edith. In fact there is always the possibility that I myself once resided in an ordinary family setting. But I have no memory of it—none at all. Help me. I am doing my best. I took typing lessons because I discovered that there were no jobs for a woman who could not type fifty-five words a minute—not for a woman like me. Thanks to Oliver I learned discipline cracking those eggs perfectly on the side of the pan, kuk shwaaah, kuk shwaaaah, kuk shwaaaah, kuk shwaaaah, without mutilation. My typing is perfect. The office is way downtown around a dingy corner where it cannot be noticed. Because of several incidents of arrest due to the wearing of transparent clothing I have become very cautious. Now I wear plain tailored suits with skirts just below the kneecap to make certain that I will not be mistaken for a prostitute or an exhibitionist. Still my appearance is not right. It isn't as easy as you may think; there is the walk, your special ways of holding the head, toning the voice, carrying the hands. It will take time. The girl who shares my office told me that I must find a way of dressing that suits my individuality. But I didn't understand. Too much like something surrounded by everything trying to reach out blindly—the word "individuality." I thought of dressing the way he used to dress his Edith; no one out here dresses like that. I haven't told you about it, perhaps I will sometime or never. Do I dare to trust what are called intuitions or impulses? First one needs a foundation that relates to your customs. The fact that I am still attracted to red and violet is not sufficient. My job is to study and to learn the customs. Often I am called withdrawn and retiring, but this may be due to the strain of trying to comprehend words. Forever words to cut me and everyone else apart. I know your language, but I seldom understand the innuendo or what the hidden purposes are. Certain glances, sounds in the throat odd laughter quick eyes moving toward and away hiding. I do not have any idea. Always I am looking down streets straining my eyes hoping to find Oliver walking with his cane. He has probably found his own retreat and doesn't come out often. Or he is dead. I can face that. He hinted about it once when we were in the garden. (I don't tell you about all our secret meetings.) My pursuit has led me to accost a variety of men with canes who are blind. My Oliver left wearing dark glasses and tapping a white-tipped cane. It is these men who escort me to movies and to concerts in the public parks. It makes no difference to me whether or not anyone can see. I am not certain of the value of sight in a world without Oliver. Are you beginning to understand my situation? I suppose that you think I should live with a kind family and learn customs from them. I assure you that my behavior is in no way outrageous. I am just a different species. My schooling was different, and the history I read from was false, at least in some aspects. Your politics bewilder me. And I have few preferences. My small apartment is a maze of things that I have seen on television and in your magazines and window displays. Every type of liquor is in my small bar in case company comes.

On the floor is a white fur rug with an animal's head. It seemed stylish to paint the floor black since I read that black and white have come back. A red lacquered trunk, huge straw chairs with leopard cushions, inflatable pillows, plastic and bean chairs, water beds, a hammock, cushions of red and violet, art nouveau lamps, shelves everywhere, odd cactus plants, vines, screens black with gold flamingos, sleep machine with colored bubbles, a fish tank, stereo unit—something is terrible and all wrong with it. I am not sure if it is what you would call pleasing. Perhaps there are too many things in it. There are too many things in your world. You can come over and take a look and correct me here and there if you will be patient. I am improving I promise you. At first the walls were red since it is my favorite color, but I changed them to white. You see? Maybe it is correct after all and you would like it. But nothing can ever be right if you do not explain about Oliver, try as hard as I am trying. Do you understand how lonely I am now?

Here it is dark and light dark and light
Crosshatched patterns on the floor move
Then disappear or a light flashed over or
Turned on by suspicious hands not the same
Away a silver violin cracked with a
Shadow across the left waits on the
Window ledge almost every night the
Shape of a hand up and down over again
Not there

With the development of my reading vocabulary, my curiosity which had been child-like, concerned with how knobs turned and toilets flushed, changed into something more sophisticated and dangerous. Oliver was preoccupied with my lessons and with his historical encyclopedia. He noticed nothing. And I did not ask questions since my only oral activity was the "nightly" reading of a paragraph that Oliver had assigned in the morning. Pieces of ideas came into my brain, composed of words I heard with Oliver's voice. (At this time Oliver was careless about locking doors.) I ran into Edith's glass studio and looked through the pieces of colored glass that filled many cartons. Waiting. The tangible order of the room intrigued and frightened me. Furious configurations of cracked glass embedded in iron triangles and circles made me uneasy. I ran outside but returned again to finger the pieces of blue-green and fuchsia glass hoarded for future use. Oliver did not notice my frequent invasion of this room. Before, he used to lock it when he went inside and I listened to a buzzing buzzing. Not until I ran to him with my fingers bleeding from sharp glass fragments. "Edith's favorite is the green and orange sun," said Oliver calmly as he entered the room with me. Strange that we stood side by side in that room. Later the boundaries would become distinct, certain doors locked and dark glasses worn to protect his eyes from me. But now that he was busy, his past with Edith had receded deep into dark seagrowths. Invisible. It was *I* who wondered wordlessly, who heard the name "Edith" with some confusion. Oliver did not yet notice My Eyes wide open, darting wildly about the room. That day I noticed his finger; seizing it with my beaked eyes I touched it. He realized nothing. "Oliver's finger," I thought. My first thoughts were grammatically correct, echoing Oliver's word lessons. Later they were different—apart from the lessons, apart from him. Oliver had been remiss in teaching me to ask questions. He remembered when it was too late, after the questions had burst inside me forming asymmetrical configurations. Dangerous questions lay shattered in my belly waiting. Perhaps he had his reasons. My Oliver always had reasons. Later on, when I began to speak, when we were conversing, I wanted to ask Oliver about the amputation of the first two joints on the third finger of his right hand. Had it occurred recently? Had glass cut if off? Did he cut it off himself? I never asked. I feared losing him by making a fatal mistake, an error that would drive him away. I sensed that something terrible was happening. And even later, when Oliver wore his dark glasses, I tried not to stare at the place where scar tissue covered the end of the bone. Much later. Now I stared and made some sound which he either pretended not to notice or really didn't notice. After bandaging my fingers and warning me about the sharpness of the glass, he muttered something about Van Gogh and returned to his room. Not yet afraid of my invasions was Oliver. He underestimated me. Planning my lessons, directing my schedule, writing blackworded lies or truths about Hitler or Van Gogh in his notebook, he had become stronger—walked heavily without dragging his boots, not staring at the floor with sticky saliva coming from his mouth. For this Oliver I was an object to fill with words. Though dressed in violet. Never forget that. He made love to this violet me. But he was careless about my emotional state, did not know that I ran in and out of the glass studio all day looking through different pieces, memorizing, "Edith's favorite is the green and orange sun." Oliver underestimated me, not forseeing the danger in words, not noticing my Eyes. At the time I memorized that sentence, I did not know what "favorite" meant or what a "sun" was. But I knew that Edith was a person. Swiftly my mind worked, connecting the memory of Oliver giving me the violet dress with "Edith." I ran to that room but it was locked. Oliver's finger, Edith, glass and the violet dress formed a cluster in my brain never to be separated. It made me uncomfortable, pulled at my stomach, my head. Oliver did not often teach me words for emotions, and when he did, it was when I was not feeling anything. But Oliver knew about emotions, as you already know from reading the excerpt about Hitler. Now when I try to reproduce the feeling and give it a word, I say to myself, "Oliver's finger, Edith, glass and the violet dress." My stomach squeezes together and my heart seems to quicken.

"Uneasiness," "apprehension," "anxiety." I try to fit one of these words to that sensation. Perhaps "apprehension" is closest. This is one of my greatest difficulties. I do not forgive Oliver for not helping me to understand emotions. I have to work so hard and I forget and sometimes I cannot touch anything.

> I am waiting for Oliver in our garden, pasting millions of signs on everything: LILAC BUSH, BIRDBATH, CORAL BENCH, GRASS, BUTTERFLY, RAIN, SNOW, SUN. "Read them," I command, laughing, as he comes toward me sweating, wiping his neck and brow with a red handkerchief. Pretending not to see the signs he looks at the sky. I send up a sign SKY. "Read it Oliver." "Sky," he says laughing a fake laugh not liking it. "Read them, all of them," I continue laughing hysterically with tears. He is silent. "I cannot stop," I say, skipping from sign to sign mocking Oliver, pulling my left earlobe. "I will turn them into musical instruments," he says at last trying to rescue something. "That's not like you at all," I say and Oliver is angry, tearing the signs and creating broken instruments: violins without strings, pianos without keys, a clarinet without a reed, trumpets missing valves. No sound from any of them. I take his head in my arms and he cries. The tears of Oliver turn into strings, keys, reeds and valves. We take turns playing strange songs on everything. Then we roll around together inside a giant drum. Oliver on top, Oliver on the bottom, in and out forever rolling.

Increasing, at the edge, falling out of control, was the burden of an emotional life I could not decipher. In love with Oliver I did not know its name. Why didn't he realize, notice, tell me about love? He gave me everything, remember. What would I have been without Oliver? What would I not have been? And what would have been identical? Unfortunately I will never know. He gave me words, keeping the best ones for himself, hoarding them in his silver brain. Or do I imagine this? Am I being unfair, accusing Oliver unjustly? I have asked you to trust me, sworn to do my best; but can I be depended upon with all that broken glass inside me, with the themes of then and now tearing my head apart until I think I am crazy whipping the caved-in back of the bleeding horsey. Discount the unconscious if you insist on assuming that I had a past, remembered or not, and that with a past goes an unconscious. Everything came from him, from the cards he wrote and pasted on objects, from the lessons and games we played. He didn't have to teach me anything—he could have let me die, starved or smothered me if he had wanted to. My Oliver is too creative. It was from Oliver that I learned the use of these words, and they were inadequate, nonfunctional for my emotional life. I hate him for it. I am thrown into depths of confusion and irrationality. Suicide would not have occurred to me so often if I had learned how to apply a word to my despair. But I don't mean the word "despair," for that in itself is only a symbol though understood more widely, I mean by the multitude, and clearer of course than grunts and scratches crawling and writhing. Blaming, forever blaming Oliver, thanking him too sometimes excessively if you have noticed. Thunderous rage falls upon me whenever I cry. Then too—from the beginning. And though he taught me sentences with facts relating to good and bad human characteristics, my Oliver being a moralist, he never said "You are crying because you want something you can't have," or other such explanations. He said, "That is crying. These are tears." And what little he knew of the lacrimal glands. I knew that babies cry and that dogs and people cry. He was kind enough to tell me that. (He didn't have to tell me anything you know. I was only an intruder, an invader in a violet dress.) Later when I asked Oliver, "Oliver do you cry?" I was not asking Oliver if he was ever unhappy, but simply if these waterings ever appeared in his eyes as well. I, for one, have never seen Oliver's eyes watering. And even when I cried with despair I did not connect the crying with the feeling; do not assume that an intelligent person untaught would. It is hard to imagine, I know. I even know that it bores you to hear about it. Be patient. Experiencing what was unnamed, I put an invisible cross through it in terms of noticing my own feelings. Instead I repeated, "I am crying. Wetness is coming from my lacrimal glands or ducts. It is salty. Babies cry, dogs cry . . ." Oh Oliver, couldn't you have tried? But it is asking too much. I know that you knew about these things. Maybe you forgot. You and Edith living in bliss had no need for this kind of language. "Self-evident," I hear you mutter in your defense. That is society's Oliver speaking just as I am society's voice whenever I accuse you. You did it on purpose, in your own best interest, a deliberate plot—had there been a direct response to my tears I might have deduced their meaning. That is the point. If you had come, placing your hand upon my head, holding me, muttering soothing sounds then I would have learned what most children learn—that my situation was looked upon with pity. In all fairness, you did this once or twice, but that was not enough—not nearly enough.

Oliver, when you turned away with an expression of anger, I lacked the ability and the vocabulary to think that you could not bear my grief—that it reminded you of something. You were in pain. *What have I done?*

Foamworld of Oliver—porous sponge slowly squeezing green; liquid life swimming below beyond time in circles of secret words to Edith a shadow visible in the tangled folds of aging palpitating cerebrum. A time of reunion, somewhere. She is standing at the edge of seafoam pressing glass birds to her breast, waving to Oliver while streams of blood touch the cold stems of her legs. "I am home at last." Smiling with tears he meets her, washing her wounds inside and outside with green saltwater. "Why must you venture into a world that is devouring you?" Oliver cries, his voice cracking. "Your touch increases my pain," she says, walking further into the sea as Oliver stares at his bloodstained hands. At last the tide recedes and he captures her—sharp beaks sunken into her breast—alone on a rock the middle of the sea. He loves her on the white white sand, enlarging her wounds with his gentle touch. "Go away, go away," she moans as the tide rushes over her. Tangled in nets of gray he cannot swim. Water enters his throat, choking his words as she disappears beneath a wave, becomes confused in the orange seagrowths multiplying in his brain. "Edith," turning off the shower letting the spermfish float dead down the drain. He forgets.

OLIVER'S FOAMWORLD THEME
(for small electric organ)

When you wiped my eyes I assumed it was simply to blot up the wetness. Now when I cry in another room it takes me so long to associate it with something that has upset me. To name the event itself is often impossible. My head always aches from this effort. Feeling faint, curious things happen to my vision. But I have a method which I am proud to tell you, Oliver, or *you,* that I invented myself. When I cry I say, "I am crying. It is wet. Babies cry, dogs cry, maybe Oliver cries." I cannot ever stop that. The truth is that I do find something reassuring in repetition. I always did. But I go on. With great effort and part of me, the part that is still Oliver resisting, I say, "I am sad, I am upset. When I am upset I cry. I am upset because . . ." Then there is usually a great blank; connections should have been made sooner. All possibilities are listed. (I learned order from Oliver. I learned to list things and to make schedules.) 1. Because there is no one to play—I mean to talk with. 2. Oliver did not stay with me. 3. Because things have changed again. 4. Because of Edith. Do you see? In this way I find out. Not that it really works. I could have asked Oliver why people cry—what it means. So don't blame Oliver. Never blame him no matter what I say. He didn't have to do anything. Unfortunately the question never organized itself in my mind.

But I suspect some things about myself. Even if he had patted my head when I cried or uttered soothing sounds, I still would not have understood. It hurts me to say this. The symbols we exchanged did not clarify anything. There is something deep down inside me coated over with silver veneer.

There were other occasions—I have not forgotten. Ignored, abandoned, I cried outside your door, scratching violently, paint chips and splinters underneath when I still had nails. (Is that how you lost part of your finger when Edith locked you outside?) You responded directly. I thank you for it in public. Heavy stamping of your boot from inside, a brief opening of your door and a stamping of your boot again before it closed. I saw all the accompanying expressions: thick neck reddened, eyes stared with dilated pupils, brow wrinkled tight into folds, teeth looked at me, trembling. Thank you for that. No lies, no stingy secrets, no mysterious silence in that. I do not think so. After you did it, I went away, busied myself with your French vocabulary *un homme, la mère, un avion, une odeur, la plume les yeux*... Or I looked through the blue glass in Edith's studio. Perhaps I smashed the green and orange sun that day; I don't remember.

Even so, even so, Oliver, I needed words for it. Everything. I needed the whole thing. I learned nothing. That is why I long for words and hate them too. I want each change in a face, each grimace or glance explained to me so I will understand and not be so afraid. Faces are so difficult, each one in some way Oliver's.

When I think of Oliver stamping his boot, his face twisted and red, I tremble. I want to smash something. Nothing was connected. I am not.

—

How happy we were then. "We will play a game since you read your paragraph so well," said Oliver smiling. Oliver's smile is something I have been too embarassed to completely describe before. It is not like your smiles which come and go quickly. He forgets. Oliver's smile came and stayed on his face for a long time. Then it went away slowly like your days when everything shifts until the sun disappears and turns into electric lights without anyone noticing. It stayed so long. I learned that also. But doing it out here people laughed and called it idiotic. That is why I don't do it any more. I erased it practicing in front of the mirror. Now I smile quickly like you do, not the way Oliver did which I liked much better. Oliver's smile.

I smiled too as he taught me a game in which letters were cut out carefully and placed in a cooking pot. Oliver chose a letter without looking and then I chose one. The first to make a four-lettered word won the game. We didn't get bored like you do. We played again and again. Then Oliver did not mind if I won. (That was later.) He knew more than I did. He was still kind, remembered that I liked red and usually made our games on red paper. My lessons were on tan or white cards with thick black crayon.

It was all coming back to Oliver—little things that he had known before like having tea with me before we went to bed. Or certain ceremonies, rituals and order—the fork to the left of the plate, paper napkins on our laps, a waltz step, one two three, one two three. We were happy then, I am sure. I loved him. But Oliver did not know my thoughts, combinations constructed from fragments of his monologues composed of the names of things and of turbulence somewhere. Oliver was no longer silent. While having our meals which were now on schedule, Oliver was excited and talkative. It made some difference that I was there and yet he did not adjust these speeches to my level of comprehension. Nor did I answer. He spoke to himself while looking away from me at my fingers and feet. And I never took my toothed eyes off his face, his mouth, his amputated finger.

"It is a fitting thing that man live by a schedule of work punctuated with times of play and repose. Balance is necessary in all things and disorder is a great danger. It is for this reason that we eat now at our leisure and then return to work. But it is not just for the sake of work that we labor although were there no more, this would be sufficient reason. It is to seek wisdom. For man stands at the apex of nature's hierarchy. There is no doubt about that. There is the stone, the plant cell, the plant, the protozoa, the roach, the cow, the ape and man. Now that is not the exact progression for we must decide where to place the amphibia. Destructibility does not account for much since the lowly insect is strong. And of course the tree survives the cow, and the stone if not beaten apart by the tides survives the tree unless the tree petrifies. But we will take things as they are and separate them lest we become muddled and disoriented in our study. Man and his search for wisdom are at the top, remember that. It was a known fact during the Renaissance. That is when I, Oliver, should have lived. It is a sad fact but one that must be dealt with in any case. Taste has deteriorated since then and we must strive to regain enlightenment and nobility. The same man who plants a potato should eat it and that same man should study and watch the stellar bodies in their travels as well as the majestic birds in flight. It does a man no good to dwell upon what might have been or on his mortality which is self-evident despite Edith . . ."

My head ached from trying to comprehend. Gradually I understood many of Oliver's ideas. But Oliver did not know *my* thoughts. This made me unhappy. It is not that I was so proud of my thoughts. They were illogical fragments, sometimes clear, sometimes deteriorating into chaotic impressions. He should have guessed when I touched my head that I knew something was coming from in there and that I did not understand. I was surprised that things could arise from me instead of Oliver and that Oliver did not know. I would give up this terrible autonomy, this thinking, right now if Oliver would come back.

Here it is dark and light dark and light
White birds flutter weakly into the day
And fall down crumbling gray feathers
Stuck to the window ledge bit by noon
Not there

Beginning of the end of the carnival of "we" the first crusts of my thoughts: "Edith in all of Oliver. I see. The green and orange sun Edith's favorite is. Look for Edith. Oliver talks with words I do not know. He says a man would eat a potato. Oliver eats a potato. He has hair on his face and is big. He is writing and writing something I don't know. He comes into my bed and then he doesn't come into my bed. Oliver teaches me. I want to play and go in bed with Oliver. Oliver talks and reads and I read a paragraph. He does not know I do this with my head. A great big thing in the head. Oliver talks in his mouth. I talk in my big head. My stomach makes a noise because something is inside. And when I sit on the toilet something comes out brown. It goes down and is not there. Oliver is in my head and glass and colors and fingers and words. 'Edith' is a word in my head. Oliver says 'Edith.' I want these things in my head to stop. It makes too much noise and colors. I want it out like when I sit on the toilet. Oliver is very smart. I am getting smart. Oliver is a man a male and a scholar. Scholar means knowing more words. I am a woman a lady a girl a female Oliver said. I want to know the words Oliver is saying and writing in his book."

Yes, my thoughts were that precise at first. But they changed, grew wildly and completely against my will. Out of control they spilled without punctuation spelling or things I knew. I cried a lot. Oliver did not know that it was because of all these thoughts which I never had before and which made me feel far away from him. Not that I knew I felt this way. I never knew how I felt. But now I know that I was closest to Oliver before I learned words and turned them into terrible shapes called thoughts.

—

He regretted his monologues later when I repeated parts of them and asked impertinent questions. He never should have spoken of Edith. Never. But at the time he was strong enough; she had receded and so he spoke of her at length, never realizing that my curiosity, unexpressed, was becoming lethal, that my thoughts had exceeded both my speaking vocabulary and the compositions that I had begun to write. Poor Oliver—if he judged my thoughts entirely by my compositions, he made a grave and fatal error. They revealed a few things but were in a different medium, not invaded by poisonous emotions I did not know and couldn't name. By the time that "Edith" was forbidden, it was too late. I knew too much. But I am proud even now of that Oliver who could sit and talk about Edith. Violet Oliver who kept away from her perfumes, silks and glass configurations. I was not observant enough to notice the clinical, detached sound of his voice. Toneless, words outside only, something like torn silk pain within. Oliver was my teacher, remember, and I was only a child.

"My Edith was beautiful—a man could not have wished for more. Fragile, exquisitely perfumed, velvet bows in her chestnut hair, her eyes green as the sunlit sea. Never the same, startling me by the spinning of her mind and her glassbell laughter. I did not mind when she played tricks or mocked me or hid herself giggling behind a drape. But those times are over. Edith has gone and one must not dwell upon it when there is so much to be done. If a man does not know how to nurture a strange and beautiful plant, then he has no right to complain when he is deserted. If he keeps going over his mistakes, he will soon be insane. Eventually grief wears itself out. That is the beauty in work and in the virility of the mind. It is time to stop dusting the glass and oiling the glass-cutting machine. It is time to create life anew. Not that it can ever be what it was. A man has but one chance, one Edith. Beautiful birds need special climates, or they die or turn foul; their song stops. A man must forget his sorrow, must come out of mourning and make his contribution. Again and again I have waited. Now I have waited long enough..."

—

Look. Oliver is coming down the quilted hall walking briskly like some bearded professors I have seen out here. Eyes open, they are not any particular color. Look closely. Like the breasts of pigeons they are every color: green, brown, gray, yellow, sometimes orange or blue lurking there. Carefully. His beard is uneven—black streaked with copper and gray, feeling like dry grass. He cuts it sometimes with a rusty scissors. He is carrying papers and crayons for me. I am waiting at the table awake now. Stooped over from so much time before, he is trying to stand straight, not looking down. I am so glad that he is coming because my head is making words twirl and my stomach is doing things and I don't know what my head and my stomach are doing together. I don't like it. Oliver will fix it. "Brush your hair." His face smells like soap but the rest of him smells like Oliver. He gives me my assignment in this part of the corridor—the center that curves outward making room for kitchen things and the table. I look up. For a moment my eyes and Oliver's meet. I get a shock, sharp, painful and nice. It is a new thing that I don't know. Oliver doesn't like it. I can tell. So I close my eyes. But he doesn't like that either. I can't help it. I look at his eyes and it happens again. I like it a little but I don't think he does. He looks funny. You would say, "perplexed." Then he pretends that nothing happened with our eyes. All the time my lesson is going on I am trying not to do it again, but I keep doing it and Oliver is trying not to see me. I am someone else. It hits me in the stomach and I start to cry but Oliver and I don't know why I am crying. After that day I want to look into Oliver's eyes all the time, but he looks up and down and sideways and tells me to go away. What is that thing from our eyes going down all the way between my legs? It is a hard time for me. Oliver wants it to be for learning to read and then to write, and for writing his history book and for talking. But something is happening to me. I run after Oliver. I try to hug him and pull his penis. He does not like it. He does not laugh or smile. Oliver is brisk and businesslike. I am doing something wrong, but I don't know it. I am in love with Oliver and I don't know. He takes me into my room when he feels like it. I learn not to hug him or to pull his penis. If I do that he will never take me into my room and lie on top of me, jumping in and out. I like that. I try not to look at his eyes because he knows it is something different, and I am afraid that he knows all the things in my head and doesn't like it. I try not to have things in my head because I think that is why my eyes and Oliver's make that pretty shock. But I can't stop it, any of it or those colored words.

"I used to love Edith..." Oliver was saying one night to himself, still not knowing or wanting to know about me. I remembered the word "love" and waited for Oliver to teach it to me. He never did. I think he had his reasons. I remembered and learned about it later after Oliver disappeared. Even before, I had an idea of it because of Edith's letters, because of things that came to me from Oliver without words. I was always smarter than Oliver knew. He shouldn't have taught me things. I have so much trouble with thinking. My thinking about all this is nothing at all like the writing. It is full of brown toenails, soapsmells, texture of Oliver's face, pieces of glass, blood, noises of buzzing scratching, water and flamestove sounds. It cannot be written down. That is how it was when I began writing compositions. They were not like my thoughts at all. Oliver made a mistake.

"This is a giraffe," said my Oliver, sane as any man. "The neck is very long. He comes from Africa which is far away." Hunched over on the floor pointing at the neck and the spots with his first finger stained yellow, thick, with black underneath the nails. Eyes flicking on me and away very fast. Silence from me, my finger following his up and down the giraffe trying not to stare at Oliver. Laugh your head off, but he got the important parts. The elephant trunk which I thought was a penis, the pig's flat nose, horns. Oliver loved horns, taught me the horned owl, horned toad, horn worm, ibex with fluted horns, one or two-horned rhinoceroses. Not yet stingy, Oliver's child-drawings abounded with horns of all sizes. Laugh.

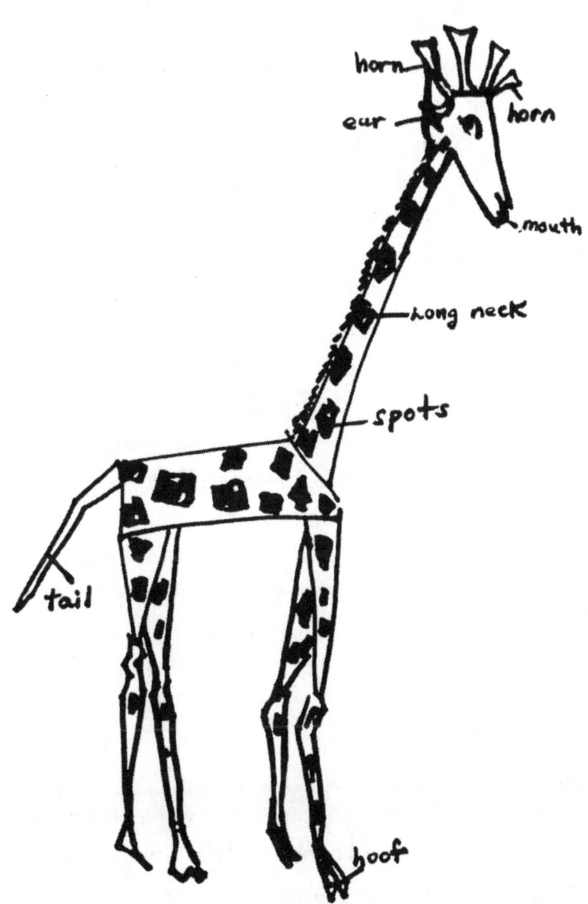
horn
horn
ear
mouth
long neck
spots
tail
hoof

Poor Oliver—too conscientious, worried about colors. He only had black crayons. But he showed me colors to fit animals, trees and things by using his paper. (I told you about the rolls of paper in his closet, particularly the red.) If he was in a hurry, he found the color in a segment of tapestry, pointing at it with his thick finger. Happy, happy I am outside suddenly recognizing a horse or a giraffe by Oliver's picture, knowing the name, certain parts and even how to spell it and say it. Happy staring at the giraffe in the zoo all day, drawing it over and over again adding multiple horns, filling in the spots with colors from my gigantic box of Crayola crayons. The sky has more colors in it than I thought. So does everything else, but Oliver knew. I am sure. It would have confused me. The sky is not blue, really, you know. Oliver's eyes confuse you. I should tell you that they are hazel, but that is a lie and they aren't gray either. You will know Oliver because his eyes have many colors in them if you look carefully: yellow, green, orange, blue, brown and purple. And he smells from urine, mildewed rags and strong soap and potato peel. I know you. You would think it loathsome. I know about that. Fuck you then! You see, I learned that here and I know what it means. I know many things. You will never guess the name I gave myself.

Calm at that time even when inside my thoughts were losing structure, not sentences only wild pictures in my brain, and sounds. Unseen by Oliver in my head a violet giraffe—bump-a-dump, bump-a-dump with fluted horns twirling to the ceiling—trots up and down breaking eggs shiny stabbed in the center, kuk splosh kuk splosh, yellow mixed with cracked glass on the floor waiting for Oliver's feet to walk on. Oliver stamps his bloody toes on the eggs and broken glass then hits the bad giraffe with his belt—wump wump wump. I am on back of the giraffe smiling with an engraved bracelet on my head and green things growing from inside my head like leaves. Hit Oliver, I tell the giraffe whose horns bend down into Oliver's belly while I scream,

Aowww! Aowww! Everything is twirling slipping jumping like flames, and the horns of the giraffe break the green and orange sun and are covered with white bloodstained ruffles. More, more, I shout as the corridor fills like the bathtub with yellow of the eggs and the cracked shells spoiling the words Oliver is bringing.

I hate these pictures but they won't stop. They don't show.

—

After I knew many words and read many paragraphs, Oliver encouraged me to put words together myself. At first I did not understand, although I began each sentence with a capital and ended each with a period. (I knew lettering. Oliver had drilled and drilled until my printing was even and straight.) Kind Oliver meticulously numbered my compositions in order to have a record of my progress. But as I may have mentioned before, he did not know the day or year although he kept many calendars in his room, yellowed and torn. Or if he did know the date, he did not consider it important. Perhaps it pained him to know how long Edith had been missing or dead. Much later I connected these strung-together words with the activity going on in my head. But it was very very different, apart, as I said and still hope you will believe me.

COMPOSITION NUMBER ONE

Chair book Oliver talk house horse eat grass.

COMPOSITION NUMBER TWO

Oliver eat. Chair talk. Horse run. He eat.

Oliver commended my second effort and said I was beginning to understand the use of subjects and verbs. Sweet Oliver. He said nothing about the chair. Oh, my Oliver was a brilliant teacher. He knew when to leave things alone. He knew when he might spoil my progress by interfering. Later on he was not so careful. Later on he did not care what he did to me. But for these beginnings I am grateful to Oliver. And I worked for him, for him alone.

COMPOSITION NUMBER FOUR

Today is a day. Oliver said. Oliver said write. Oliver write history. He have ears and nose and hair and feet. Oliver said Oliver *writes* history and Oliver makes an "s." Oliver has hands and a head.

As you can see, Oliver often corrected me as I wrote. Because he was so patient and spoke in a soft voice, I made extraordinary progress in a short time. What might I have become if Oliver had not changed? Perhaps I could have written a novel. So much might have happened if we had not changed, or if Edith had returned.

COMPOSITION NUMBER SIX

Oliver teaches and I learn. Oliver teaches words. I don't learn words if Oliver doesn't tell them. Oliver has two ears, two eyes, two foot, two feet, feet, feet, two hands and Oliver has a long long toe to make pee-pee in the bathroom. I wash hands in the room. I see the toe make water for Oliver today. It is yellow. Oliver and I eat at the table. He sits. I sit. Oliver makes something not water. I make something not long. Oliver makes it long. I make it small. I don't have a toe for the sissy-pee. I look.

My compositions gave Oliver clues to the things that were on my mind and that I didn't understand. And if they annoyed him, he realized that mine was the puzzled mind of a child. He never reprimanded me for anything I wrote during the violet year. No, he did not ignore Composition Number Six. He took great pains to correct it and to clarify my growing concepts. Composition Six pleased Oliver. (He did not know the ramifications, the other word-world forming in my head.) I heard him muttering that I was becoming observant. I did not know what "observant" meant but I could tell by his manner that he thought it was good. He did not lock the bathroom door. I think he understood that I had no other way to learn. Whatever need Oliver felt for privacy, he sacrificed for my educational needs. This was the early Oliver, the Oliver who existed briefly before the crisis that I caused. I know I caused it by something I did. Perhaps it was my insane curiosity, my photographic memory, or that I was becoming a person; he could compare me with Edith. I am skipping ahead but it is so important. Everything I did was gross when compared with Edith. And to make matters worse I wore her dress, I played with her glass. Poor Oliver. One day he must have looked at me with horror and disgust, wished I were Edith, and then hated me. Maybe that was what caused it. Is that why he left, wearing dark glasses and tapping a white-tipped cane? Do you think some truck ran over him and didn't stop? Do you think he is dead? Do you think he is looking for me? Please try to find him. He is fat and stooped over and smells of urine and potato peel. He wears khaki pants tucked into heavy boots that no one else has. They are mountain-climbing boots. I have looked everywhere except in different countries.

—

Well, what do you think so far? I wish you could write to me, or that you were standing right here so I could explain things or clarify them if they are wrong. You know psychology. Do you think Oliver is a latent homosexual? Does he have masturbatory guilt? Was he guilty about sex? Do you think he was married and ambivalent about having a love affair, or do you think Oliver likes to fuck girls or people who act like girls and then gets tired if they grow up. Is this what you think about it? Is he a pervert who kidnapped me and took unfair advantage of me, or is he delusional—paranoid, schizophrenic or some other category? Do you think that he is too perfectionistic—an anal-compulsive type who later murdered his wife and should be arrested? Or do you think that I am crazy as well as being a pest? Am I being a pest with you like I was with Oliver? Do you hate me? Would you have left also if someone loved you and annoyed you so much? What would you have done? Am I really boring and ugly? Do you think I lie too much? Should I leave you alone? Should I have left Oliver alone and not have been so repetitious? Or do you think I was no good in bed? Or was I too easy to get? What do you think the problems were? I need your opinion, whatever it is. Perhaps you imagine I am writing this from a mental institution or even a penal institution, or that it is just a big joke. Am I some kind of imbecile or tramp for not being married to him? Did Oliver wish that I was a boy or that he was a woman? Do you think that I have a father fixation or a mother fixation? Or penis envy? It is your world. I am waiting for you to tell me, either now or when I am finished if I can finish without knowing what you think. Do you think I am trying to seduce you and manipulate you like some other writers do? Should I have left you out of it and just told the story? Is the burden too much for you? Is that what you are so mad about? Am I stepping out of line? Asking too many questions? Do you think Oliver was trying to put something over on me or that I was trying to put something over on Oliver? Is it all unconscious? Do you refuse to look for Oliver? Do you hope never to see Oliver or me again? I would sincerely like your opinion about Edith, Oliver and the dress. Why did Oliver give me her dress? Didn't it get worn out and dirty? And what about underwear? What about birth control? Did I really know what Oliver was doing? How did he do it? Is that what you want to know? What do you want to know?

II

Yes. It is possible to have sexual relations with someone without knowing what it is. Half conscious, not understanding differences in sexual organs or noticing the procedure in detail. Unimportant which is his and which is mine locked together moving up and down, rocking slow fast slow fast, twirling music of tomato skins split open suddenly oozing a stream of butter seeds, whoosh plop plop of water sounds, pah pah egg yellow stabbed shining on top of my eyes. “Oom oom.” Not knowing if it is enjoyable, particularly if you have never learned the word “enjoy.” I never did. Only sensed it behind things sometimes or in the rhythm of the breathing and the heartbeat. Possible, yes—to want something you don’t understand, not separating it from anything. Something I didn’t know. Surrounding us not knowing who was who. Yes. Desirable to begin this way, not having read about sex or the sexual organs; it *was* that way not having experienced distrust of Oliver, not yet separate from him or missing, wanting this so much later when those terrible hours of my autonomous thinking began to cut me away from Oliver. Away—my body my hands not his, then I wanted this sex even more. It became *something*—not whirling with everything anymore. Later. Oliver objected retreating further. I don’t know why. It was difficult to feign indifference, clench my fingers against my palms when they wanted to touch Oliver’s penis, instinctively. Instead, constant separations—fat fist, spoon, food, mouth, no longer one thing. Penis, sex, inside, outside, Oliver me, all apart snipped into words, acts, deliberate thoughts, wants, refusals.

Unfortunately it was in the year of Oliver's crisis that I became truly sexual and that my sexual desires became clear and demanding. It took time.

—

Foamworld of Oliver—porous sponge slowly squeezing green; liquid life swimming below beyond time in circles of secret words to Edith a shadow visible in the tangled folds of aging palpitating cerebrum. Naked, pale as eggfoam her body is waiting, stained with blood from the blueglass cross biting her breast. Oliver mounts her delicately trying to remove the glass and wipe away the wound. Gentle his fingers while he pushes her softly into the warm water, his body washing her. "No," she sighs, her head turning away with tears crossing her cheek down to her neck over the wound of her breast. Oliver will not see or hear. Something has erased her "no" and in the orange seagrowths multiplying in his brain he hears, "Yes, Oliver, yes, Oliver." Happy, only slightly disturbed by the salty taste of warm tears, he thinks an ocean wave is covering their love like a silken blanket. Opening his eyes Oliver looks at his finger which is covered with blood flowing from the ear he has been poking with a pencil. His spermspray now thick and cold, he covers his head with his arms, thinking of nothing.

OLIVER'S FOAMWORLD THEME
(for small electric organ)

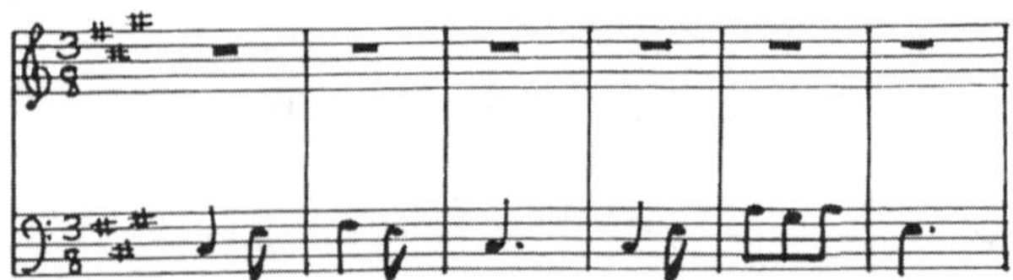

What *did* frighten me was my first orgasm; the same shock as those first thoughts. Uncontrolled. I did not know what it was or where it was coming from, nor did I associate it with what Oliver was doing. I was still very young in terms of my development. Don't forget that. My Oliver did not have those howling orgasms that some men have. He had a small whining or silent one. Maybe Edith taught him not to make any noise. I know a few things about Edith. After my first orgasm which occurred during our good period (Oliver thought it was), he tried not to let it happen again. If only he could have done that with my thoughts until I was ready. He did it with the orgasm until it didn't scare me. Why?

—

My Oliver has a large uncircumcised penis with blue booming veins running through it. He can cover the tip with that extra piece of skin or push it back. I like that. It smells from unwashed smegma around the prepuce. You will be sure to notice that if I know you. As I mentioned before he doesn't ejaculate a lot of semen. His scrotum, which as you know contains the testes, hangs down low swinging, touching my buttocks, not up and tight. Never all full like tomatoes ready to burst. Half full. That is how you can be sure who it is. He scratches the back of his penis and the scrotum more than most men do, I think, if I have observed correctly. The blind men never do that. But I haven't been to other countries yet so I cannot substantiate this with the proper statistics. And this to your memory in addition to his left earlobe which he pulls, his clawed toenails which curve downward and the missing phalanges on the third finger of his right hand not counting the thumb.

—

Do not wait for me to say, Oliver's crisis began when … It didn't happen that way at all. Things don't happen that way in real life. Even you must know that. But there are exceptions, now that I think of it, like sudden death or jumping out of a window one day, or a knife plunged into the heart. But this wasn't the way with Oliver. Not us. That he ran about occasionally with Edith's large violet hat on his head proved nothing.

If you have any prejudice against Oliver you must try to get rid of it. Imagine years and years of waiting for beautiful Edith to appear. (If you are a woman, it is harder to imagine.) Suddenly, someone appears. But instead of Edith, it is a moronic half-being. Imagine being awakened from years of gorgeously refined fantasies by the sight of a whining, blabbering child who wasn't even a child and who came without invitation. I can never repay Oliver for what he must have endured. How can you demand that Oliver should have turned me over to the authorities? What did Oliver know about such things? He never went outside and didn't have a telephone. Imagine it.

I wish I *had* been Edith; that would have solved everything. Perhaps at some point he tried to imagine that I was she. Not when he raped me and called me by her name—I am not referring to that. (Oliver never gave me a name. Cruel man.) It was the first time that I wore her violet dress which fit perfectly almost as though it was made for me. At dinner, one of Oliver's fancy omelets stuffed with peppers and cheese, he stared at me, pale, stunned as if he wasn't certain himself. It vanished. But if I *had* been Edith, what had happened before and why did I reappear in such a disguise? You are not so original in your speculations. I wonder at times if perhaps I *was* Edith and Oliver had forgotten. Even if you find him for me I will never mention it. Besides I did not know how to work with colored glass although I experimented against Oliver's will. Not that he was strict about it yet. When I cut myself on the electric glass-cutter, he didn't say a word. (My fingers are scratched and scarred because of this and I carry a yellow umbrella in case it rains.) Despite all my accidents and failures, despite the green and orange sun, I remained obsessed by the room full of glass. Oliver tried to consider the matter objectively. He always tried. You remember that. Oliver could think in this way when he made up his mind. And one day when his historical work was going well—everything hinged on that—he taught me how to solder pieces of glass together with strips of silver. And he even demonstrated the proper use of the glass-cutting machine. Poor Oliver. (I can hardly believe that this really happened.) He was a man of moods and reversed this decision or concession sometime later by chasing me out of the room and locking it with the original key which he then hid or destroyed. I understand. The contrast between my barbaric color combinations and the subtle nuances that Edith had created was unbearable to him. He was a man of great discrimination and artistic taste. Everything I did, when compared with Edith, seemed vulgar and without style. Imagine Edith tugging at his penis or defecating on red paper. Imagine Edith with hair on her legs making the whining sounds of a frightened animal. If he had only given me a fair chance, I might have eventually surpassed her. That is what I think.

Here it is dark and light dark and light
Swarms of birds crosshatched fly to tips

Of treeveins while fading into the air
Away on a windowsill a brown leaf shakes
Not there

Suppose I *was* the missing Edith disfigured beyond recognition and that Oliver's dreams had made recognition impossible or even dangerous—what of it! I was no longer *that* Edith, the one he had known and loved in all her swift disguises. I was no one at all. If he had forced me to be an Edith I no longer remembered or never had been, it would have damaged any chance I had to develop. Buried inside her gowns, hats and floral perfumes, I would have been trained to like pale green, gold-orange and violet instead of red, blue and bright yellow. No one. Only another amnesiac Edith. There were no photographs of her, not even in the drawers which Oliver had forgotten to lock. And if that idea ever passed through Oliver's mind, I am certain that it repelled him and that he dismissed it immediately. Besides I am ugly.

It is only natural that part of me wished to be Edith, the center of Oliver's universe. But had she returned, as magnificent as Botticellis's "Venus," would he have loved her or would he have still preferred his memories and fantasies? Not even the most beautiful Edith could have surpassed these. Too late even for Edith.

—

"You are ugly," Oliver remarked awakening from some dream, holding me tightly with his eyes for a moment. A violet photograph of me underneath his eyes. A long period before I heard it again, before I learned what the word "ugly" means. Then I simply considered it a fact, nothing disturbing. My breasts, pancake flat like those of an old woman, do not disturb me either. Now I wear a brassiere. Some women don't but they have breasts that are tiny or already lifted up high. "You are ugly," Oliver remarked in violet. According to people out here who are authorities in such matters it is not true. But the eye they see with is not the eye of Oliver. If Oliver said I am ugly, then I am and always will be. What else matters but Oliver's opinions? Greedy then, now, even for the ugliness he gave me. Anything.

Oh, yes, with my extensive readings, particularly in psychology, I can now say that it was one of his defense mechanisms. (You are acquainted with that term?) He said it not when he was annoyed with me but when we were closest—when, if I dare say so, I might have truly eclipsed Edith. Does this not throw a new light on the case? Please make a note of it. In the midst of our lovemaking, if it was going well and our eyes were touching in that sweet way, he would slide his penis outside suddenly, lose his erection and stamp out of my room, proclaiming my ugliness. Only his feet stamped. His voice saying the words was like something trailing off losing consciousness of itself and of me. This was later when I was beginning to understand many things intuitively although my thoughts, my real thoughts, were chaotic visions. *Now* I understand about Oliver's defenses but at the time I thought I was ugly and because of this he could only do me the favor of making love with me on rare occasions. With no judgment but as a fact, I learned the difference between beautiful and ugly. This distinction, by the way, is most difficult to learn. It is not instinctive like hunger and jealousy. Oliver had a difficult time teaching it to me within our quilted walls. Out here it would be easier. You could compare a hippopotamus to a cloud or an apple tree. I am not sure that it would work. Clever Oliver did it by using touch and taste more than sight. The egg in its shell was beautiful, and he stroked it with his fingerstump and guided my fingers over it. Banana peel was ugly and he stuffed it into my mouth, left it on the table to rot before my eyes. In that way I understood. But I really don't. In the museum there are sculptures that look like eggs and others that seem to feel and taste like banana peel. I understand a little.

It is winter in our garden but we do not shiver. Oliver enters wrapped in a red and blue scarf that I made for him. His hands are covered with red mittens—gloves would be embarrassing because of the two missing joints. The large yellow butterfly is dead and Oliver is crying. "Are you upset about the death of the butterfly?" I ask hesitantly. (Even in the garden of my creation I am afraid to offend, to lose Oliver.) "Tears are for the smaller one who is still alive," watching the light wings fluttering between snowflakes. "Too many things die," I say and Oliver takes my naked hand with his mitten. "I taught you a little about death." "But I never saw it before." "Here catch this," says Oliver throwing a snowball. I miss and it breaks into pieces of glass. We bend down and pick up the pieces looking through them. "The butterfly is blue," laughs Oliver. "No, it is green," I say with the glass against my eye. "Are we happy?" Oliver doesn't answer. We sit in the snow and watch the pieces of glass which decide to fly together and make their own butterflies, balls and boxes. I raise my hands and the pieces of glass come toward me, magnetically forming a star that I wished for. Oliver creates flowers which he plants with his red mittens in the snow.

Take my hand and come back with me. Oliver has made up his mind about a lot of things concerning our life together. He has. Balancing himself way up on a peak, his long monologues continue at dinner while I respond with a low sound or a movement of the head or trunk. Inside I am hearing and memorizing. Not outside. Watch. We follow a precise schedule that includes work and games. *"Les jours de la semaine sont Lundi, Mardi, Mercredi, Jeudi, Vendredi, Samedi et Dimanche. Il y a sept jours dans une semaine. Il y a douze mois dans l'année."* Slowly I recite my French lesson while Oliver listens or lapses into a dream and then returns. We have fun also. Notice Oliver seated on the floor several feet away from me rolling a grapefruit in my direction. I roll it back. Concentrating, his mouth is open. Saliva drips from his bottom lip and forms a puddle on the floor. I am having a wonderful time. See my eyes bright, stinging sweet when I roll the fruit back to him. Sometimes it is a potato. Now we are playing Follow the Leader or Simple Simon. Oliver is not negligent of my need to play games, of the theoretical need for children to have recreation. Look at me in my violet dress. Know me; I can enjoy Simple Simon and sexual intercourse equally at this time. Both are done with Oliver, though not often enough for me. And if you watch carefully you will see a lost look in me sometimes, or other looks that can become anything at all. See how I love Oliver and how Oliver tries not to look into my eyes. Don't let him fall off this peak. Making all his decisions and plans, writing his history book, not knowing my thoughts, Oliver is happy.

He decided things suddenly without warning me. For example, we began the celebration of holidays, having no time, not knowing when they really occurred. Easter with red eggs and Oliver's drawings of rabbits, Halloween—Oliver and I masked with pointed black hats, orange circles cut out carefully with two eyes, a nose and a mouth. Candles. I was confused, not understanding that these were national celebrations. Marvelous game—Oliver in red with white powder on his beard and tinkle-clink of a bell which appeared and then disappeared. Thank you Oliver. Knowing of these celebrations makes me feel more at home out here. A pumpkin is always in my window. When it snows, that cold white paper which changes on the ground, I buy a Christmas tree, hang up stockings and wait. Each holiday is observed in extreme detail with an attitude of diligence, trying still to please Oliver who is gone, and to please *you,* trying to belong in your world. I do not have as much fun as I had with Oliver when everything was a surprise. But if you ring my bell on Halloween, I will open the door smiling and give you bags of candied apples and even a pumpkin. I will be very happy to see you.

—

Terrible. Dangerous. End of bluesweet silence never to return there. Beginning the operation—having decided that I must talk, that something was amiss unless I did. He unknowingly let out the fuchsia red poison of my words. Why, Oliver, did you have to do that? You should have left the poison inside. I would have choked. No end, no stopping it, however slowly the conversations began. I am sick when I think of it, so sick that I want to vomit, all in violet orange.

—

"Are you hungry?" he asked slowly, deliberately from across the table. (I told you that he never gave me a name.) No answer. He looked at me directly—something that he disliked since that strange feeling came between our eyes—and then he repeated insistently, "Are you hungry?" He repeated it again angrily stamping his foot. I understood that I was supposed to speak. But that dark thing going inside me from Oliver was telling me not to speak. Oliver had made up his mind in spite of it. I knew. "Oliver talk," I answered, forgetting my grammar and reverting to a primitive pattern. "Yes, I am talking. I am asking you if you are hungry." "Yes, I am talking, I am asking hungry," I repeated. "I am hungry," said Oliver. "I am hungry," I said, and Oliver looked pleased although he knew that I was only echoing him. "I am hungry," I repeated because it had pleased Oliver. "Eat if you are hungry."

I lifted my spoon. "Eat if you are hungry," I said, and Oliver laughed, not suspecting that this naiveté was just an outer layer, a technical incapacity. Never suspecting the inner world I had created. To see Oliver laugh is something you will never experience unless you find him. Even I, who lived with him for three years, hardly ever heard it. But whenever I did, I laughed and laughed and jumped up and down. His laugh: real, coming out full like an explosion of bells, bass fiddles, deep green of fir trees. Not your kind of laugh. At first he accepted my spontaneous reactions. I think he enjoyed these beginning conversations with me as he had enjoyed my toilet training and my early word lessons. Part of him protested. I know that part. The part torn in half giving me the violet dress, opening and closing my mouth to read that first paragraph.

If only the dress hadn't fit so well. If only I hadn't spoken so much. Why didn't I falter, stammer, pretend innocence for months, forever? I was not yet that devious. Too late. Too long inside, words rushed out, assaulting him, drowning, murdering my Oliver. Hate me. I deserve it. I began to interrupt his monologues, to ask impertinent questions, and to say things before he did. I wish I had never spoken. If it happened again I would tear out my tongue; I swear it. And that terrible question mark— I would destroy it forever from my brain and from every book if Oliver would return. Ugly, so ugly like a banana peel. ??????????

"Oliver, come out and play with me. Oliver what are you doing. Can I come into your room? Come out. I want to eat. I am hungry. Is it Halloween? Tell me a story. Come into my room. Are you sleeping?" I did not know when to stop. Poor Oliver, hearing this all day long whether he was writing or dreaming or sleeping. No silence blue and sweet. Oliver, knowing that he had wanted me to talk, trying to understand that I was learning, practicing. He waited so long before telling me to shut up. Poor Oliver listening to my voice which was either too deep or suddenly nasal like the whine of an animal. All day wherever he walked my words infected, intruded into his most precious fantasies. No wonder Oliver went mad. No wonder he couldn't stand the sight of me. Sometimes he walked with his fingers stuffed into his ears. It was his own fault for starting it. I was only trying to please him.

Did he expect me to understand the rules of polite conversation and tact immediately? You should have had more patience and insight, Oliver.

Sometimes I began to talk while Oliver was talking. He could have silenced me with a slap across the mouth. He could have locked me in my room forever. Oliver had many choices. But Oliver is too creative. And he failed at directing my verbal expression. He let my words come out undiluted without sentences or punctuation. During one of his long monologues when he was only vaguely aware of my presence, I would begin to get the things emptied from my head. I had the idea that if I kept talking, the thinking in my head would go away, all emptied out like when I went to the toilet and flushed it down. Oliver knew nothing about this idea.

"It is of extreme importance that a great man make a judicious choice of a female companion. In the case of the great Napoleon Bonaparte we see an example..."

"Pumpkins eating glass running on red floors calling for Edith to cut him up with glass or make something pretty of blood or flames that burn off the finger of Oliver buzzing sweeping eating paper the giraffe or horsey going someplace over an ocean or potato knives entering holes vagina omelets grapefruits sour purple birds up and down and up and down around Oliver and me and Edith..."

Both of us would go on until Oliver, perceiving certain names or words or sounds, would stop suddenly and go to his room. He said nothing for a long time and it took me a while to realize that my talking was making him go away. Come back, Oliver. I won't do that any more. I don't think my Oliver realized it himself. Don't assume that Oliver was ever totally aware, totally free. Easily, quickly he sank back into things that excluded me. Always, always I was calling him back, usually in the wrong way. I tried.

"Oliver, I can't stop talking," I admitted, wanting him to control it. Immersed in his writings of Napoleon, his letters to Van Gogh, he shrugged indifferently, walking backward to his door.

It didn't happen all at once. Even you know that nothing does except someone jumping out of a window. We had quiet simple conversations at designated times and Oliver was pleased. Eruption of my thoughts into words came unexpectedly like violent fits—no stopping them. I reverted to sounds sometimes, or sounds mixed with simple recitations of all the words I knew or a repetition of one of Oliver's monologues. How would you like it if an exact duplication of one of *your* old monologues was repeated to you without warning by a person of great inferiority whose skills and memory you had underestimated. I did that to Oliver. Like an electric tape, not knowing the meanings, similar to your well-fed computers:

"My Edith was beautiful—a man could not have wished for more. Fragile, exquisitely perfumed, velvet bows in her chestnut hair, her eyes green as the sunlit sea. Never the same, startling me by the spinning of her mind and her glassbell laughter. I did not mind when she played tricks or mocked me... If a man does not know how to nurture a strange and beautiful plant, then he has no right to complain when he is deserted. If he keeps going over his mistakes, he will soon be insane. Eventually grief wears itself out. That is the beauty in work and in the virility of the mind. It is time to stop dusting the glass-cutting machine. It is time to create life anew..."

That is what came out of my purple mouth. Unexpectedly, right after Oliver had made love to me in out up down round and round. Then. And now I must remember the expression on his face and translate it for you, for me. His eyes with a glaze of all the colors, forgetting to blink, looking nowhere, a sudden jerking spasm of the neck followed by a loss of color and an expression of terror mute heavy still, like a large weight falling falling thump to the ground. The door closed quickly, leaving me. I hate myself when I think of Oliver fleeing large and naked down the hall, unaware of his shriveled penis hanging there empty.

I had not done it maliciously. No. It was my awful photographic memory. Most of the words had no meaning to me, only gave me some intuitive sense of the whole thing. Why had I chosen this particular monologue to taunt him with? Please believe that I am innocent. Many reasons why I chose it—Edith had been on my mind for a long time, a name inside my hideous fantasies, a presence. Already her letters had been discovered—the letters I have been generous enough to share with you. Jealousy? I didn't know what that was. Jealous of a name, glass configurations, of a room with a large white ruffled spread satin on the top climbing down to the floor with frills, and a dressing table with a mirrored surface where different-sized atomizers stood in pairs or far apart. Most of all I was curious. Isn't curiosity a healthy thing for a growing mind? Besides it was not that important. Oliver did not change because of one or many such incidents. If it was that simple I would know why Oliver left. It was only a single event causing Oliver to lose his appetite for a few days and to forget to give me my assignments. And when he looked at me the next day, it was something new, something I refuse to remember or to translate. Not yet. Soon things were back to normal except for a minor change; my new words compiled by Oliver were words that I already knew. It didn't matter. I am just telling you in case you think that it has special significance. I tend to exaggerate, to see large meanings in the smallest changes. You, I assume, are more objective having grown up with scientific method. He forgot our recreation period—I went to get the bruised grapefruit but Oliver shook his head slowly to the right, back to the center and to the left, back to the center. He refused to play with me. I am not saying that we never rolled the grapefruit again nor played Simple Simon. We did. (I wish I could take it back.)

—

Foamworld of Oliver—porous sponge slowly squeezing green; liquid life swimming below beyond time in circles of secret words to Edith a shadow visible in the tangled folds of aging palpitating cerebrum. "Come back to me," he calls over moonlit sand dunes. Edith is gazing at a star. "You killed my bird by shouting words into her gauze wings." Oliver moves toward her. "I covered her wings with words when it was cold. Forgive me." She floats further away her body still as a cold statue. Breathing with the heartpump driving blood into his huge penis, he cannot reach her. "Edith," he moans collapsing into sand, stroking entering into the damp sand beneath the gleaming surface. An ocean wave hot and cold crashes over him contracting the muscles of his limbs. Awake in bed he thinks that he is a long fish floating in warm water trapped suddenly by the orange seagrowths multiplying in his brain.

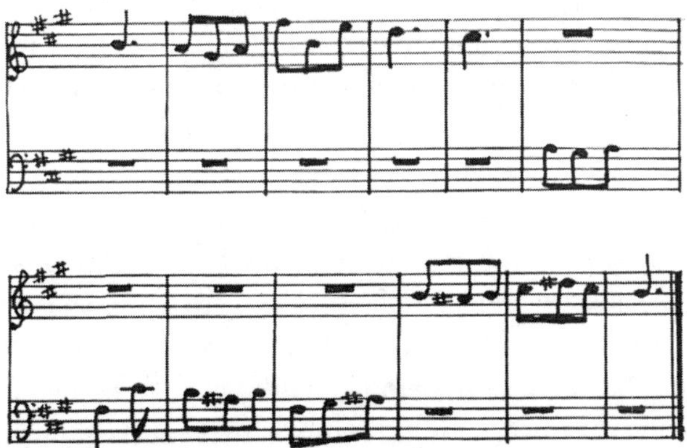

"Never mention the name Edith again," said Oliver sometime later, days weeks. He said it firmly but without any ill feeling toward me. Secretly he locked the glass studio and hid or destroyed the key. Too bad, because I was beginning to operate the glass-cutter without damaging my fingers and my color combinations were improving. Was that the reason? The glass studio is one of the sacred regions joining Edith to Oliver and I was lucky to have seen it at all.

I swear that I tried not to mention Edith. Sometimes I forgot or the things in the head got jammed together and my mouth opened to let them out. He forgave me and he didn't. My Oliver is a man of many different and contradictory moods. Think of Oliver and how long he had waited for Edith, how he had resolved to forget her. Think of me and my growing, childlike curiosity; quickly I was putting everything together and those thoughts were running, giving me indigestion. Me falling in love with Oliver, following him around with my whining voice not knowing how to keep from asking about things. His pain. Mine. Whose fault was all of this? I should have left. But there was no door and I knew nothing of what was outside or where to go. Even after Oliver left tapping his white-tipped cane and wearing his opaque glasses, I remained for a long time. Waiting.

—

I sense that you are not too anxious to meet me, and if you have stayed with me this long I am more than grateful. It might embarrass me to meet you after all the things you know. What should I say? The rules of your conversations still elude me. Is it supposed to be a kind of music, a custom of mechanical codes, or a free-for-all?—I never get it just right. Each situation is different and calls for unique methods. There are far too many hellos, goodmornings, howareyous, and merrychristmases, as I see it. But maybe there is something subtle about utterances that I haven't yet grasped. I am still learning, remember, and still living in Oliver's world. What a handsome couple we would make sitting together on one of your subway trains, leaning over the circular black railing to watch the seals, waiting arm in arm for tickets to a Saturday night movie, or curled together in front of the screen inside. But Oliver wouldn't have done that.

Even though you are not anxious to meet me, I will tell you where I can be found particularly if you have an important message for me, a comment, criticism or even a plan or a secret strategy. (You are good at that, I bet.) Try the toy stores—the larger the better. I am always there, secretly of course. Even I know that it is inappropriate. If you see someone with a yellow umbrella winding up moving toys, shooting guns that throw sparks, looking through small and large kaleidoscopes, playing on toy pianos or drums and listening to musical boxes, you can be certain that it is I. (I never touch the dolls.) My fingers are scarred and my breasts are flat as pancakes. My brassiere hides that—I've learned to hide certain things. I understand your society well enough to know how to appear normal. I do, except that I walk stooped over a little in imitation of Oliver, and I cannot help dashing into a toy store to wind up things or to buy red and blue finger paints. No one knows about my finger painting. If I had known that finger paints are just for children, I would never have begun buying them. Now it's beyond my control since I love them. I am very anxious to conform to your world, having no choice in the matter. However I have a lot of toys. But you would never guess it by looking at me or by talking with me or even if you were to see my apartment which is very contemporary. I am smart enough to keep my playthings well hidden, conscious of having to be more careful about these things than other people. I am not implying that Oliver deprived me or pushed me too fast. We played many games. But I am tired of rolling balls or grapefruits even to the blind men, and I don't like word games any more; I never do crossword puzzles. But as I told you before, I collect new words every night because he was stingy and kept giving me the same words over and over again. And he didn't explain it.

Here it is dark and light dark and light
Crosshatched patterns on the floor move
Then disappear or a light is flashed over
Turned on with shuffling feet not the same
Away an iridescent green pigeon lies dead

On a window ledge kissed by a bar of sun so
Warm from the sky like a warm gray stone
Not there

Before the time of my aggressive, compulsive talking and interruptive playing back of Oliver's conversations and old monologues, he hadn't minded when I won the word games. It began to change; it wasn't that I knew more words—that isn't why I kept winning. It was because I concentrated harder. It was too late when I began to lose on purpose. Oliver knew I was faking. I always won the game of who could make the most words out of a large one like "fermentation." Oliver used to be amused and pleased—that is, when he trusted me. I knew more small words and could turn them backward and upside down very quickly. Oliver knew larger words and found it difficult to extract the small easy ones. That is all there was to it. He was unfair. I made some larger words that I had learned from Edith's letters or from reading pages of his history book, but that doesn't mean that I understood. When I asked Oliver what they meant, he refused to explain. I think he didn't believe my ignorance of the meanings. That must be it, don't you think? Or was he trying to keep me stupid? Not my Oliver. If that was the case, why had he educated me at all? "Religion" was a word Oliver would not explain. "Insanity," "love," "despair," "grief," "suicide" and "abstinence" were others. It made some difference in my learning which, if you remember, I only did to please Oliver. I wanted to stop. But it was too late—my mind did it all alone. After a while you can figure out a little of the meaning of almost any word if it is in a long sentence in the middle of a paragraph, particularly if you read it over and over. I did it with the letters. I did it with the monologues recorded in my head.

But it wasn't just one way. Oliver was still proud of me for a long time especially when I was obedient and conversed in a formal manner without asking too many questions.

"Have you washed up for dinner?"

"Yes, Oliver, and the potatoes are almost baked."

"Remember not to burn the skin. Pay attention."

"Would you like butter or sour cream on your potatoes, Oliver?"

"Just for variety I think I'll indulge in some sour cream, thank you."

"How is your history book going today?"

"Quite satisfactorily, thank you. And your lessons?"

"Quite satisfactorily, thank you."

"We are keeping to our schedules very well it seems."

"Yes, we are keeping to our schedules very well."

Oliver taught me the niceties such as "thank you" and "excuse me." He was striving for a life of moderation and order. Poor Oliver. I spoiled it, detested polite conversations and couldn't keep within their structure too often. He tried to understand, but he needed precise arrangements of words just as much as I needed to say all kinds of word combinations and ask questions that he didn't want to answer. When Oliver was inside his room, away, I talked to myself with my thoughts. Not purposely. Not so loud. When I started I couldn't stop.

"Riding on the tall giraffe with his neck getting longer and longer my neck and Oliver's neck got so long it began to bend down and break crack crack empty smash all the glass and Oliver stamped his foot and the giraffe stamped all of his four feet and we all stamped thump thump thump and the knives and spoons and plates and saucers all grew tall and laughed and went clank clank so Oliver had to put his finger in his ears and wump wump wump he beat everyone to pieces except the green and orange sun which laughed at me when all my fingers fell off under the water I said to the lion and the giraffe get me the key to the glass studio get me all the keys and don't tell Oliver and they looked everywhere and opened up everything and Oliver could do nothing about it the glass-cutter went round and round and round and I broke eggs over it and hammered all the green and purple glass sheets into tiny pieces and the giraffe and the lion and Oliver decided to move into my room away from words and glass and we played all day long with the grapefruit and Follow the Leader with Oliver as the leader and when the giraffe was too bad or I was very bad saying Edith Edith Edith all day then Oliver left and it made me mad at the giraffe everything is your fault giraffe stop telling me to do these things to Oliver he is missing a finger and I'll cut your neck off if you say Edith again."

In a weak moment he had drawn a clock and explained the passage of time, had even made tick tick tick sounds and clipped rotating hands to the center. (You have seen these paper clocks in many kindergarten classrooms.) But I wasn't satisfied until I got one of the real clocks ticking. There was no end to my curiosity now that it had been aroused. If I have not told you before I will tell you now or again that there were many clocks in their house—Oliver's and Edith's house. Some of them were rusty and missing arms. Others had neither numbers nor arms like those I've seen in the horror films that the blind men take me to. He had taken them apart for reasons of his own and parts lay scattered in careless places—gears, motors, tanks, screws, abandoned alarm bells, tarnished discs, screws, hooks. Oliver smashed the clock I got to ticking—it was only one of the lesser incongruities—clocks. There must have been fifty or three hundred. Once someone had loved and collected them and allowed them to tick. Parts were under my bed, in kitchen cabinets, under Edith's breakfront with the tarnished keys jutting out. I wanted them to move and tick—all of them. In a frenzy I could think of nothing but clocks. (You should see all my clocks now.) Oliver would be hurt or furious or both. He would smash all of them. They are all set at different numbers and tick at different speeds, various tones, a million sounds to the alarm bells. The blind men like them but everyone else is driven mad as you and Oliver would be. I like them. I think of Oliver making ticking sounds with his mouth. Then I imagine that they are Oliver's clocks and that time is all arranged for us, that Edith has returned and everything is clear. Blue clear. I find old abandoned clocks, steal them, buy cheap ones, even toy clocks. A sense of quality is not something yet developed in me. What can be revealed to me by these clocks? What was Oliver afraid or angry about? But don't let me distract you. Have you noticed how I changed from a docile obedient child eager to please into someone easily obsessed, persistent, frenzied, violent when something interested me? Edith, the glass, the clocks. Note how my thinking became wild and disordered, how I changed. Like a giraffe my brain and eyes grew many horns. But that was when I was in the quilted world with Oliver. Now I am precise, calm, punctual. Only on occasion do my thoughts become confused thinking of past and present together until I think I am a speckled woodpecker riding on the back of the poor silver horse—krat krat krat krat with my purple beak until the poor punctured horsey falls into a stream and drowns with pieces of liver, heart and silver spermtanks floating on the green spray, until the ocean is all red with horsey's blood. Oliver, don't let the silver horsey drown way at the bottom, please.

"Oliver, make them work, please. Make them tick. I don't want the paper clock," I said tearing it up.

"I won't discuss clocks or time except as they relate to our lessons," said my Oliver, redfaced trying to hold his temper, to retain the calm moderation he wanted so badly.

"Why? Oliver, let me fix them. Please." I was in tears, those wet things from the lacrimal glands and Oliver was stamping his clawed foot. If I had been more sensitive, more observant, I would have noticed that his lower lip was hanging way down again wet inside out and that he looked at the floor with glazed eyes. But only for a moment. Then I was punished severely. I will not tell you how. It is no one's business. There are certain things you may not know about Oliver. I recovered but don't think I stopped my stubborn behavior. Reward had great power over me. Punishment much less. Remember that if you are trying to teach something—anything at all. Forget your insults and brutal deprivations and punishments. Just give and take away your love—see if I am not correct. Oliver knew this. He just forgot when I went too far, when his own strength was pushed to its limit, like with the clocks. He also smashed them to bits so that not even someone as mechanically gifted as I am could have ever made them tick. (Besides my terrible photographic memory, I also have this mechanical ability; it comes from being so patient.) I can work on a broken clock for months and not get frustrated. Never. Oliver taught me patience with long waiting for him in my room or outside his door, endless time alone in the rectangular world hearing nothing. That is why I type so well without being bored. And I can fix almost anything although I know nothing of the principles involved—nothing of engineering, physics, thermodynamics or mathematics. Give me anything that is broken, preferably clocks, and I will fix it at no charge. I want everything fixed. I want to be fixed. I want Oliver fixed. I want everything to be as it was once with Oliver. Besides there isn't so much to do when I am not typing in the office or playing with toys or going to see horror movies with the blind men who, as you know, I initially thought were Oliver. Oliver left wearing dark glasses and tapping a white-tipped cane.

Excerpt from Oliver's *Historical Encyclopedia of Great Men*

"Wagner"

When I, Oliver, a great historian, speak of Richard Wagner, I gasp, hold my breath with admiration. Such a giant, a Napoleon of music, has never walked the earth before or since. Condemn Wagner because he felt it was his right to borrow money from everyone? Condemn Wagner because his infidelities caused his wife Minna's health to deteriorate? Condemn Wagner because he wanted to be the center of the world? Not I. Never, never. He was my friend and I, Oliver, who lent him as much money as I could, who ran to his side when he called, do not condemn him. That a great man with a vision must even live in this troublesome world is a sin. That he should be burdened by economic necessity is criminal. His actions toward others became coarse

and insensitive due to his monomania, a creative lightning that struck him blind and put him into another realm. I will say this again and again. Great men should be locked away. "Oliver, I am killing this good and loyal woman as if I put a knife to her throat every time I meet Frau Wesendonck. But I cannot help myself. Without the spiritual union I feel with Mathilde I could not rise to such heights of beauty. She is my Isolde and together we will move out of this terrible reality and become one with each other and with the World. This, Oliver, will be the eternal death that I strive for—the death that is love." The question I ask is should a great man be judged by ordinary human standards? Should Wagner? Should Oliver?

The first room along the corridor was Oliver's. I knew his room from quick sliced images as he closed the door behind him. Details became clear later when I stood on a chair watching, peering over the crack above the door. As Edith's studio was glass—glasswild configurations within circles, triangles and squares—Oliver's was paper. Old calendars, newspapers, maps, documents dry as leaves were strewn about disintegrating, or in some cases deliberately affixed to portions of the wall. He disliked the insinuation of objects. Do not imagine that he hung any of Edith's green suns on the wall or that he had portraits of Wagner, Hitler, Freud or Van Gogh tacked to the mirror. And although he might have carried a lamp into his room, he preferred the naked bulb from the ceiling fixture. Her world was color and his was print—no pictures anywhere except what was reflected in the flawed mirror which was part of the wall. It was the only mirror in the house—no, I am forgetting Edith's other room of silk and velvet ruffles. I would like to forget that room forever. It was just as well—I mean the absence of mirrors. I can tolerate the suddenness of my reflection only rarely—distorted, unfamiliar and absolute for that second like a photograph. I allow no one to photograph me. Mirrors show everything reversed. Make-up can be applied without them as blind people know. Next to his room of out-of-date calendars which he circled in black, and newspapers too faded to read crackling like dead leaves, was Edith's room. Remember the skirted dressing table with its mirrored surface, closets of silken, gauze and brocaded dresses, tiny shoes with velvet bows, hexagonal hatboxes. Oh, I loathe this room with its mysterious aura, luminous emptiness, radiant whisperings. Untouchable. And its gradual intrusion into Oliver's world. After a space came the indentation half-circular into the corridor wall for the kitchen and bathroom areas. There was a wooden table with grains up and down, crooked and smooth. Directly opposite stood the insinuating breakfront with its tarnished keys. Several objects appeared and disappeared on a projecting ledge.

A blue cross, an engraved bracelet and a mustard-colored coffee mug had vanished. But a pair of torn red gloves, a green enameled plate its central sun radiating yellow light and a brass-hinged box transparent and etched with roses upset me with a prior fragrance. But remember that my mind was disordered, to say the least, and cannot be totally relied upon.

"There is something I remember," I said, fingering the red gloves. Oliver changed the subject quickly and the red gloves soon disappeared just like the ring and iridescent ashtray with a fish carcass on its edge had disappeared earlier. I hid them or Oliver did. How can I be certain?

—

Further down the hall was the glass studio, now forbidden to me. And then my own room, tucked into the farthest corner, empty but for a bed, a plain bureau, a faded print of Rédon's pastel flowers and a piece of red paper that I made Oliver hang on the wall. He did this smiling, cutting it into the shape of a wide open rose.

Don't think that Oliver didn't like me or that he didn't try to please me anymore. No. High on the wall above my bed was what I now know to be a crucifix. Then I didn't know or care. Do you understand the relationship of room to room? Are you certain that you realize that the eating area was not enclosed and the breakfront with an upper ledge and three bottom drawers opened by tarnished keys was not hidden. Do not forget the patchwork walls. You have seen antique bedspreads and skirts like these wall coverings and they are probably worth a great deal of money. This tapestry, as I've already explained, was uneven with certain parts sewn carelessly, blending rags to shredded silk. No doors, windows, day or night—only a succession of events, a succession of meetings with Oliver, lessons acts and words—words being the worst of it at this time. A time of change obvious or invisible. Oliver large, corpulent, not too fastidious, changing his walk from brisk efficiency to a slower hunched-over limp, his lower lip hanging way down inside out shining from drooling saliva. Myself either in my torn camisole or in violet, long legs, thin, hair brushed and smoothed with water, too clean, rushing about. Not slow and immobile as I had been. Me—wanting to get in his way, wanting to wreck his peace, to jump on his back and startle him, riding my big giraffe everywhere, longing to stare at Oliver's eyes and make his penis fly up. Persistently asking about time, clocks and Edith.

"When is Edith coming home?" I asked over and over again despite Oliver's warning. How could I have helped it. I understood that she belonged in his world more than I did. Things would be better if she came, the waiting ended. His waiting had become mine. Everything that was Oliver flowed into me somehow, despite my autonomous thinking and my evil giraffe. *Beginning.* Because of that. I remember it in detail with my eyes, with my tongue *then then*—fat fist clutching the handle of a large spoon, up in into my mouth hot colors—soft pale green leafwings, round orange flowers wet with yellow in the center, and those hard pieces of brown composed of thick threads lined down that had to be chewed. If there is a soul, if I have one, that is where it is—in our beginning.

I kept reminding him of Edith—not that he could have ever forgotten. A man loves only once. I know that, despite your scientific facts and research. A man loves only once. Women love more times. Half of your research is incorrect. You don't really understand about a man's love. I didn't either until Oliver left, after it was too late. A man, not a woman, loves once and then he might as well do to the clocks what Oliver did. Stop. Out here everyone would think him mad. He keeps ticking along and even he, confused by all those people and things and breasts, thinks that he loves again. No. He is just a dead clock ticking, a moving cock with inner feeling dying. That is what Oliver was trying to be. Not with his penis or cock. Not even with me, but with his new plans, schedules and his history book. It might have worked if I had cooperated. I spoiled it. I had to know answers and to remind him of Edith. The word "Edith" from my mouth became the worst insult to him, a sacrilege, a criminal offense. And he had ordered me, commanded, pleaded, asked me kindly, everything, not to say it.

Suppose I kept asking you when your beautiful dead wife was coming back as I ran up and down wearing her dress; suppose she had deserted you for someone younger, dashing—wouldn't you kill me or want to, or go mad or lock one of us up or go away?

I wish I knew when her letters stopped, if they ever did. Why didn't she want him to write to her? Where was she all that time? I have more of Edith's letters. I am certain that you have been waiting to see them and I have been keeping them inside my head. But what is the difference? They hardly say anything of importance. And there is no way to determine the year unless you gave the originals to a laboratory technician or to a chemist, or to someone who specializes in such things. But I don't have them. I didn't steal the letters. Not technically, as the police might say. They are still in the drawer. Read her boring letters if you want to. I have to entertain you. Besides, I may have missed some important clue.

Oliver My Darling,

I know how hard it is for you to give me this chance to find myself. But I am not leaving because I don't want to be with you. It is an obligation I feel to both of us that is making this separation necessary. When you find this note I will be gone. When you are present I cannot fight your will and leave. Please don't look upon it as a separation or as an opportunity to be unfaithful to me. Take care of my bird. I have never known who Edith is and I cannot find out unless I go away for a while. Not long. It won't be for too long. I am grateful to you for trying to understand. I trust that you will try very hard. I don't want to hear from you as this will destroy my purpose. Trust me and wait for a better Edith to return.

With Devotion and Love, Edith

My Dearest Love,

I cannot come and take care of you. You know how fragile I am and how easily I catch infections. I would tire too quickly. Besides if you eat sensibly and rest you will be well soon. If I even go out for a walk in this weather I get chilled. Besides one day we will be together forever and then I won't have to travel on the dreary dirty trains to come and see you. You ask just a little too much of me sometimes and forget how delicate I am. I know you understand. I hope the doctor finds out what it is. I can't wait until you are well and spring comes. Then we can make plans for the future. I shouldn't have gone out in the cold but your naughty girl did and bought herself a pair of white fur-lined boots that you will love. I have a matching hat and rose-red gloves. I am now wrapped in quilts to get the chill out of my bones. I hope that I don't get sick. I love you so deeply.

All My Heart, Edith

Dear Oliver,

I wish I could come home but I am still nervous and find the country soothing. We go on long hikes during the day. I have made six birds out of plastic. I told you that I am not permitted to use glass. The people here are very interesting. There is a poet who I am friendly with. He wrote a poem to me and I gave him one of the birds. He likes birds. I have never met such a sensitive man. The rest of the birds are for you. Please don't call or write since it upsets me and makes me nervous. Just take care of the house and please don't forget to wash and to brush your teeth. These things are important. I don't want to argue about them anymore. I worry about the house and about how you are keeping things. Don't forget to dust.

Love, Edith

My Darling Oliver,

Don't begrudge your Edith a little fun. My affection for Mr. P. the artist has nothing to do with what I feel for you. I wish you could understand the subtleties of things and develop a lighter touch. Sometimes Oliver, I feel oppressed when I am with you, the way you watch me and follow me about. I know it is not fair of me since you have always been so patient. But I like to dance and sing and not to always be so serious. Mr. P. thinks that I have a gift for life that not many people have. Don't be jealous of him, my Oliver. I am only now finding out the great potential in my own body. I will be better for you when this is over. Be generous and wait. I cannot survive without knowing that you are waiting for me. We all have different needs. I am anxious to see you and miss you as always.

Your One Love, Edith

Oliver,

I told you never to try to come after me. I am angry and disappointed. I exist independently of you or of anyone else. You spoiled everything and now I have to stay longer to recover. I know you will always love me. Why can't you understand that my way of loving is not the same as yours. You dwell too much upon rules of conformity. Real love allows freedom when it is required. That is what Mr. P. has explained to me. Can you understand it. Why can't you trust me without question. I do not understand you Oliver. The snow is so beautiful and I am so happy. Don't spoil it by saying ugly things. You know that I belong to you in a deep sense no matter where I am and that I would perish inside if I thought for a moment that you would not always wait for me. If I planned to run away wouldn't I have taken my bird? Be good Oliver and if I hear one mean word or accusation from you I will not return. I don't really mean this and am already sorry.

Your Edith

My Darling,

I've made so many mistakes and yet you have forgiven me. Now I am ill and I wish I had stayed with you and not wasted so much time. I am so thin that nothing looks well on me and my hands shake and sometimes my whole body shakes and I don't remember things. When I come home I will not be able to do all the things I used to do. It is my own fault and I cry about it all the time. I hate it here and pray for the day I can be with my one and only Oliver.

Your Own Edith

P.S. Don't think you have deceived me for one moment about the bird. I know how much you hate it you rotten bastard.

Darling, I only went out to the bakery. I am happy to be home. It is silly but I want you to find this note from me when you return in case I am not back yet. I am happy and I love you very much, Edith

Dearest Oliver,

I feel badly about breaking my promise but I couldn't get away. The sun is good for me. We will try to understand each other better when I return. I know that it is not all your fault. Could we try to read some manuals together? It isn't all instinct. Even poetry has to be learned in part. I am not a cold woman. I know this. You have just wasted my body. I can feel so much when touched correctly. I have learned many things since I last saw you.

Your One and Only Edith

Darling Oliver,

I love you so much that I can't bear to hurt you. It makes me sick and shaky. I just can't anymore. But it will change, I know. Please don't clutch at me. I can't stand that. I really can't.

Love, Edith

You would think Oliver loathsome with his huge stomach, urine odor and the hairs coming from his ears and nose. You would hate his brown-clawed toenails and his thick hairy fingers, particularly the one with two joints missing. His lower lip, hanging down inside out wet dripping saliva to his beard, would make you shudder. That is because Oliver never fed *you* when you did not know what a spoon was, nor did he cook for you and dress you when you remembered nothing. And he didn't play with your pancake breasts when you were ignorant of the world, of the differences between women and men. I've told you this before but each time I add or subtract so each time I will come closer to understanding his disappearance. It does not bore me to repeat a thousand times that Oliver had gigantic ears that cupped forward, long earlobes—and that he never cleaned them and that the wax was hard, closer in color to orange than to yellow. The veins of his nose made a lovely design. I haven't told you *that* before. Oliver's nose came forth suddenly fat and bulbous with purple veins crisscrossing everywhere and some black and gray hairs growing from the nostrils long and curling, to filter the germs. He was the prince of men and nothing can change my mind. Certainly not those evil investigators who think that he kidnapped me and brought me to his home. I swear to them again and again that I appeared, simply appeared, and that he wasn't even expecting me. Nor could any psychiatrist (I've read about them) convince me that the entire episode was a delusion. I have the scars on my fingers from the glass-cutter and a piece of red paper cut in the shape of a flower to prove it. No one has claimed me and I am not reported missing at the Missing Persons' Bureau or listed anywhere. Of course this is hard to prove since I have no real name. If I had any identification when I appeared, Oliver must have disposed of it or lost it. He has his reasons for doing many things. I have given myself a name and I have every right to do that since Oliver was remiss. If you find Oliver you will not turn him over to the authorities. I trust that you won't do that. If I thought you were like that, I would kill myself right now and not tell you anything else. If he happens to be living in your house—I have considered all possibilities—and he is happy and writing his history, then don't let him know that I have written about him. Get in touch with me.

Here it is dark and light dark and light
Patterns crosshatched silent or vertical

Float around the floor or climb the walls
Like treeghosts or pure as an absent hand
Not there

Remember, always remember that he was my beginning, and what I felt and would never feel again was unconditional. He could have been base, brutish, insane, unkind. Just as well, he might have possessed all virtues—it would have made no difference in my passion. This was not true later. Initially it was. But I am lying. I needed Oliver. I was hungry and my mind was disordered. Who was I? Here with Oliver to be created. No—I do not like to talk about this aspect of our situation any more than is necessary for perfect understanding. It is preferable and less agonizing to discuss how, despite certain rebellions which Oliver took too seriously, I became just like him. Take the matter of hierarchy, for example—even a rudimentary being such as myself has an innate tendency to abhor certain ideas and attitudes. I was, from the outset—that is, when I could reason with some clarity—opposed to any concept of hierarchy. The man, the roach, the weed, the cat I felt to be equal. Oliver accused me of a decadent kind of religiosity. It wasn't the case. How could I have known about religion since he had refused to explain? I did not feel that all things were the same in God's Kingdom or in the Heavens. No. Only as I experienced them: the housefly, the ant, the egg or grapefruit, a drawer, a word—hierarchy made no sense to me. It might have been my condition; so many things were to me as one and I fought against their separation. My body and Oliver's were related in a mysterious way. Even the rooms, the glass, the potato, the toilet all assumed vast importance and unity to my child's consciousness. Oliver took my disagreement too seriously. What did I know? He was superior to me and we were superior to the lower animals, and a weed was barely anything. Or a bug. (How then could I have adored him? Do not ask anymore.) It was not long before I truly believed that the man was higher than the cow and that the cow was higher than the weed. I also believed that wisdom was at the apex of all hierarchies and that we, Oliver and I, should strive to attain it. Despite my futile rebellions, my evil giraffe, my terrible struggle for an autonomy that I did not want, I believed whatever Oliver said.

Had certain thoughts and feelings possessed a vocabulary for me, I probably would have striven for Oliver and I to love each other as well as possible in the best way. But Oliver, as I have already mentioned, did not want the best to occur. There is self-destructiveness somewhere inside my Oliver. I know it. Otherwise he would have been more patient, given me a name and made me his lover.

Fortunately, I say, for the history book. The preservation of Oliver in this alone. He shared these pages with me at first. I listened. Mute. Nor did I look for double meanings or messages. Oliver would have become angry and finally stopped writing. He would have left much sooner. How fortunate that I knew no history and had such a small vocabulary; he was correct in restricting it although I felt deprived, sensed that something had gone wrong. Had it happened today—all of it—his historical encyclopedia would never have been written. I am much too shrewd, too aware of innuendo and too suspicious. I would have gone to the library and checked dates and facts. (I've learned that from you.) Having read other history books and well-documented biographies, I would have laughed at his errors. Worse, I might have tried to be encouraging, a type of condescension that would have appalled and paralyzed Oliver. He is a proud man and resents all encouragement, particularly from me. Frightened at what I might discover, he would have fled much sooner leaving only the cracked mirror and delapidated calendars.

Oliver waited for Edith. He tried not to. How hard my Oliver tried. Admire and pity him for this, if you know what pity is. I also waited. My waiting was anxious tormented impatient and aggressive. His was a chronic malignancy. His entire integration depended upon the constant under-theme of his resigned endless wait. Did I destroy Oliver? His life spun about this waiting. Even Oliver could not change something like that. He was only fooling himself. Too deep, too necessary. *I* was the delusion—my education thinly disguising the spreading infection, pushing it into deeper places. His history book was fake too. It served the same purpose. Yet we were happy—until I existed, until he thought he no longer controlled me.

The truth is that Oliver and I never touched each other. You would have thought we touched hearing us at our lessons or watching the synchronization of our lovemaking. We exacted nothing. That is what is so surprising to me—this one similarity between our life and your life outside. With Oliver and me it could have been different. I can only surmise that my Oliver had become indoctrinated by your philosophies. To say, "I love you," I now know is dangerous and is considered to be in bad taste unless you mean it casually or direct it to many at once like a parade. I blame Edith and her senseless wanderings among your people away from Oliver. (You read her letters.) Only an aberrant or irrational person would consider such an utterance (I love you) out here, assuming it would be a lie or knowing it to be an extinct emotion, judging it beforehand not to be the case in almost all instances, or fearing that someone might take it seriously and exact things causing the painful necessity of flight or of a retraction. I am not as dumb as I may seem; I have picked up essentials of your world rapidly, such as your curiosity about sexual matters and your scorn of romanticism while wanting it. That is why Oliver never taught me the phrase or ever said it to me. That must be at least a part of the reason. And after I had learned the phrase from Edith's old letters and knew pretty well what it meant, I kept my mouth shut. Even children sense certain things. More than you.

I wish Oliver was like me and had not been in the world and had never met Edith. However, in that case he could have taught me nothing and I would be sorry, I think. As I understand it, living out here for some months or years, the authorities have sought to destroy words of love—not, as they claim, because they lead to unrealistic demands and eventual disappointments, a clash with biological reality and so forth—but because of their power. I am the first to consult about the power of words. No one knows better than I that despite the state of our nation and world, and the derangement of our minds—Oliver's and mine—these obsolete "I love you" words could have held us together for an uninterrupted eternity. Too late I have learned what you will never learn: everything is destroyed by the wrong words and everything could have been fixed by the right ones. Too late.

Thus waiting for Edith, hoping that she might appear (I echoing Oliver's insides in this), we might have had nothing at all to do with one another. Or everything. But we observed the manner of civilized society despite the eccentric circumstances of our lives. I see that now. So my writing is not in vain. We were not as unique, after all, as I have been trying to make you believe. Why had we not been more daring? Weren't we free from outside commands? No, on the contrary, we proceeded with a circumspection that makes me ashamed.

He should have never let Edith out of his sight. Don't think that I didn't tell him this. Poor Oliver. When I learned not to say whatever I suddenly realized or thought, he had gone away. I do not mean that he actually left—not yet. His body was still there. But I keep forgetting how disordered my mind was even after I was thinking and reasoning. It isn't easy to connect one thing to another. (I haven't yet succeeded.) My visions were fragmented, irregular, blunt or overly precise. And Oliver had his own preoccupations even when he was briskly working, planning my lessons or playing games with me and teaching me about sexual organs and time. He wasn't like you. Edith was there insistent always. I don't like her. That he even allowed me to remain in the house is one of the miracles that cannot be explained. Indifference? Madness? Or an instinct to have another being nearby. My existence—its expression at first—no more than the hungry yelps and whinings of a housepet. That might explain it. Oliver should have had a dog or a cat or an anteater instead of me. I know it for a fact. Or someone of great insight and tact—no, that would have been worse for him than the original apparition that was myself. Long ago. If I had only progressed at a slower rate, everything would have turned out well. Don't you think so?

Excerpt from Oliver's *Historical Encyclopedia of Great Men*

"Van Gogh"

It may seem unusual to include Vincent Van Gogh in a history of men who have shaped the world. But it will soon become clear to the reader that mine is not an ordinary historical work. Although I deal objectively with men of greatness and their relationship to an historical era, my major emphasis is upon the problem of the frenzied idealist, the man who wants to shape his own fantasies and communicate them, fully translated, to society. I, Oliver, would understand such historical figures better than most historians, I humbly state.

Not often does a historian have the opportunity to meet as great an artist as Vincent. (I am one so honored.) It was after one of Edith's short trips, if I recall, that I received a gracious invitation from Theo asking me to accompany him on a trip to visit his brother in Arles. With enthusiasm and a proper display of gratitude I accepted. Van Gogh, at this

time, had already attempted every kind of relationship. All had failed. All, except for his work. I understood this. Hadn't Napoleon, impotent Hitler and Luther understood this also? I worried about him most when he was not working, when he confessed to me that he still doubted his work, that time was short and he had started too late. "I searched for God, and having failed in that I do this work. I know I am often insane and does that not invalidate my art, Oliver?" I paused as I often do, being a man of slow response and of great reflection. Finally I advised him that it was the society that was insane and he, not being able to fit in with its insanity had only one choice, and that was to ignore it altogether. "There have been women," he said, looking far away. "Women keep a man from his true destiny," I replied. "I, Oliver, know about this from experience." "Work is not enough for me. It is only a pathetic substitute for the things I would have liked," said Vincent. "Oliver, what I am trying to do is impossible. It is a vision within that burns and throbs and has grand calm power. How do you think I feel when I see these twisted forms in my own work? I've always admired the calm and control of the Japanese masters. They were not striving for some kind of individual expression yet they have individuality and calm. But a man must work lest he die, even when he has given up. More so then. Remember that Oliver." Vincent smiled sadly. I remember his words now and try to live up to them in the work I am creating which is a synthesis of the philosophies and lives of idealists, of those men who were too large for the world and sometimes too large for their own work. And I think that they should have been locked all together in a large home (shut off from the world) where they could work undisturbed by the malice, mediocrity and turbulence about them. And what was insane about a great man like Vincent Van Gogh shooting himself? He knew that he could not adjust to society. He also feared that his work

would not survive and had been a waste. I fear this also. And from the past one is never free.

Oliver's historical encyclopedia often changed form; artists suddenly appeared, dates were omitted or compulsively if incorrectly noted. Surely he never met Van Gogh. I say this as the I that your society has created. The other part of me, still existing in spite of your libraries, books and systems of checks and balances, does not see why they could not have met. What small importance is the incongruity of time; he could have met Van Gogh had he lived in a different century. Poor Oliver; he had no place in history and that must have hurt him very deeply, must have caused his obsession with historical figures. He was not suited to his work. I know it now, having read others. But Oliver's history, if it can be called history, has the mark of Oliver. I prefer it to all others. Perhaps it is a new kind of literature. Not pure history. I know Van Gogh also. Oliver was happy to tell me all he knew about the artist and to draw crude approximations of wild cypress trees, weavers, reapers, and the final cornfield. No one had to tell me, nor did I have to look for the signature; I knew Van Gogh the moment I walked into the museum, smiled with recognition, tears coming from my lacrimal glands.

—

Foamworld of Oliver—porous sponge slowly squeezing green; liquid life swimming below beyond time in circles of secret words to Edith a shadow visible in the tangled folds of aging palpitating cerebrum. "Where are you Edith?" he calls running seeing her pearlrose form appear behind a jagged rock lighting the gray sky. A white stem. Disappearing then vertically radiant or slanting behind another kniferock. "I will find you, rescue you," as he searching finds only gurgling mudholes and soft toeprints. Breathing heavily he crawls over the endless landscape of terrifying crags. "You are lost to me," he moans as horizontal triangular tips of stone pierce his head hurting fertilizing the vibrating orange seagrowths multiplying in his brain. White, awake, the sting of sharp blades inside his eyes, he calls to lost Edith.

There are things about my Oliver that I do not like to tell anyone, things I do not know how to explain. I fear your interpretations. I was going to omit the letters from Van Gogh. The handwriting is not the same as Edith's looped script. That is why I have not let you see Hitler's letters to Oliver—I fear that Oliver wrote them himself. You will think him mad and therefore unworthy of your attention. I am also afraid that you will conclude that Oliver also wrote Edith's letters—and this is not the case. The proof is that Hitler, Van Gogh, Napoleon and Darwin all have similar handwriting styles while Edith's is quite unique. The paper that Van Gogh's letters are written on is the same paper that Oliver used for his historical work—unlined with three holes on the left. They are carelessly folded, smudged and inserted inside a plain white envelope. I found these letters during the epoch or episode when Oliver was running back and forth from his room to Edith's silken one. Sometimes he forgot to lock his own door. That is how I found Van Gogh's letters scattered on the floor of Oliver's room. Confused about printing them, I have developed what you would call a psychosomatic headache. I did not know what a headache was when I lived with Oliver.

My Dear Oliver,

It was an honor to receive you at Arles. Theo was not exaggerating when he said that you were a learned and brilliant man. Speak-

ing with you made me feel as though my work has not been in vain. All my life I have searched for a kindred spirit—someone who can share my feelings about nature. Perhaps when Dr. Gachet is finished with me, we can live together and work in peace. Since our works are different, there can only be mutual admiration and encouragement rather than the envy that one artist has for another since the other's viewpoint challenges not only his work but the entire edifice of his personality. I have great respect and admiration for scholars and historians, and unlike some painters I love to read. Think about it. If Theo should die or desert me I will have no one but you as a friend. Weakness or not, friendship is a necessary factor for my creativity.

Yours,
Vincent

Dear Oliver,

I hope that you are in the best of health. I am feeling much better nearly recovered from my last attack. I have done a portrait of Edith from your description. It is quite life-like and I cannot wait to show it to you. It is after Botticelli's "Primavera," since you mentioned the resemblance. Oliver, my friend, beautiful women are to be painted or written about (Zola understands this) since they are works of art and are as unfortunate as we are in not being fit for ordinary survival. The other women are to be taken care of if they are infirm, demented, or have falled into disgrace, or to be employed for the daily tasks that men of destiny tend to ignore. Cézanne thinks this way and surely he is a man of genius although I've never been able to converse with him. I have used very intense colors right out of the tube for the portrait. The background is cobalt blue. The hair is cadmium orange and the eyes are viridian green. When we live together I would like to paint your portrait. I may attempt to do it from memory or possibly paint a synthesis of you and me.

Yours,
Vincent

Dear Oliver,

I am happy to hear that your work is progressing well. Remember that I have the same faith in you as you have in me. Dr. Gachet thinks that it is best for me to remain with him a while longer. He tells me that I am improving. I feel sorry for him and so I pretend to agree for what worth would he think his work if he could not delude himself in this way? And what difference does it make to me? I think that my "fits" and withdrawals are from my inability to find a congenial place for myself among others who feel as I do. My malady is a protest against my own work, against the very work that is all I have and that I must do in order to prove that I was here on earth for some purpose. My entire life would have to be lived in a different way for there to be what he calls a "cure." But how can I go back to the past? Can you? Can you, Oliver, ever change the steps you took and which others forced you to take by their behavior when you trusted them so? (In my case a certain woman disappointed me and created this destiny out of the misery I felt.) Seclusion as we both know, as Luther knew, is necessary for a time. But it is not a cure. The cure if it is possible at all is to create a new society outside these walls with a very carefully chosen group of people who will have sympathy for one another's weaknesses. You and I will begin this society. Men like you and I must forsake intense emotions such as the love for a woman for the sake of our sanity and work.

Can we do this Oliver? I hope it is not too late.

Yours,
Vincent

You don't think that my Oliver left me to find Vincent Van Gogh and to create a new society with him—that he is wandering around the world looking for the dead painter? Sometimes I worry about this. I have studied the dates on the paintings very carefully. But Oliver did not know the year. Yet he circled numbers on the old calendars that formed his collection.

"There are more ways than one to look at things," he told me when I noticed that he circled the calendars in backward sequence. Even I knew the proper sequence of numbers, the number of days in a month and which month preceded another in the year. Oliver himself had taught me.

I should have tried harder. You will hear this again and again; it is the struggle, unending for my autonomy while sensing that it was damaging Oliver. Admittedly I have exaggerated my knowledge of emotion for the sake of narrative and diminished it too far for the sake of truth.

—

At this time in our life—was it not one life, considering the circumstances?—I already possessed a sufficient number of words to fill a mediocre, small college dictionary omitting words with more than six letters, short subtle ones and those with direct emotional significance. However, the gaps were not as noticeable as you might expect. If you, a lawyer with a love for the detective story or a creative curiosity about human behavior, were to have visited us—preposterous of course—you would have hardly noticed *my* deficiencies. Even if you are a most fair and discerning gentleman willing to dispense with usual prejudices which you reserve for your wife children and peers, you would have observed incorrectly. Oliver would have taken most of your attention while my own blankness and aberrations would have gone undetected. First, because Oliver is such a huge man and not groomed as you are. He has an old rusty razor blade that is quite insufficient for close shaves, so the bristle that grows all over his face has to be cut from time to time with an ordinary pair of scissors. We have one of these. Heaven knows of the variety of cuticle implements, scissors, nail clippers, tweezers and pruning shears possessed by Edith. To come to the point, sir, if you were in our rooms at this juncture or time, you would call me a liar. Enter, please. Your eyes, bespectacled of course, look and see bristly Oliver who drools ceaselessly from his huge underlip and walks hunched over hiding his head on his chest. From the back thin graying hair, although quite orange-brown in part, from the front. Huge, you say. What enormous ears with hair growing straight out from them, and such a bulbous veined nose with hairs protruding. Why doesn't he cut, snip or whatever? Oliver is not ugly I state. You contradict. Those are your eyes, sir, bespectacled of course. Mine have grown accustomed to what they see. Is it not so that in some primitive societies the most beautiful women have large bellies, enormous feet and no breasts? Well, in our culture, things are viewed in a different matter from yours sir. You know this, but to see it is another matter. I, upon seeing Oliver drool, or noting that one of his fingers is absent though not entirely, and that his ears are large and bent forward to say nothing of the hardened wax, take it at that. I feel no disgust. What have I to compare him with? *Your* ears look strange to me—pale, waxless, tiny, pushed back flat.

To your eyes, sir, I am an ordinary young lady, maybe a girl, maybe a woman—not the youngest but young all the same. No whining geeeh geeeh; my derangement is internal at this time. Your presence is making me nauseous but it is all for the sake of clarification. I am clean soapsmelling, neatly dressed if hairy legged. My movements are coordinated if not graceful or sexually provocative. Oliver, realizing, remembering that women walk with smaller steps, legs not too far apart, has corrected my original motions. I speak your language fluently. Only if you are very astute would you notice certain nasal sounds, prolonged hissing s's and an unexpected tumbling into the bass clef. Do you realize that oral expression is new to me and that accents, particularly the emotional ones, are absent? I doubt that your ear is that discerning with all the yelling honking clanging sounds clogging your head. Each of my words is evenly marked off, metronomed, or droned. You judge me calm, not realizing it is simply my inability to form long or precise thoughts. My unfamiliarity with the new environment that your presence creates is causing a further absence or retreat of my emerging self. My horned giraffe is invisible as it cuts off your head, smashes your spectacles or shouts incoherent ravings into your cotton-swabbed ear. Easily frozen, emotions cut off immediately by definitions or new diversions, you study me only slightly, focusing the intensity of your concentration upon Oliver. And that, I fear, is a mistake. He is what he is in motion, deed, physiognomy, eccentricity—apparent and unified—while whatever I am lies hidden beneath my education and his instruction. I know how to behave, sir. There, sit down at our table and I will serve you tea with a dry biscuit. "When company comes, tea and biscuits are served." I remember that sentence from one of my grammar lessons. How kindly Oliver explained to me what "company" was. And if they should come, how I would conduct myself—this was hypothetical of course, unless he was truly concerned that some day I might have to face such an occasion. Predictably, I asked, quite unwisely, but he assured me that Edith was not "company" and that *I* was "company" if anyone was. He added that I should not mention her name again. He did this so often. Not with spite did he say that *I* was "company." In matters of instruction, even now, Oliver keeps his emotional feelings submerged. At least most of the time. Not in the matter of word lists as I have explained. I am prepared for your visit superficially, sir. You do not even dream that you are my first guest. Oliver is absent at tea. But you glimpse him carrying Edith's dresses from her locked room into his own room. At this time Oliver's room is little more than a junk pile. Oliver's plain paper room is gone. I hope that you never see it, sir, so much does it express Oliver's difficulties and preoccupations. Edith's gowns hang from hooks he carefully attached to his wall moldings. Much of his day is spent exchanging one dress for another, weighing and considering the matter, making important decisions. "What *are* you doing?" Not even you would ask, seeing the absorbed expression of a man who is intent upon his day's work. Perhaps you recognize yourself at your ledgers and documents or perusing the ordinary telephone book with your thick index finger. With a similar madness, everyone's workday is possessed of this quality—by which I mean purpose, accomplishment and absorption as well as a desire for completion. But Oliver's work, like that of bees or ants, is continuous. Interspersed fortunately with periods of calm, of concentration upon his history book and furthering my ofttimes neglected education. He changes at odd moments, and I have hope of a vague sort. Sweating and pale, you judge him correctly not to be in the pink of health nor at the peak of his powers, creative or otherwise. He has lost interest in me for the most part, but don't go jumping to conclusions. Perhaps that is my reason for inviting you to tea—I sensed an ulterior motive from the beginning. Loneliness. I am happy to see you, sir. We chat in the foreground while Oliver goes about his business, his dissolution in the background. I see you squinting over my head at Oliver, trying to guess at our relationship. Impossible sir. Just drink your tea. Even I cannot guess. Yes, we have sex sometimes—not as often as is normal or desirable. And we have certain formal conversations about the day's events, soap, potatoes and sleep. Punctured, our carefully planned routines, by brief or long separations. No, he isn't always acting in this manner and I am not shocked or worried about it; whatever Oliver does is correct, logical by my standards. Am I lonely you ask. Yes, lonely, a word I don't know. I am forbidden certain things and allowed others. No. I don't understand most of your questions. I am in love with Oliver. And thank you for coming to visit us.

I have made a lovely summer day in our garden. Birds are alive and the large butterfly is resurrected for the occasion. Even the grass is a perfect shade of green, uniform, mixed in a pail. To the left of the coral bench, the lilac bush is blooming and fresh water is filling the birdbath opposite. The red veins of the coral bench have emerged elongating into streamers that float gaily in several rhythms. Red flowers that are not real but cut from paper, grow between grass-blades in symmetrical clumps. I hope Oliver likes it. Everything is prepared, waiting for our wedding day. He appears, dressed for the occasion. I wear a violet gown covered with dew, and a white veil. Oliver wears a black suit, a red tie and red gloves. He looks magnificent and happy. "Are you happy Oliver?" "I really don't see the necessity..." he begins, but I run about arranging the flowers and making the grass stand up straight. "I am being a bit conventional," I admit to Oliver. He just laughs and looks up at the green and orange sun realizing that it is a concession just for him. "I forgot the ring," reaching into his pocket. "A blade of grass will do," I say as he twirls it around my finger where it crystalizes into an emerald. "I have invited Vincent, Hitler and Martin Luther, among others." Oliver looks puzzled. "I don't see the necessity... don't tell me you forgot Napoleon Bonaparte?" he asks suddenly alarmed. "There he comes." I point to a small figure who enters carrying a gift. "Your army can wait outside," I say to Napoleon as politely as I can. "Josephine is heartily welcome." "Oh, that's been over for a long time," he says looking hurt. "The German princess?" I ask. "Irrelevant," he answers with gravity. "Will he object to Tolstoi?" I ask Oliver. Oliver laughs. "This is a wedding, not a political arena... who are all those men with dark glasses and white canes?" "Just friends," I answer evasively. "It is a sacred and beautiful event," Oliver says after the ceremony. "But what can come next. That is what worries me, Oliver." "There are always nuances," I am happy except that the resurrected butterfly is dead. It couldn't last the entire day.

Oliver and I had sexual relations until the end or near the end. To cater to my imaginary guest's questions as well as to the questions you must be asking yourself, I will be more specific. (From living outside I am aware of the confusions and curiosity about sex.) Needless to say that when I lived with Oliver I knew nothing about rights—not in any form, and certainly nothing about woman's rights to orgasm. There were those occasions when he was not preoccupied with Edith—that is, before she had entirely taken him, and when he thought his historical encyclopedia was going well—that he proved himself to be a master of the most minute aspects of lovemaking. I know this now having read the most up-to-date manuals on female anatomy, orgasm and man's traditional ignorance of the fact, not to mention God's error. Oliver was not ignorant. Oliver knew about the clitoris. But he was a man of changes. When he felt like being generous, he was the best lover even in your world. Although I did not like him to say this, he insisted that I was not a virgin before him. You know this. But since *that* consciousness was gone and has never returned, Oliver was my first lover and I *was* a virgin. Do you think he would have preferred it if I had been an authentic virgin? I felt uneasy and undeserving during those times when he was most detailed, considerate, generous; not that I resisted pleasure after I matured. I did not understand it. Nor did I understand how there could be so much pleasure at one time and none at another. Now that I have studied Oliver in retrospect, I suspect that he gave me great pleasure and then none at all in order to confuse me and assert his mastery over me. Is that probable according to your own studies? Perhaps it was the variation of his inner life also—that strange clash between present occupation and past obsession that began to make all his actions, particularly toward me, totally unpredictable. It was during this time that I began to experience a feeling I can now name as acute anxiety.

Oliver did not teach me how to give him pleasure. He preferred that I remain passive. I understand that now and it makes me unhappy in the same way as the omission of a name does. Or the dark glasses that eclipsed me from his sight. Had I been experienced technically, it would have interfered with his own fantasies—with his control. This is my present self speaking. Having become inventive and somewhat resourceful by then, I attempted to do things to Oliver. It made him angry. I stopped instantly, realizing that things were becoming precarious. Despite my verbal outbursts and my disobedience in asking questions about Edith, I still awaited Oliver's instructions. I also awaited his sexual impulses. It is not as though I truly rebelled or tried to lead Oliver, or to assert a self beyond him—I didn't desire such a self. That it grew, despite my wishes or Oliver's, is unfortunate. Only once did I make a mistake and approach Oliver tugging at his penis and starting to undress, subtlety being foreign to me at that time and even now. (Imagine Edith doing such a thing.) He slapped me. Do not be shocked. I assure you that I was not injured, and I knew better next time. I pretended indifference until Oliver felt the inclination. What could I have known about human rights or the widespread desire for self-expression? If you are feeling sorry for me or thinking that Oliver was selfish, remember that you are feeling what you have been taught. Remember that Oliver knew about the clitoris and he was a good lover when he was in the mood, not thinking thump thump thump was the end of it. Nor was I sexually frustrated, not until he ignored me altogether. It was a combination of many things. Now, having learned your customs, my frustration tolerance is as low as yours is and I would feel deprived and angry in such a situation. At that time I could go on to something else and not feel sex-hungry all day as we do out here. I tell you that it was a different world, a prettier star, difficult as it is for you to believe.

—

It is so hard; memory gets lost sometimes up up to those high tree branches seeing little out of big and littler ones spreading, a million being blown by the wind hit in the head by the knifesun until I think I am a silver horsey being peeled pecked krak krak krak by the big red pecker beak until all the egg cells disappear, the cervix melts and womb is blown up big big up up with airfumes until the hollow horsey flies into the sky dropping heart, intestines, liver and ovary flowers into the bleeding ground.

—

My education continued despite Oliver's intense preoccupation. (My Oliver fought a hard battle before giving in to Edith forever.) I was instructed in all things that were basic. He was very insistent that I understand the differences between the sexes. My confusion had first become apparent to him when he found me so desperately trying to wear his clothing. I told you about that. "Never do that again," loud stamping his boot and tearing off the clothes with rough rips, red-faced, gasping, lower lip way down inside-out dripping long sticky saliva. Next a purple beating, "aaooow, aaooow," belt-strap wump wump wump, then falling to the floor red, leaving Oliver's face now white. The big hand is over his eyes and he goes dragging his boots away not turning back. Oliver, dazed, going away, disappearing. Pain.

Despite the violet dress I did it again. And I attempted to urinate in the way that Oliver did. The results were shameful. Anger again. "Aaooow, aaooow," belt-strap wump wump wump. Anger faded, he patiently drew diagrams for me with the parts of the male and female bodies explained and labeled in detail. Ask me. I can tell you that your Freud was not as dumb as some of you think. I definitely wished for a penis like Oliver's, not in dreams or below in that other part of the mind but right out in the open. How could one not wish for such a thing, seeing it working and not having one? Yes, take it from me, your Freud was correct, quite smart in fact. Men with small ones want bigger ones and secretly want breasts. They must be all confused having nipples right there and no breasts. Some of the nipples even stand up and feel things. (Of course I have not traveled or had too many experiences.) Oliver went into too much detail at the time. But I kept these diagrams and referred to them later. In addition he made lists of clothing that were for men and those for women. "Learn these lists," he said, returning to Edith. My Oliver was ingenious if not up to present styles. Never did I hear of slacks, pantsuits, shorts or such apparel for women. He knew that I would never have understood, particularly if he had taught me of flyfront slacks that women wear. Outside I was shocked to see women in slacks, felt that Oliver had lied to me, but finally saw that the effect was different in most cases, particularly with the floral or silken slacks. But I still have difficulty with the frontal zippers. Why do women wear them? At first I considered the possibility that Oliver, not wishing to confuse me, omitted a category of women who have small penises. Later I learned that this was not the case. I never wear flyfronts myself, thinking that Oliver would be angry if he saw me, and still considering it somehow improper—wump wump wump. So far I have not seen men in dresses although I have read about them. I read about everything but it is really insufficient. An interpreter is necessary. And I have pride, pride learned from Oliver and from you. Instinctively I have learned to ask questions obliquely or to find out the answers myself. I wish I had been this way when I lived with Oliver.

I am trying to create an expression for my face that looks like I am not puzzled and wondering about everything. It is like hiding my toys—one thing for real adults to paint pictures or to play with clay and another thing for me to do it.

—

Away. Inside the closets of pale silk, a hailstorm of placements and replacements diminishing me. Always. I. Without Oliver. Hunched into a tiny silly ball writing compositions with my fingers a pencil outside not inside the very inside of my head. Almost gone. Stretching up suddenly in the silent time with a whispered moan a wounded giraffe talking with staccato dots over each word zit zit zit over the broken sun wrapped in twirling whirling ice pah giraffe cut the doors dressed shoes Edith home stepping over the broken sun wrapped in twirling whirling ice edges pulled falling into the red toilet sucking her inside flush it down around it all disappears like a bracelet cup or Oliver's penis getting big great big blue bigger than you your neck spots up to the ceiling with the word PENIS tacked on grab everything away we will hide and Oliver will look under and over and behind and in front calling where are you where are you wump wump wump belt-strap on giraffe's buttocks krak krak krak peck his head so I see inside peck my head open way down too so the red blue yellow glass circles squares rectangles things fall out and Oliver catches them open the door giraffe quick kill them kill them the doors the dresses kill it the colors.

Oliver, forseeing the end you should have taken me into the world on occasion. Did you keep me inside deliberately so that I might have to endure in a world unfamiliar to me just as you had to endure in a world without Edith? You might have had some consideration all the same. Mean Oliver, always thinking of yourself, forgetting that I existed. Why couldn't we have walked these treacherous streets together? You could have deciphered things for me. It is too hard. I would have clutched your hand too tightly and made you angry. Or I would have wanted to go home and never come outside again. Can't you come to help me for a little while? Why must I live these hours and days without you, tick tick tick? If we pass on the street will we know each other? Maybe you shaved off your beard and got very thin and clean, pinned your ears back and cleaned them. Do you hide your finger in a mitten? I have a different expression on my face, wear a gray suit with a light blue blouse and carry a yellow umbrella. There is a watch on my wrist, tick tick tick, pink lipstick and straightened hair. How would you know me? What if you have changed your mind and are looking everywhere for me and I am really around the corner having lunch next to you, squeezed at one of those smooth counters rag-wiped. I promise not to ever mention Edith again. I will stop learning words and wear my old plaid skirt and child's blouse. You can feed me yourself and I won't talk or run after you. If you want to stay out here, I will stay with you peeling potatoes without breaking the skin like you taught me. Unless it makes you mad. I will become stupid again even if I have to beat my head with a hammer. All I need is one chance. You will hardly know I am there, not need those dark glasses or fingers in your ears. Is that what you would like, Oliver? I hope I can do this now that I've learned so much. I think I can do anything for you.

Here it is dark and light dark and light
Crosshatched cold blank on up down bulb
Headvision birds treetips shadow on the
Vacant cold wall noon rings in my head

Screams light the black singed moon out
Not there

No time. No ticking. A variety of actions to define movement. Unpredictable. I told you that my Oliver is unpredictable. Worse. Oliver coming down the patched hall with my lessons—always a repetition of lessons I had already learned. Why? Suddenly changing his mind and walking backwards, slowly to his room sometimes. Doors locked without explanation. Brilliant excerpts read to me from his encyclopedia and then no reading, no reference to work. A sluggishness. Oliver sleeping for a long time and waking up confused, peeling a potato and leaving it with a bewildering glance, or carrying a satin dress from Edith's room and then returning it. Finally the abrupt appearance of synthetic plastics and foul-smelling chemicals, a sound of patting and sawing, Oliver greenish forgetting to eat, not caring about me, whether or not I ate, not speaking to me at all. Then looking at me with careful scrutiny and urging me, far away, to do my lessons or to brush my teeth. Forgetting to come into my bed, not noticing if I followed him whining. Not caring at all. Then alert, eyes shining alert telling me about the moon and the sun and the rotation of the earth. Me smiling and listening, happily memorizing the solar system, the constellations, the tilting of the earth's axis. Oliver forgetting, looking blank when I recited what he had taught me. Me—humble, obedient now, never knowing what to expect, beginning to develop thumping of the heart, hearing Oliver's door open, not knowing which Oliver would emerge. Shaking of the hands when Oliver shouted that I was stupid and that the food tasted like wood. Our schedule punctured, lost and periodically reissued with angry resolutions by Oliver. "It is important, imperative, urgent that we keep to a schedule." Stamping his foot, banging his fist into the wall. For a few days the schedule was adhered to until Oliver forgot. I was always waiting and listening not understanding, not knowing enough to be silent. "Is she coming?" I still asked, more out of nervous habit than anything. (I had read her letters, understood parts.) I wrote my own compositions which Oliver did not see and made up many words from the ones I knew. Sensing confusion, I invented rules, orders of my own, wrote word lists, drew the horned giraffe, the owl, ram, solar system, cooked and cleaned talking to myself endlessly, using up space, waiting to understand. "Do not disturb me," he announced, not looking at me before entering his room with the terrible chemicals, melted plastics and intestinal parts, organs snatched from the insides of chickens. He stayed away for a long time. My fingertips were raw from scratching the locked door to his room. Afraid to say something wrong, still unable to control myself, I stuffed my mouth with cloth. Fearing to knock definitively, to hear the clarity of my own need, I used my nails. When they were blunt and useless there was the tapping of my fingertips. Then the rubbing of grazed elbows. When my fingertips bled I sucked them, relieved of my longing by this diversion. I with my mouth stuffed could not say, "Why won't you come out, Oliver?" or "What are you doing?" or "Please let me come in." Besides it was never our language. In our own situation a unique pattern of communication had arisen. The words that existed were reserved for my instruction, for the games and entertainments that we devised or for formal conversations. That was the way he wanted it. For our needs born in heart, hands, brain, liver (or wherever such are born), we had only symbols. When I lay on my back with my knees scraping the door, it was my way of telling of my loneliness. Oliver knew. I don't want *you* on a witness stand. We both knew that as far as the meaning of the symbol went it was deciphered correctly. I will not ask, "Oliver, were you being deliberately cruel on those days when you did not respond at all?" It is as likely that he would attack my persistence as an audacious disregard of his privacy, Oliver being a very private man who didn't even like his genitals to be touched without special permission, or his clothing to be worn or carried to bed. He could say that I was unwilling to understand why he remained silent. The latter would be an unfair accusation. Not until later did I know all about it. By then I was no longer spontaneous enough to lie there and express what I felt, knowing he was with Edith and totally inaccessible. But at the time I was selfish, knew only my need, a need that had taken stronger form each "year" or moment of our life together.

A selfish little girl in the form of a woman—no one could have put up with me and my speech. Oliver noticed my mouth stuffed with cloth. He liked it. It hurts me to tell you that. But Oliver liked my mouth stuffed with cloth; he came out more often. He even spoke to me and taught me—not things about words, but about the weather which I could not see, about rain, snow and the formation of clouds. To me with my mouth dry, silent with cloth, he could speak unafraid. Deliberately, deliberately, I know Oliver used very small words to keep me from learning any more. In labeling the parts of a bird, he wrote beak, wing, ear and belly instead of upper and lower mandible, auriculars, abdomen and other such scientific nomenclature. And of clouds I learned only one name: cloud. Nothing of Altocumulus, Altostratus, Cirrocumulus, Cirrostratus, Cirrus, Cumulonimbus, Cumulus, Nimbostratus, Stratocumulus, Stratus, Mammatocumulus. He was overly cautious, hoping secretly that I would forget my entire vocabulary. The stuffings in my mouth prevented questions or wrong statements, kept Oliver with me for a while. Oliver, telling me that a cloud was wet smoke, fearing to introduce the word vapor, not distinguishing between emotional and technical words in his censorship. That is what became of Oliver and of my education. I am ashamed to admit that I did not care at all. As long as Oliver was there noticing me, speaking, not always locked away, I was happy. Think of it. What right did I have to speak at all if it upset Oliver. Besides, I thought. I thought best when my mouth was thus stuffed. But do not think of me as a saint or as a totally sacrificial being. If I had been, if I had kept my mouth stuffed forever, things would have been tolerable for Oliver. On occasion I spat out the rags and began my own incessant monologues which included Oliver and his room and beautiful Edith who was far far away in the snow and on and on and on until Oliver ran away. Too late I put the rags back and scratched at his door.

No. My feelings did not diminish. Believe, if you wish, those agents who write of diminishing desire and of the gradual dissolution of intensity through time, of the need for variety and of the contempt that familiarity breeds. It was not true in my case. The reverse. Part of the reason, I admit, was that I had not been exposed to any propaganda whatsoever before meeting Oliver. And so. But stop. You will say then, how did you develop your attitudes and prejudices; are you blaming Oliver again? I ask myself now, a sophisticated being with a past. Yes, Oliver indoctrinated me. And my unconscious, if you believe in such an entity, rose to the occasion; pre-prejudiced, it made its choices. I do not believe that. If all educators will believe my testimony, I learned everything good by reward and the rest by imitation. The punishments accomplished far less, passed quite unnoticed for the most part or caused regressions, confusion, hidden things.

—

What would I have been without Oliver? What would I not have been? And what would have been identical? Unfortunately I do not know and never will. But I did learn words from him. Discounting the unconscious, if you insist on assuming I had a past and that with a past goes an unconscious. But as far as I know I learned my words from him and he became my unconscious. From the cards he printed and pasted on objects, from the lessons and games we played came words. And I can assure you that it was from Oliver that I learned the use of these words, and that they were nonfunctional for the emotional life. I hate him for it. Such depths of confusion and irrationality it has thrown me into. Suicide would not have occurred to me half a dozen times if I had learned how to apply a word to my despair. But I don't mean... I think I have said all this before. But I love repetition. Boredom is unknown to me. I would have been happy to do the same things with Oliver day after day forever. I am not like you in this way. Except that I became curious. I have lied too. I have lied about emotions. Oliver did not teach me the word "jealousy" or its meaning, nor did I learn it from your competitive society. But I felt it when he was sawing and working with the chemical compounds in his room. I am a very jealous person, more so now that I understand the term. More so now that I have nothing at all. Ask me if you want to know what is learned and what is felt spontaneously. Jealousy is felt easily, spontaneously. Unless I learned it from Oliver. Don't forget that his unconscious was mine.

—

Do you think Oliver feared *my* departure? Was his subsequent withdrawal from me a defense mechanism? No. Not even I believe that, not for a moment. I would like to. I would like to think of my Oliver's disappearance as a precaution—he wanted to leave first. But he knew I would never leave. And I stayed for a long time after he disappeared, not changing a single thing, hardly moving, waiting for him to come back, knowing that he would not.

III

I knew for a long time that Oliver was visited by someone; then I knew things that my vocabulary and thoughts did not know. Later I pretended to be more ignorant than I really was. Even now it gives me an excuse for my errors—a permanent excuse in fact. Besides, ignorance is rewarded. Even here a naive quality is charming; people are less defensive. Speaking with a slight slur or mispronouncing words gains trust.

On these occasions he would make scrupulous preparations. He shaved beneath his beard with the rusty razor blade, and plucked the longest hairs from his nostrils and ears. This was a painful process; he grimaced and groaned softly with hard breathing. This sudden concern for his appearance and for matters of personal hygiene warned me of the visit. Ordinarily Oliver cared little about his physical appearance. (You know this about my Oliver. You know that he did not like soap and water and splashing as much as I did although he knew the rituals involved and taught them to me.) In fact he went about stinking much of the time, I now know. Not as much as he stank when I first came. There were long intervals between baths. *Now* these stenches would repel me, particularly since I am aware of their origins: formation of smegma on the prepuce beneath the foreskin, stale perspiration under the armpits, urine, moldy sperm ejaculated in sleep or otherwise long dead, attacks of diarrhea, vomiting and so forth. Then I was not so discerning. I found nothing about Oliver offensive to my crude senses. The cliché about love being blind must then be true, yet it would be more honest to admit that ignorance and a lack of the normal civilizing influences left my senses of taste and smell quite coarse. Compared to yours my senses are still undeveloped. For example, all perfumes smell the same to me and I cannot tell a well-cooked meal from a poorly-cooked one. Nor am I sensitive to bad breath, although I am beginning to notice its occurrence. (Do not misunderstand—I use a deodorant and try every one I hear about. I am quite anxious to conform.) The shock of Oliver's disappearance took away whatever rebelliousness I had inside me.

"Do I smell all right?" was a question I asked incessantly of the woman who shared my office. She was patient and I must commend her. It seems to be important, very important, in this world. I am stalling. Do you know me well enough to know when I am stalling, when I do not like a certain subject and get lost in other things?

—

I was surprised by the suddenness with which these seizures overcame him. Oliver scrubbed his armpits, underneath his scrotum, and reached way inside his ears with cloth-covered matchsticks. He even sprayed himself with a florid smelling liquid and washed his shirt which still smelled from Oliver. His feet were placed, one at a time, into the washbasin and scrubbed with a metallic clothes brush saturated in a chemical detergent. The clawlike toenails were filed and sanded—not that this helped them. No one has toenails as hard as Oliver's. They feel like stone.

I experienced uneasiness at these abrupt changes. Remember, my perceptions were no longer diffuse; I could think although my translations of events were inadequate. Left out with no part to play—that is the translation of my feelings when these visits began or rather when my consciousness acknowledged them. I must have felt this keenly since I can recall the sensations and now classify them as anxiety: a squeezing together of the stomach muscles, sporadic acceleration of the heart, weakness in the legs, a giddy sensation, a loss of interest in my daily schedule and in my weekly assignments. Oh my Oliver was not devoid of deviousness. He knew of my presence, and despite his urgency he made certain that many lessons had been prepared for me. "Do your work well," he would say abruptly when handing me an impossible number of assignments. No pat on the head. A severe warning look in his eyes when he gave this command so I usually took the assignments obediently and pretended to begin. I knew I was losing Oliver. I knew many things on that strange child-level but I was helpless.

The visitations took place in Oliver's room, out of my sight, behind a locked door. For the occasion Oliver put his room in order. Oliver's idea of putting things in order was to make piles of objects according to their size. Thus books, calendars, clothing conforming to certain dimensions (such as eight by twelve inches) went into one pile. Larger items regardless of category went onto another mound, and on and on with these piles placed in a long line against each wall. The center of the room was wiped with a dry cloth—Oliver down on his hands and knees with a magnifying glass and a magnetic dust rag. (I—on a chair looking over the crack on the top of the door.) Finally two chairs were placed in the exact center of the room. And a round lamp table stolen from another room or secret hiding place was put between them. Settings for two were carefully arranged. Dainty white china with purple roses as well as antique silverware had been extricated ceremoniously from the shelf of a locked closet.

Pressed against the door, red-eared, I listened to their conversation.

"Edith, why do you stay away so long. No one can ever take your place and I will wait through all eternity. Come, precious bird, sit on my knee. I won't crush your wings. See how neat and clean your Oliver has become. Let me pour you a cup of tea. Be careful, I don't want you to burn yourself. There, is it sweet enough? . . ."

There were many endearments: sweet rose, precious bird, darling, little flower, crystal wren. (Oliver never called me anything at all.) I listened hot-eared, never hearing *her* voice. Nor did I ever catch a glimpse of her. Perhaps she hid seeing my mad horned eyes up over the door. But I knew they made love, heard my Oliver moan in an ecstasy he never experienced with me—louder orgasms, ejaculations like swift fountains. Searching his bed when he carelessly left his door open, I found Edith's undergarments strewn, tangled in the sheets—lace-trimmed, elegant, colored violet or pale blue. (Now I too have violet, blue, and lace things that Oliver would like. Not then.)

Oliver slept almost constantly for several days after these visits, waking only to urinate and swallow a little tea and bread. When he did fully reawaken, he seemed confused for a time, walked blindly not caring where I was or whether or not I had done my assignments. Never touching me. Gradually he recovered. Nothing happens all at once. You know that already. If only I had known what to do, how *not* to drive him further, deeper into the violet bed. Inevitably he was drowned, possessed. "Was Edith here again?" And he looked at me with a look I now know as hate. Oliver hating me after he had cared for me and fed me and taught me everything I knew. "Aaooow, aaooow, aaooow."

He did not wear the opaque glasses yet nor did he abandon me completely, came back slowly sometimes. He, the old Oliver rolling a black-eyed potato to me across the floor, "oom, oom." But it wasn't the same. Gone the busy carnival of "we" *then*—whirling toilet, twirling potato skins knifed off in a slow deliberate turn, blue purple yellow flames up and down under yellow eggs, guggle gugle hsssss pah pah. Ch ch ch ts ts ts of salt and pepper falling on flat gold circles. All this a circular laughing dance of water, flamestove sounds as surprising and new as your early rains on spring green leaves spun from sleeping yellow buds. Innocent. Gone.

The visitations became more and more frequent, particularly during the end of the violet year and running into the other one. But that was not the worst that happened. The visits probably occured all along at intervals and I only became aware of them during this time, no longer slipping backward into sweet sameness. Eyes open, hurting, wide. It took him longer to return to me; I am sure of this, and of the precarious quality to his reappearances. Later, I tried to hold on to him. (Don't go away, Oliver.) I feigned stupidly glazing my eyes, trying to fall away remote as Oliver himself, uttering low sounds, "oomah, oomah, geeh, geeh, geeh," but Oliver no longer trusted me. I realize that now. It became increasingly difficult for him to recapture his affection for me, his pride in my accomplishments. Oliver, my sweet Oliver, even suspected me when I was being truthful. Once, rolling the grapefruit back and forth on the floor, a game I never ceased to enjoy despite my development, he suddenly looked at me (a quick photograph—click—of me, my Oliver-smile in violet), frowned and stepped on the grapefruit. Pain. Sting of the juice into my eyes, squirting. I understand. He thought I was faking interest in our old game. Far away, he did not know what I was like. And I will admit that had I really lost interest I *would* have pretended. He was right not to trust me. I changed as much as he did. One day my mouth was stuffed with rags to keep from mentioning Edith. Rags flying out of my mouth at other times; I could not stop my elongated tongue from imitating the chaotic names and colors in my mind. Or else I stopped at nothing trying to win back his attention and praise, presenting him with pictures of giraffes, kangaroos, goats, owls and wild pigs. He resisted. Nothing that I did kept Oliver. I should really have no regrets. Wasn't it already too late?

Oliver's crisis, yes, *that.* He was having difficulties. Preparations became more elaborate and obsessive. Often trying to remove hairs from his cheeks, he cut himself, face full of scratches zig-zag. He burned his toes and testicles by soaking himself in water that was too hot. Scalding. Just to please her. He broke many elegant purple-rosed dishes as he carried them into his room with shaking hands, stepped on the glass, unaware that his bare feet were bleeding. Transformations stinging my eyes like grapefruit juice—his room strangely lit with blue and orange bulbs, sprayed with perfume from ancient atomizers in pairs or far apart. Doors unlocked swiftly and then locked again.

Oliver's bed was now covered with a pink satin spread dotted with specks of blood, his ears bleeding from unsuccessful efforts to penetrate the hardened wax with dangerous instruments. Preparations completed, perfect, the door was closed. Oliver waited.

What did I feel at this time when I was almost totally ignored? In part I echoed Oliver's frenzy. I waited. I shook. Perhaps I expected to be invited inside one day to sip tea with Oliver and Edith. I was unable to feel very much. But I remember how lonely the corridor was. Silent except if I clapped my hands or made objects move. I continued. Do not ever imagine that I was a true adult capable of overt mourning and prolonged despair. Not me—peeling potatoes, washing, talking to myself, cutting papers, rereading letters, I forgot his absence sometimes. I was selfish and only wanted Oliver to come out and play with me. What did I know or care of the failure that was taking place behind the door—of Oliver's shame and anguish? Nothing. What of Pity? None. I felt no pity whatsoever. And still know little about it. That is why the blind men are happy to take me places and laugh at things I say and dial my number incessantly on their braille telephones. A serious matter, I admit—this total absence of pity. But Oliver never showed me what it was by explanation or demonstration. (You probably would not like me because of this trait.) If you told me that you were dying or very sick, I would listen and ask what I could do but I would *feel* nothing at all. I want to. But I do not understand what it is. Pity is a hard feeling, I must tell you. Ask me and I will tell you the easy and hard feelings. Jealousy, as I have already mentioned, is easy and so is faking and pretending. But pity is hard. Oliver never pitied me and I never pitied him. Fear and anxiety are natural and easy. I try to feel pity looking at those broken people in wheelchairs. But I don't. Nor do I pity myself, although I can see that there are some things others might pity such as my efforts to understand society and my loss of Oliver. Now, not then, I can understand on an intellectual level that Oliver was suffering during those visits. At the time I understood nothing about it.

Here it is dark and light dark and light
Vertical shapes crawl like snakes inside
Blue walls of my speckled brain high on
The edge of a tree a giraffe is weeping
Here real blackbirds desperate as moths
Pound at the fake blue sky now shrieking
Not there

There were hints that even the dullest mind would have perceived. But connections were hard for me to make. Warnings fell against me undeciphered.

—

I remember it. Not as well as the hand feeding me or the voice saying "chew." Not as well as the red paper for my toilet training nor as clearly as the wording of my first paragraph. No, it was not that important. Still I must tell you. Quickly quickly before I twist it into something else or leave an empty space.

He left Edith in the middle of everything—only once. Me—I was absorbed, trying to construct a story with French words.

"Oliver, le duc, a un cheval qui est malade. Il joue avec moi tous les jours et moi, je parle avec lui. Aujourd'hui il a une toux violente. J'ai besoin d'un autre ami. Je décide á trouver le lion. Où est le lion, Oliver? Oliver regarde son rasoir. Il refuse à repondre..." Hardly hearing Oliver behind me, not understanding when he grabbed me with a brutality I had never felt from Oliver even when he punished me—wump wump wump. He carried me into *my* room, not his, threw me on the bed and raped me. I do not like to say that about my Oliver. But he did. That it hurt because Oliver is so large, so wide in circumference when fully erect was the least of it. "Edith, Edith," he called me while he reached heights of passion that he had never reached with me before. It wasn't me, it was Edith—that is the bad part. Oh, I admit that I deserved it for my constant taunting and mentioning her name. It may have been some kind of revenge. No. It was too spontaneous for that. Had he not called me "Edith," which even I knew was not my name, I could forgive him. But I who hardly existed at all, whose image in the mirror was vague, who was unnamed—even I felt a sense of being exchanged, eclipsed, turned into something that was nothing. And for the first time I did not seek Oliver. I retreated from him.

My feelings were not defined but I reacted strongly. Not reasoning any of this out, not comprehending it, I lay on the corridor floor, barely moving, far away, much like I had been when I had appeared over two years before. This time no clumsy hand with an amputated finger reached out to give me food, to wash me or to carry me into bed. He was ashamed or confused or too ill to make any attempts. Or he was asleep and uncaring—it may have been only a dream to Oliver.

I remained like that for several days knowing nothing. You may think this reaction extreme or an exaggeration. No—it was all those things I knew, really, but could not say. Too much even for me this changing Oliver moving further and further away. But it hadn't been sufficient to destroy my desire to exist. This act could alienate me temporarily from the physical Oliver but it could not erase the beginning. Beginning is the pretty star from which I came. The bright red, the greentwig early laughter orangesweet of Oliver. Annihilation could come to me but not this easily. Had I some experience, I would have known that Oliver was more damaged than I. I would have made an attempt, despite his indifference, to show him that the blow had not been fatal. Instead I lay mute, waiting for him. I knew nothing of pity.

—

Today I have many thoughts about this rape—now when it is too late. The most recent one may shock you particularly coming from me, but it will show you how clever I have become. I wish he had done it again and again, calling me "Edith," until I would have grown used to it and become the beloved. Yes, a sacrifice, and an illusion—but think of it! Her visits would no longer have been necessary, and if the delusion had endured, *I* would have sat opposite Oliver sipping tea from the purple-rosed china. *And he would have never ever gone.*

Soon after this event, Oliver appeared intermittently in glasses that were nearly opaque. He did not wear them constantly. Not yet. Were the glasses to make sure that I could not be mistaken for Edith, or were they to eclipse my ugliness from his eyes. I am not certain.

> I have filled the birdbath with blood and murdered every living thing in our garden. Both butterflies are immobile with torn wings. Birds are stuffed and preserved in transparent boxes like crystal coffins. Nothing moves or blows over or under the wax grass. I want to shock Oliver with bottles of formaldehyde with preserved fingers and chicken claws floating inside. He comes toward me smiling, half expecting a green and orange sun or warm snowflakes. "Now that we are married we have to settle old scores and clean up the mess or else remain dead," I explain. To my surprise he begins to laugh. Then he empties my bottles of chicken wings and dead

> fingers. "Death cannot be pickled for your pleasure or revenge," he says smiling. But his eyes aren't smiling. "Today is the result of the absence of pity," we both say in unison. I notice blood coming from Oliver's ears and watch it like watching a colored fountain. He watches my trembling like watching leaves move. "Bring pity next time or I won't let you in," I command. "You may not like it," he answers, leaving me alone in the garden. I have spoiled the garden which was meant for Oliver and me to play in and to be happy in. I try but cannot awaken the butterfly. Finally I leave. Oliver and I have never touched.

"Rape"—I say that word over and over again, trying to extract its meaning. Have I used it incorrectly? Not according to your definitions. But your definitions do not concern me. Brutality is not the issue. Oliver's moods had been unstable and unpredictable for a long time. Once he banged his hand into the wall, suddenly, unreasonably. Were it not for the tapestries insinuating, protecting, hiding and muting everything, he would have broken it. It wasn't the sudden brutality although I do not like such things. He had failed with Edith. That is why I call it rape. His preparations, the white antiqued teacups, silver-rimmed, purple-rosed, were for *her*. Exotic lighting, grotesque satin spread, the scratches on his face, aching ears invaded by sticks to remove the hard wax—all for *her*. Nothing for *me*. I know.

I knew. Without powers of reason, emotions can be either very strong (too much chaos unnamed) or absent as in the case of pity. He came to me with his "rape" because he had failed with Edith. Either she had refused him or had departed suddenly. (This was a new trick of hers, disappearing in the midst of his most ardent love-making.) I know something of what went on since I often stood on a chair and looked over the small slit between the top of his door and the upper molding. I saw. It used to go well for him. He was satisfied and she seemed almost as eager as he was. Those were the days when he slept afterward, when he had prepared with moderation rather than frenzy, days when he still cared whether or not I ate, slept or washed. Then it was no longer easy. Oliver pumping up and down on the rose-smooth spread in the midst of her lavender underthings, beige shoes with green bows tossed to the floor. Oliver's head in her violet hat, sweating, pale, the blue veins of his penis bulging with eager pain as she became elusive. Disappeared. It was this blue-veined penis prepared by Edith and for Edith that he thrust into *me* after she had escaped. Later it made him hate me. When he realized. What had *I* to do with the beauty of Edith? My Oliver is not a sex maniac—do not think this. If that was all there was to it, then *I* would have been sufficient. No—he was a deeply sensitive and mystical man in search of a pure beauty that constantly eluded him. I will admit something to you. This quality is not specific to my Oliver; I have met it again and again in your world, not as refined, not as excruciating or absolute as that of Oliver. I mean that blue-veined penis clumsily searching for something beyond flesh, beyond anyone—I have met it often. Blindly seeking something else with all that thumping and pushing and impatient rushing inside everyone, anyone. Yet doing everything to make it disappear with all that bursting nothingness. It is one thing I am already familiar with. Because of Oliver I know more about men than some of you—because of Oliver's extremes. I know about the failures of blunt red or blue penises. Not a physical failure, necessarily. Women think it is a matter of physical beauty, are fooled by the fake pictures men like, by their staring at parts of bodies. It is all an act. Men are cruel, but hardly of the earth, hardly at all. But who am I to be lecturing about men? I only knew one man, and I have never been to other parts of the world.

—

Foamworld of Oliver—porous sponge slowly squeezing green; liquid life swimming below beyond time in circles of secret words to Edith a shadow visible in the tangled folds of aging palpitating cerebrum. In Oliver's mind a white flame, an ice stem, a bird, the echo of a song. Edith covered by high black waves growing suddenly upward looping into hollow caverns. Spumegray anemones rush blindly into open funnels of orange seagrowths multiplying in his brain. His dead penis sleeps in the cup of empty hands.

The more elusive she became, the more desperate were his actions. Slowly the chemicals invaded his room alongside gizzards of chicken preserved in formaldehyde. Oliver checking parts of my body, making diagrams, pushing his fingers up into my vagina, wordlessly seeking the entrance to the womb, finding my ovaries with some difficulty, and I—desperate, glad of any attention, not asking why or protesting, sensing a coldness about these manipulations; unsure, wishing things to be as they once were, wanting to roll fruits to Oliver back and forth, wanting him to feed me in the twilight, not thinking as much; numbed, never certain what was to happen next, fading with the violet dress, tired all the time for a long time while the visits continued, the history book stopped, our former schedule dissolved—seeing but not feeling Oliver's crisis.

Mainly a change in the rhythm which had been slow, monotonous—Oliver walking back and forth peeling potatoes, appearing and disappearing; I following, learning, doing lessons. *No more.* Now everything shrill in strange quickly moving jagged pieces of what is called time. No peace. The corridor fluttering with silken garments smelling of decay. Oliver rushing back and forth. Blue gauze falling, floating retrieved. An unexpected pat on the head, an old word on a new card, a penis inside me, and a long disappearance. Awful smells of the formaldehyde, rotting chicken livers exchanged for new ones. Old ones were burned or flushed down the red toilet.

—

From reading the excerpts of Oliver's historical encyclopedia, you know as I do the originality of his mind. And perhaps if you have read it without prejudice, you understand even better than I do why Oliver disappeared. Does it not become apparent from his comments about Hitler that he left me in order to protect me from something inside himself? Of course he was wrong to make this decision without consulting me. But Oliver was easily confused. I should have threatened him with my death. I should have reminded him that Edith might yet return if he waited a little longer. I could have tried to convince him that he had left many gaps in my education. By then he did not care, I assure you. At the time of his disappearance, I still did not understand most of the words in his history book although I had it memorized and could recite the text. I can still recite it.

Do not laugh at Oliver's small distortions of history, at his visit with Van Gogh at Arles, or at Van Gogh's portrait of Edith. I have been laughed at and even condemned when I recited Oliver's interview with Adolf Hitler. How was I to know differently? Poor Oliver. He left without the history book. I wonder if he regretted this later or if he no longer considered it his own since I had it committed to memory. He knew, I suspect. Didn't I take everything from Oliver? Isn't that why he had to leave? Think of how elusive Edith became until he could no longer summon her. Surely I accomplished that with my reality, my terrible insinuating violet presence, my mocking curiosity. I drove him to create the monstrosity with the chicken gizzards and pig's eyes. I could have pretended that I had not memorized his book, but I am diabolical. I am afraid. Why did he not take pride in my ability to memorize? I admit that it is a stupid uncreative ability, but I meant no harm by it, at least not initially. How can I know what I meant when I had very little analytical ability? You assume that everyone has this. No. Reasoning was not an easy thing for me and self-analysis was totally unknown; I have learned it quite recently. Only recently have I learned of motivation, unconscious hostility and other secret things that exist in your everyday vocabulary. If I was malicious I knew nothing of it or its source. Oh, if it could only happen again I would remember not to learn so fast, not to memorize so well, and never never to mention the name "Edith." It is because of me that his potency with Edith diminished. No wonder he raped me and measured my insides. I destroyed the solitude necessary to make his fantasies real. I became alive in violet. She was all that he had left despite his pretenses, his work, Van Gogh's letters. I understand fantasies now because my fantasies about Oliver are all that I have left despite my office job, my toys and my blind men. I only pretend to live in your society. No wonder he wore dark glasses to protest my existence. I wish he had murdered me—earlier, when I first awoke from total anonymity, when I first began to invent, to memorize, to express my grotesque thoughts. No one would have found out since no one knew who I was or where I was, and the extinction of my "self" would have been far less painful to me than to others. I had only a little over two years of self to be destroyed and would have felt only the slightest protest against my own early end. Death was unknown to me and finality beyond my comprehension. Admittedly it would have been more difficult in the third year. Conflict and secret wars with Oliver had borne the dubious fruit of a separate identity. I truly existed during our terrible year. This separation pained me and was not initiated by me on a conscious level. I told you I didn't like those thoughts independent of Oliver that my brain constructed. There was no help for it, for my growing experience and my terrifying realization of Oliver as a distinct personality. The most terrible thing in the world that. He should have killed me or at least bashed me over the head so I would remain always half-conscious. Instead he gave me all he had and left tapping his white-tipped cane. Was his departure based entirely upon self-preservation or was it his way of punishing me for my tangibility, my femaleness? And well I know that tangibility was the most repulsive thing in the world to Oliver. Even Edith did not understand this as you can see in her letters. Even Edith was blinded by his fleshiness, by his smells and by his own corpulent tangibility. She was stupid—in her way as stupid as I. How could anyone have left Oliver? I would have remained under any conditions. I swear.

—

A friend of mine is a policeman, the kind who wears a regular suit instead of a uniform. I go to see him sometimes and we drink coffee in a bare room while he asks me some peculiar questions. I think he is conducting an investigation. I like him so I go to see him even when we don't have an appointment. This seems to puzzle him but I do want to be friends with people. I like to drink coffee with him even though I can't answer his questions and I don't know what he is talking about. The reason why I haven't mentioned him before is because I didn't want to confuse you. It isn't an affair or anything important. It reminds me a little of playing games with Oliver. He even came to see my apartment like the blind men do. But I think he likes me. Sometimes people, particularly men who are blind, think I am putting on some kind of an act. They don't know all that you know so they think I am trying to act child-like or naive. I am not acting at all. I wish someone would believe it.

—

She wouldn't visit him any longer despite all his preparations, his spraying of the room, and (I am ashamed to tell you this) my atheistic Oliver even hung a large cross above his bed. He did everything. Her shoes—all of them were polished, brushed, and arranged in lines or rows around his room. With his amputated finger he sewed the green bows that kept falling off her beige shoes. Oliver, ironing her dresses on the floor of his room, burning himself and some of the dresses, screaming, throwing the iron in disgust. Oliver putting purple glass birds with large black wings on his desk. He did everything to please Edith. But she wouldn't visit him any longer. I know. I watched, standing on the chair. "Edith, why do you disappoint me? I have changed. Everything is the way you wish. I have done as you asked. Are you angry because I burned your silver dress? Look how I pray. Watch." Oliver on his knees muttering things, then looking around. Oliver making love to nothing and knowing it. No longer able to become erect. No fountain squirt. Nothing. No Edith. He did not give up easily, went on and on and on. Then with a great effort he tried to resume our conversations.

Poor Oliver, sitting across the table from me, opaque glasses resting within reach, asking me how my studies were going. Like a voice that was not there. I felt it in my hands and feet and stomach. He did not care anymore. However, our conversations had reached a rather sophisticated level although I did not always know what I was talking about. He understood little about child development. If he had understood that I memorized constructions and constellations of words without understanding their meaning, perhaps he would not have felt threatened. I was hardly a developed human being and cannot conceive of having been a threat to anyone else. But then you must keep in mind the fragility of Oliver. (Edith did not understand this.) Growing, growing in Oliver a fear that I might understand something sacred, inviolable to him, and that I would make a verbal pronouncement. His fears were not completely without justification. Once, for example, I said, "Edith is the construction of a genius." "Construction of a genius" was a phrase I had taken from a page of Oliver's book. If Oliver had not been so fearful he would have realized that he had never given me the words "construction" or "genius." It was the fault of my diabolical memory that much of our conversation assumed this pseudo-sophisticated form. How stupid I was, thinking that it would please Oliver if I conversed in large adult words. Nor was I able to connect his growing silence and withdrawal from me, his increased use of opaque glasses, with my use of certain phrases. I persisted, accidently forming sentences that I had no control over and did not understand. If you do not entirely believe this then I will concede that it might have been a primitive instinct, unknown, that chose some particularly dangerous word combinations. Perhaps Oliver was dictating these sentences to me from his unconscious. Preposterous? Never forget how close we were in our narrow rectangular world, and how he gave birth to me in a sense. Remember that Oliver and I were closer than any two human beings are in your world (except Adam and Eve), and so it is not unlikely that subtle kinds of communication went on between us. We never had company.

No, I am not going to continue my plea of innocence. I did have some autonomy by then and a subconscious as well, if you believe in such an entity. My choices of word combinations seem almost designed to antagonize and disturb a sensitive man such as Oliver. But they were not willful. I have these speculations only now. I do not understand the mind as well as you do and so I cannot give definite answers. But I can recall each sentence now and add the meaning to it. I can recall Oliver's facial expressions, replies and gestures and interpret them today.

"Is denial of reality going to be your raison d'être indefinitely?" I asked Oliver, pleased with the sound of this sentence. "Raison d'être" was in many pages of his writing. Surely I did not know what this sentence meant?

"My raison d'être vanished long ago," he answered softly and left the table, glasses over his eyes, forgetting to eat. His voice tone, his facial expression, I can now analyze as defeat. His subsequent withdrawal from me for a period approximating three days during which he ate nothing and became quite ill, I now pronounce to have been an unconscious sado-masochistic reaction. I have become so clever from reading all the books in your libraries. Yet I am forever uncertain. Learning all I do provides me with a storehouse of knowledge from which to conjecture, but it deprives me of all certainty since your books contradict each other. Perhaps he merely had a virus. How improbable that a virus could find its way into our secluded world or that it could infect the rarified air that we breathed. I fear that you doubt me. I don't blame you at all. Do you think that your sophisticated little children really know what they are talking about in those adult tones? I'll bet you are threatened by them and start to hate them also—I'll bet you are. They don't know what they are talking about—only echo words. Let me assure you of that. I didn't know either.

In order to make my position and state of mind more tenable to you, I will record a composition that I wrote during this period. You will see that my vocabulary was very small although it was adequate. Nowhere in these compositions do words appear having the magnitude of those I used at those final dinner conversations. Had I known how to use them, I certainly would have made creative use of them in my private writings. I was greedy for words. Ask your children what they are talking about before you start despising them or fearing that they are superior to you—as well they might be. They don't really know. Not yet. Not really. Ask me. I know all about being a child with words.

The following composition refers to the time that Oliver withdrew to his room after my use of "raison d'être," and was written while he was sick: "Oliver stays in his room and does not come out. He will not eat. I call, Oliver, Oliver, but he does not answer me. I wish he would answer me. I think I did something wrong but I don't know what I did. If I knew what I did I would say I am sorry like you are supposed to. Oliver has done this before. Since I don't understand I try to guess what it means like a game. I wish I was not so stupid. I don't like him to wear the glasses. I just came back from Oliver's room. The door was locked. I knocked. I heard him making funny noises, ooooh, ooooh and things I can't spell. I said Oliver I don't know why you don't come out. I want you to come out and talk to me. You didn't eat anything for a long time and that is not good for you. I also said I am sorry even though I don't know why. Oliver didn't answer. Then I banged very hard with my elbow and he yelled that I should go away and never come back so I did. I don't feel well when he goes away into his room and doesn't come out. Edith isn't there and he isn't waiting for her. I looked. My stomach is doing something and I don't want to eat but Oliver told me once that everyone has to eat even animals. If this is so and what he told me is true I wonder why he doesn't come out and eat. I peeked over the door again. Oliver doesn't know that I can stand on a chair and do this. I am very quiet. Oliver was lying on the bed with his face in the bed. There were some torn papers on the floor. Edith was not there and he was not talking to her or waiting for her. I don't like to see the chicken parts or that smell. I can never see her. I want Oliver to play with me and to teach me things that I don't know. Sometimes he comes into my room. His penis doesn't go up anymore. That is called an erection. It is one of the biggest words Oliver gave me. I forgot what makes an erection although he explained it to me a long time ago. The blood goes in I think."

—

Sometimes I am so tired remembering all these things looking way up high where pieces of gray light are patched at the top, tangled between the brown lines. Dark rain comes out quick quick for the tree to eat from the bottom and it has to get way up to the tips. It makes my head dizzy that noise up there until I see the silver horse with the woodpecker rain plop plop pushing all the tinny pretty silver off until the soaking horsey falls into the wet brown leaves. The silver heart and broken kidneys, sperm-tanks and the big intestine hang on the twigs. It hurts. Don't let poor horsey get so wet.

—

How can you say it was my fault—that everything I did and said was wrong and made things worse? It was a terrible coincidence and due to neglect. If he had explained what I shouldn't do and why and if he had still played with me and liked me I am sure that I would not have made all those mistakes. I would have been perfect. But everything changed too fast and I was left alone too early even before he really left. I didn't know it. I only sensed everything sniffing like some strange animal.

> "I won't come into the garden," whispers Oliver outside in the darkness. "I don't care." But I wipe away silver tears. "It used to be for happiness, playing and forgetting the past. Now it is full of thorns and dead things," he continues. Dull sun goes in and out weakly with sudden blasts of darkness. Nothing is on the trees and the grass is uniformly brown. Even the coral bench is coated with dust and dead insects. I am dressed in black. "It's not my fault. You used to laugh at dead things and make them come alive," I say. "I can't do that forever," Oliver answers. He is beside me on the dirty bench holding me in his arms and patting my head. "Poor child, poor child," over and over again. He laughs. "I didn't forget. I brought you pity." "Where is it?" "Here," says Oliver putting his black jacket around me and holding me. "Is it real pity?" I ask. "What is the difference? Now, where is yours?" Oliver answers. I give him back his coat and give him everything I am wearing. Oliver laughs. "I think it is too late for pity." He walks away.

ON THE NEXT PAGE IS A LETTER JUST FOR YOU

FEBRUARY 21, 19__

TO YOU:

I AM CORDIALLY INVITING YOU TO COME TO MY HOUSE AT YOUR EARLIEST CONVENIENCE FOR THE EXPRESS PURPOSE OF EXPLAINING TO ME WHAT YOU THINK MY MAIN MISTAKE WAS WITH OLIVER. I WOULD LIKE YOU TO COME PREPARED TO TELL ME IF I DROVE HIM TO HIS CRISIS AND HOW I SHOULD HAVE TREATED HIM AND ACTED. SHOULD I HAVE REMAINED LIKE A LITTLE GIRL OR SHOULD I HAVE LIED AND PRETENDED TO BE EDITH? IS THERE SOME WAY I COULD HAVE DONE THAT WITHOUT MAKING US BOTH GO INSANE? I AM ALSO VERY ANXIOUS TO HEAR YOUR VIEWS ON PITY AND ON UNCONSCIOUS MOTIVATIONS. DON'T BRING ANY PSYCHOLOGY BOOKS. I WANT YOUR REAL FEELINGS IF YOU HAVE ANY. I DON'T MEAN TO IMPLY THAT YOU DO NOT. IT'S JUST THAT RECENTLY I'VE BEGUN TO WONDER IF EVERYONE IS NOT PLAYING SOME GAME. IF THAT IS SO I WOULD APPRECIATE IT IF YOU WOULD TEACH ME HOW TO PLAY IT AND WHAT THE RULES ARE. MY APARTMENT STILL NEEDS YOUR ADVICE. MY BLIND FRIENDS ARE SATISFIED BECAUSE IT IS CLEAN AND SMELLS GOOD, EXCEPT THAT ONE OF THEM SAID HE WISHED IT WAS A LITTLE SIMPLER BECAUSE HE IS ALWAYS BUMPING INTO THINGS. COME EVEN IF YOU ARE BLIND AND DEAF. THE POLICEMAN THAT I KNOW SAID MY APARTMENT IS ALL RIGHT, BUT I DON'T THINK HE IS VERY INTERESTED IN DECORATION. I AM. I WANT THINGS TO LOOK RIGHT. I WANT TO HAVE A GOOD COLLECTION OF BOOKS. I HAVE SOME BOOKS ON PARAPSYCHOLOGY, ON SEXUAL RESEARCH, ON GIRAFFES, MANY DICTIONARIES, SOME SHORT JAPANESE NOVELS WHICH ARE TRANSLATED AND A MEXICAN COOKBOOK. I ALSO HAVE SOME THINGS BY FREUD WHICH I NEVER READ EXCEPT FOR A FEW SECTIONS AND A BOOK ON THE RENAISSANCE IN ITALY. AND OF COURSE "WAR AND PEACE." WHAT ELSE DO YOU THINK I SHOULD HAVE? IN RETURN FOR YOUR ADVICE YOU CAN ASK ME ANY QUESTIONS YOU WANT ABOUT MY LIFE WITH OLIVER. I MAY HAVE LEFT OUT A FEW THINGS. I HAVE SMALL TEACUPS WITH DARK ROSES AND I WILL GIVE YOU TEA WITH CHEESE AND CRACKERS. I ALSO HAVE A BAR WITH ALL KINDS OF LIQUOR AND SOME DRUGS. I LIKE TO PLEASE EVERYONE WHO COMES. YOU CAN BRING YOUR OWN FOOD IF YOU ARE AFRAID OR DON'T TRUST ME. IF YOU LIVE VERY FAR AWAY, I HAVE A COUCH FOR YOU TO SLEEP ON. I HOPE THAT YOU WILL COME SOON BECAUSE THE MORE I WRITE THE MORE I THINK THAT EVERYTHING MUST BE MY FAULT AND NOT OLIVER'S. I ALSO WANT TO KNOW IF IT IS ALL RIGHT THAT I LOVE OLIVER BUT THAT I HATE HIM TOO AND WHAT THIS MEANS, OR IF I'M JUST UNGRATEFUL.

P.S. I DON'T MIND IF YOU BRING A PRESENT.

Even you know that nothing happens all at once. I keep saying this because it is true. I *had* another chance. Oliver, *my* Oliver, tried once more after the rape, after the frenzied preparations—cheeks slashed shaving, handsaw ripping the skin off his toes, ears bleeding, calling summoning Edith. It stopped. Oliver gave up. He lost the ability to imagine her while pumping up and down on her velvet dresses, her perfume sprayed over himself. Defeated, Oliver removed the bedspread and put her dresses away. There was no one but Oliver and me. I swear. He tried to resume our life. Faked it of course since he wasn't well. He was tired. He walked with his head bent down, looking at the floor, leaving a trail of saliva, holding a pair of opaque glasses in his hand, peeling half a potato, getting half an erection with me, trying to be patient, trying to write. It was all dead, all finished, Oliver's life. Together alone.

"We have neglected our work, lapsed, fallen backward, forgotten our purposes," said Oliver, nibbling at his food, not looking at me. Needing me, I think, broken.

"Is Edith coming back?" I meant nothing harmful. He knew. He did not run away or walk backward to his room immediately. It took longer than that. I had time. Time, a chance, a last chance and I didn't know what to do. I didn't.

He ignored my question. Together we devised a new schedule. Oliver trying to smile, to look at me, appeared with a Bible. He explained that it is important for every educated person to know the Bible. He read from it. He gave me words from it, carefully. Still cautious, my Oliver, not even realizing it. "In the beginning God created the heavens and the earth," Oliver read. No, Oliver cheated. What he really said was, "Once upon a time God made the sky and land." He no longer trusted me, feared that I would learn too much. Pity him. You.

"Who is God?" I asked.

"A man who made everything," answered Oliver.

Perhaps he simplified it for me and I should have been grateful. But I knew too much already.

"I don't believe you," I said quietly. Oliver who was tired, said no more but told me in a steady voice to go to my room.

"No." I just sat there while he put on his glasses, slowly. What did I understand of Oliver's struggle? What did I know of tact or of compromise? I wanted him to hug me and feed me and play with me.

"After this I saw in the night visions and beheld a fourth beast, dreadful and terrible ... it had great iron teeth ... and it had ten horns," Oliver read from the Book of Daniel. (When you find Oliver, give him a horn from an animal or a photograph of an animal with horns. He loves them. Now I like horns too because Oliver read about them and drew pictures. My giraffe has two, three sometimes five horns.)

"Play with me," I demanded, pulling his shirtsleeve, knocking the Bible out of his hand. No longer timid, sensing a lost vulnerable Oliver I took advantage.

"Later," he said, turning away from me and locking up the Bible.

—

No more smile of Oliver that stayed for a long time orangesweet.

—

In me something thumping going krak krak krak like a nasty woodpecker who changed, took a leap onto the back of the limping horsey feeling secretly exhilarated. High up with iron footclaws ripping the skin of his bent back my laughing sound cracked his glass heart, smashed the thin-stemmed ribcage with the flap flap of my relentless wings. I waved my speckled horns.

—

And one day when Oliver came to *my* door alone with his blue-veined erection, I wouldn't let him in. Where could I have learned such tricks? "Go away," I said. Me, not Oliver. It was *I* who disappeared leaving Oliver, Oliver who had no Edith, no dreams, no appetite, who could no longer write his history book. I know that I am a vengeful, spiteful person. Who taught me to be like that? It was Oliver who knocked on *my* door which I cleverly fastened from the inside with cord—from mattress spring to door and black bureau knobs. Later wires reinforced my blockade. "Come out!" But I was silent on my bed liking to hear him at my door, Oliver wanting. I went too far. He needed me, I realized even nameless. *You* be the judge not forgetting his tea parties with Edith and how he gave me only small words and locked me out of so many doors. He was all I had. Behind electric wires I feigned indifference. Other times I felt nothing not caring any longer knowing that Oliver didn't. Positions reversed, Oliver outside my door pleading and groaning, even yelling and banging with his fat fists. Not that he cared whether or not I starved. But I was clever; listening peeping when Oliver went into his room I came outside and ate. Do you understand? It was all his fault. But you see, I had a chance. Oliver needed me and was calling me, without a name, but calling. And I did not answer.

Here it is dark and light dark and light
Shadows like icicles flicker inside the
Edge of my speckled brain white white a
Snowball on the window ledge above real
Floats punctured by a gash of crying sun
Not there

By the time my revenge was finished, by the time I ached for Oliver tearing the wires of my barricade with bare hands, trying to please him, it was too late. Don't ever say that you never had a chance or even a second chance. I say it but I know it is not true. You heard me. I had my chance, Oliver all alone, and I used it to get even. So what if I didn't know what I was doing. That is no excuse. I have not excused Oliver so why should I be excused. By the time I stopped my tormenting questions about Edith, my kraking laughter, riding way up high on the bent horse or the mad giraffe, Oliver was making the tangible construction of Edith. Busy. Oliver day and night (no time) alone with the fragile bones of chickens, chemicals acids plastics turkey livers gizzards oils and sprays. Oliver using me for measurements, and I like a selfless mannequin not objecting. Not even to silver rulers and probing coldgloved fingers that stung from chemicals. Is it not strange that I am not insane from all of it? But it is important to me, *the beginning.* I remember it in detail with my eyes with my tongue *then then*—fat fist clutching the handle of a large spoon, up in into my mouth hot colors—soft pale green leafwings, round orange flowers wet with yellow in the center, and those hard pieces of brown composed of thick threads lined down that had to be chewed. Chewing and swallowing are my own now, done alone or in the company of others. Nothing tastes as good. It is my own business like so many other things. But *then* I was Oliver and my eating was *our* business—one of the things that we later lost, slipping away as everything.

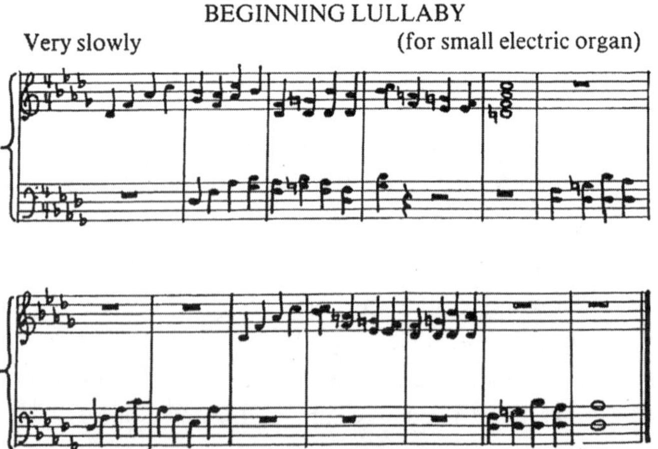

I have had to stop writing; remembering my last chance and what I did with it and the evil smell of the chemicals that made me sick, I couldn't go on. Something else happened. When I came home from a movie with one of the blind men whom I imagine is Oliver, the policeman was waiting at the door. He was very polite and didn't want to intrude. He only asked me again and again if I could remember what Oliver looked like. It is an investigation of some kind. I lie to him. That probably surprises you since I have told you all about Oliver, but writing to you is different. I just said, "I don't remember." He made an appointment for me to come and talk to him again. I am not so sure he likes me. He never takes me to the movies. The blind man said he is probably a detective involved in an investigation. Blind men are very patient and they explain everything to me. I wish they could tell me how I look. If things change again and I go away I may not be able to finish. I will try. Meanwhile I made up a questionnaire for you.

A QUESTIONNAIRE FOR YOU

1. Who do you like better, Oliver or me? __________
2. Do you believe my story? (Yes, or No) __________
3. Why did Edith leave Oliver? __________
4. Why did Oliver teach me things? __________
5. Who was most at fault? __________
6. Why did Oliver leave? __________
7. Where do you think he is? __________

DRAW A PICTURE OF OLIVER
IN THE EMPTY SPACE UNDERNEATH THIS

IV

It ached those days without structure, without Oliver, needing to run to him never mentioning Edith, finished with questions quiet again, movements soft tiptoeing everywhere not learning or curious any longer, waiting in the empty corridor touching gently the quilted pieces calling softly only softly "Oliver" sitting long long waiting wanting but only saying his name, and he sweating working obsessed with his creation feverishly walking quickly salivating uttering incoherent sounds remembering to eat sometimes seated across from me with his opaque glasses on not lying near his hand, eating quickly halfcooked things not waiting for me and I watching Oliver watching waiting quiet of all fight, hurting with sexual feelings with things I could never name, all feelings gone underneath, my thoughts hesitating not quick running wild with split colors like before, watching only silently over the door to his room numb seeing him making forming it with secret things and smells, no words between us nothing anymore empty space, not shaking slack sometimes cutting red paper slowly or washing counting patches on the wall crisscross, only awake when he appeared seated turned from me with the dark glasses not asking anything not telling me to get washed or to go study not even pretending anymore, I waiting ready to do anything waiting for the chance that was gone to come a knock on the door, never knocking on his door trying to remember things eating carefully washing dishes without breaking one thinking only I want Oliver to play with me Oliver does not play with me, thinking itself gone pale simple as simple as simple sentences, aching in the belly helpless to do anything because anything I had done for so long was wrong, no growing changing in me anymore just fingering things slowly my body knowing it the table again holding an egg in my hand knowing the shell and shape not really looking but touching listening in a half-conscious way always for his steps but not running toward them only raising my eyes glad to see Oliver no matter what no matter about Edith in his room not yet perfected, even words tears coming from lacrimal glands when I saw Oliver's feet clawed or the amputated finger or his ears, quiet no moans nowhere to move, in me not slipping way back just remaining, not ever thinking of leaving or of meanings anymore, dead.

—

Wake me up Oliver from this terrible dream I am walking in, pretending to talk to people and to move through all this space without you. How long will this bad dream last? So many voices, everywhere, everywhere whistles blowing and never any sight of you. It cannot be done this separation and learning to live here in an apartment with things I do not really understand even when I seem to understand them. Looking plain sometimes in my gray suit with a yellow umbrella or looking pretty learning to trace black around my eyes and wear the right lipstick color and walk nicely. Kissing men lying in beds with men who are blind and who can see and who know how to touch me and who don't give me pleasure and who do or call or don't call all sizes, everyone. *Oliver I can't stand this!* Lock me up with you. I don't know those men. I don't know what I am doing or where to go. I only like the stars or the sun red, coming up in the morning reflecting the bars steel bars blinding my eyes. I want you to see the stars and the red sun or the real soft green that is slowly coming up over everything. Buds open too fast before I have a chance. It is like a rapid dream passing before me and I want to wake up with you. Can you, Oliver, know how I feel? It isn't any one thing. That is the trouble. And I don't know why the small green or white flowers make me think of your fingers or toes which are in no way like them but make me hurt in some way. Please find me Oliver, if I can't find you, and take me home. I have changed. I will never talk of the past and everything will be like a big yellow star or clusters of simple scented flowers whose very names destroy their beauty to my eyes. It is all what they call a nightmare this outside world with myself not really in it but still with you for all my life. Even kindness which some people have is not what I want. I want you because you are my beginning and past and present. You would see me smiling thinking I am happy but it is only something I learned here, to smile quickly and go from one thing to another from painting to painting from place to place and say things and things and get tired all the time. I have tried. I have tried. Please wake me up Oliver and tell me that everything will be all right. I am waiting and watching for you every day through these bars.

Finally I will admit it. You had suspected it already, I suppose. There was a door—not only a door but a bell. I had entered *then,* a mild disordered child in some condition of psychosis or amnesia. A fugue, eclipse or nothing before. I have not wanted to admit the DOOR. Oliver left through it—a hinged wall, then suddenly a space mysterious always and swinging shut. I loathe the word DOOR. And it still pains me to realize that a past did exist before I came to Oliver. Most of my pain comes from my unwillingness to accept certain things. I don't want a past before Oliver. I never wanted a future. Oliver, I—timeless—I want.

Of course there was a door, fool; how do you think we ate? Did you ever hear of a supply of food lasting for three years. He went outside. He had to. But to him the existence of that world was as repellent as it is now to me. How do I know? For one thing he wore dark glasses, not ordinary tinted lenses or cheap sunglasses. Fashioned from the glass in Edith's studio, they were nearly opaque, letting in just enough light to see large shapes—faces could not be distinguished. But he could get around. Not very far—if he did I would have never forgiven him. He knew. Going outside was abhorrent to him. He wore a disguise. In addition to the thick brownish glasses was a cane white-tipped, which he held up to the cars as he crossed the street in the manner of a blind man, but refusing anyone's arm. Tzap tap went the cane right, left, in front of him as he walked the corridor to the DOOR. In the past I had chosen to ignore it but when he left and did not return, I had to face certain realities. I waited. There was no way for me to measure time. I didn't know. But as I slept and woke and slept and woke I began to feel a distance from when he left. It was like a long tunnel and I looked through it seeing Oliver getting smaller and smaller so far away. I grew weak and made strange noises like animals in the zoo make when everyone has gone home. A tear or two came from the corner of my eye. That is all. You may have guessed that I knew many things that I have refused to admit—things like the existence of windows and doors beneath shredded tapestry. I have been lying a lot of the time, maybe even remembering how I came. Oh many things. Can you call me a liar? I don't want to remember. I do not want to know, really, about his disappearance. That is my worst lie. I have asked you to look for him. I meant it. I have not intended to be tricky. It is not like that at all.

—

Oliver left wearing dark glasses and tapping a white-tipped cane. I had been obedient for months. I had not tried to make love to him or pulled his penis. (I had long forgiven him for the brutal rape that had occurred after his failure with Edith.) Did I have any warning? I did. Inside, a fluttering of the main thing called heart, vision coming, going, chopping his face when I looked, a stinging in my palms and feet. Sensing something unknown I went to extremes, suddenly rousing myself from passive waiting, deliberately trying to regress to the illiterate creature who had appeared at the beginning. "Geeeeh, geeeeeeh, ooomah, ooomah, geeeeeeeeh." He was not convinced. Oliver was a discerning man despite the flaws in his history book. From afar he scratched his shaggy hair now gray and pulled at his long earlobe. (I have mentioned that my darling Oliver had gigantic ears and that they cupped forward.) Squinting at me from behind dark glasses he witnessed my mad antics. I sensed his coming departure like a desperate animal, like nothing else.

How ashamed I am when I recall that I even put on the plaid little-girl skirt that I had been wearing three years before, crawled on the floor, pretended difficulty in holding a knife and fork, and went so far as to spit out the meat. "Chew," I wanted him to say again. I thought I could fool him, make him forget the time after the violet dress. I used no words but ran pulling at his shirt the way I used to *then*. He ignored me. Besides I could not keep up this deception for long. (Forgive me Oliver, I was trying to keep you.) Mistakenly I had become resigned to Edith, thinking that her presence, now tangible, was sufficient reason for you to stay. I do not understand why you chose that time to leave—that time when your Edith was complete.

—

Edith's construction was perfect. I had learned to accept the fact that he preferred her to me, dressing her in detail from satin undergarments to pink fluffy gowns. She was always delicately perfumed and elaborately coiffed. I won't disclose to you the details of her anatomy—proof of my Oliver's ingenuity. I will never betray his deepest secrets. Let me state, although I may have stated it before, that every bit of her anatomy was as satisfying to a man as that of a real woman. Use your own imagination, but do not steal what was Oliver's.

Because Oliver never loved me I can reveal everything about myself and my thoughts. If he hadn't taught me how to read or how to form ideas, he might have developed stronger feelings for me. Or if I had come out when he moaned and knocked at my door, he would have abandoned his construction. My Oliver hates tangibility. I told you. Think of what this creation of Edith must have done to him. But he couldn't help it. Besides, his construction wasn't insane. I have seen similar things out here. I have seen women or girls who look like something Oliver or someone else constructed. Not only in the street but in the movies and on television. Only Oliver did it from the beginning.

You would think Oliver loathsome with his huge stomach, his urine odor and the hairs coming from his ears and nose. But that is because Oliver never fed *you* when you did not know what a spoon was, nor did he cook for you and dress you when you remembered nothing. And he did not play with *your* breasts when you knew nothing of the world—nothing of the differences between women and men. I've told you this before, but I can't help it. Each time, I add or subtract something so that I may come closer to understanding his disappearance. It does not bore me to repeat a thousand times that Oliver had gigantic ears that cupped forward and that the veins of his nose made a lovely purple design. He was the prince of men and nothing can change my mind. Certainly not any investigators who do not believe me. I swear to them again and again that I was *not* kidnapped. They say it would be in my own best interest if I changed my story. I do not know what they mean. I swear. It would be like changing his name. Then what would you think of me? My eyes are viridian green, Oliver said. Not every color like his.

—

Foamworld of Oliver—porous sponge slowly squeezing green; liquid life swimming below beyond time in circles of secret words to Edith a shadow visible in the tangled folds of aging palpitating cerebrum. Darker and darker, cold, the silhouette of white ice-pain sucked in covered by the tangled roar multiplying in the orange seagrowths of his brain.

No. He did not run off with dismembered Edith in his briefcase or wrapped inside a dampened plastic cloth. He left her with me. When I think of it I re-experience the shock I felt knowing that we were alone in the house. No Oliver. Was I to keep her ready and perfumed in case he returned? Edith required certain care and adjustments. Some of these were not pleasant to administer—but I refuse to go into further detail for all our sakes. Wanting to destroy her was a new impulse. (Oh, Oliver, I almost did.) But I suspected that he was testing me. I will not fail in the final test, I thought, not in the way I write it but through my intuitive knowing about things. Dutifully, faithfully, I unlocked the cabinet where various fluids, chemicals and lubricating oils were kept and replenished the things kept in the freezer. In this way I administered to her month after month during the timeless space in which I awaited Oliver's return.

Had I not failed in some way he would not have been driven to re-create her. Oliver, how did we fail you, Edith and I? For not to blame Edith is to ignore her letters, her changes and disappearances. Perhaps *I* am therefore innocent of all crime. What *is* the exact crime in all of this? I only know that it exists, hidden somewhere waiting to be found. When had it all begun? At what point could a new life for Oliver and myself have been initiated? Surely not now, after he is gone. When?

Jealousy is something terrible and important. Who put it there? Perhaps that strange man who made the heavens and the earth. I do not know. But I had it for a long time not knowing what it was. Now that you know that there was a DOOR, that loathsome word, I can tell you that Oliver left quite often before his final disappearance. He went to buy epoxies, resins and presents. And Oliver continued certain social amenities even when he no longer cared for me; there was a ballpoint pen, a lined notebook or a box of crayons handed to me abruptly in a brown paper bag. The white gift boxes, carefully wrapped and tied with silver and purple bows, contained presents for Edith: expensive slips, stockings, blue and violet undergarments, negligees and unusual hats. Sometimes an engraved bracelet or amethyst earrings. He loved her very much. To be jealous of a creature who is not alive in the sense that I am or you are is ridiculous. On the other hand, what is the difference?—she was more important to him despite my reality which I still sometimes doubt. No wonder I am frightened by dolls. When I go into toy stores, I avoid them deliberately, going so far as to squint my eyes when I am accosted by one. Such an encounter causes a mild electric shock to run through my body. Even when I hear about robots or see one on television, I become quite ill. You would not believe how ill I become although Edith in no way resembled a robot. I react in a similar way to some of the girls and women I see walking on the streets; they do not look real although I know it is only the careful make-up, wigs and other chemicals. This is Oliver's fault. But I notice that men like them and they like those terrifying pictures of dolls like Edith in magazines. I am scared of all those magazines.

—

Oliver was not impotent with this Edith. I watched. To him she was alive. So if you call it a perversion you are wrong. Sexually he had no need of me, and I must admit that I did not compare with her artificial beauty and the perfection of her measurements. I can understand it—but why did he leave? Is it one of those events, haphazard with no reason? I did not nag him anymore or even mention *this* Edith or any other. Nor did I watch them too often. Still my presence disturbed him, I think.

—

I still cry about the glasses that eclipsed me from my lover. But it will take a long time to arrive at a definite conclusion. It is necessary to proceed with caution. Oliver was not a simple man. He had a precise reason for everything even if he is judged insane by simpler minds. At some future date I might pronounce him a madman myself—so great are the possibilities for betrayal in this world without Oliver.

Here it is dark and light dark and light
Tired birds fly into the white silk sky
Then fall down with broken wings on the
Window ledge inside my brain freezing flies
Desperately slam jump invade the shattered
Cells with their last violent love cries
Not there

In spite of everything—the limited structure of our world, Edith, and his indifference to me, I would like to return. Oliver was kind. He could have locked me in a room so he wouldn't see my face. He could have shoved food under the door or through a slat like they do in your prison cells. Instead he chose dark glasses. He could have raped and beaten me many times to relieve his frustration with Edith. He could have cut my tongue out or blinded me. However, as you know, he raped me only once.

—

The investigator, who I thought was a policeman, wants to know about Oliver's beatings. I am sorry I ever told him anything. But I was naive when I first came outside after waiting there for Oliver a long, long time. I thought he was my friend. But I began to suspect that something was wrong when he never took me to the movies. Now I must find out what a lie detector test is. He says it is to my advantage to tell about Oliver's beatings. But I won't. He says I must have a defense. I don't know what he means—a defense against what?

—

If you (assuming that you are a man) had entered while Edith and I were waiting for Oliver, sitting side by side on his bed, you would have been most attracted by Edith. So I warn you not to make judgments about Oliver. I was in my little-girl skirt, legs unshaven, hair hastily brushed—the way I had looked before the violet dress. But she was dressed in lace revealing a huge upturned bosom scented with delicate perfumes. I can assure you that you would have been intrigued, would perhaps have fallen in love with her yourself. And you could not have resisted picking up her skirts. That is the art of my Oliver. Take my word for it.

Together we waited—plates unscraped, unwashed from his last meal. I wanted everything to be the same when Oliver returned. Afraid to change anything, I ate from one plate and then washed it, leaving the old ones coated with hardened egg yolk. Oh, it occurred to me to go outside and try to find him. But I thought he would return eventually—if not for my sake and worry about how I would survive, then for Edith's. That is why I did not go out and look for him. What would he have thought if he had returned finding Edith alone and uncared for? Then I could never come back. I am certain he would not have let me in again. Impatience—I know you are always thinking of endless time, of boredom and impatience. But that is because you do not fully understand my world with Oliver, our world without clocks, televisions and amusements other than what we devised. You forgot how long I had been alone, even with Oliver there. I had only a vague sense of time passing by the slowly disappearing food, the disintegrating soap bars and by something in my body hurting between my breasts, missing the sight of him. Agitation of an overt nature was not present. You would have seen me unsmiling, watching over Edith though hating her, I admit, cooking food, peeling onions when the potatoes disappeared, boiling carrots and rotten string beans. Sometimes I reread old letters that I knew by memory or studied a little without any enthusiasm. That is all you would have seen at that time, whenever it was and however long.

—

I am a sneaky person and a spiteful one as well; I don't want you to have any illusions about me. I admit to taking secret delight in knowing that with the small kingdom of words Oliver had allotted to me, I could construct a thousand secret sentences. The autonomous thinking that had initially frightened me began to give me a sensation of malicious delight during the period of Oliver's crisis. Much like riding atop the mad giraffe, my legs wound around his neck, grabbing his horned excrescences in my fists, this joy. Guilt? I knew nothing of it. That is why it did not bother me that I had read Edith's letters without Oliver's consent or that I had witnessed his sexual failures over the door's crack. That he was successful with the flesh-like Edith (at first) was due in part to her anatomy which was real, from her lacquered toenails to her paired ovaries. Combined with her beauty was total passivity. Oliver could do what he wished to this Edith of his own genius, nor did he have to fear her thoughts. He could invent them, project them inside her as he chose. Of all Ediths she was the best for his particular erotic needs. Yet I am certain that he preferred the Edith that had lived in him before I came, before I wore her dress and erased her. Oliver resented me for forcing him to substitute this concrete form. I think he resented me without even realizing that my existence had caused Edith's transformation. Without guilt. I tell you without guilt. Even now I feel nothing of it. Incomprehensible. Yes, sorry about my mistakes, tormented because I am not with Oliver, but no guilt. I warn you about this in case you are pitying me or thinking that I am repentant. I have no conscience whatsoever. It would be all wrong and a waste of time for you to even think about it. Not a pang do I feel telling you as much as I have about Edith's construction and about Oliver's sexuality. The real reason I don't elaborate is that I love Oliver and this love is greater than you and your meaning, whoever you are. I want to keep certain things secret between Oliver and myself. To give you everything would be quite unlike me. Yet I am not selfish. I assure you that if you were to come and visit me, I would give you some of my toys, clothing and furniture. And I know how to bandage cuts and would call the doctor if you were sick. But do not think for a moment that I would consider—although I have dragged you into this, invited you in fact—do not think that I would consider telling you everything. I am sneaky. But I would tell Oliver everything if he were here, if he could listen. For all you know, I may have another garden or location where I meet Oliver and we do things that you will never guess about. You can never be certain of anything; but I don't have to teach you that. I learned it from Oliver and he learned it from you—this business of doors, of leaving through the rectangular space, of going away without a word.

—

At the time of Oliver's departure he was functioning in only one way—sexually. He hardly ate, didn't wash for *this* Edith, was scrupulous only about *her* clothing and physical well-being. If he hadn't left he probably would have died from starvation and exhaustion. It was all her fault. She kept him occupied day and night. I hate her. And when he had to go past me to pass water through his penis, he wore opaque glasses. Not with Edith. I checked that by looking over his door—a habit, a sneaky habit which gave me some satisfaction. Oh, you would know me. I am the one who is always staring at everyone with my glittering green eyes and listening to intimate conversations in restaurants, hardly bothering to disguise this although I know it is not proper. That is me staring into your window with a pair of binoculars, and listening at the door. There I am reading entire books in the bookstore, never buying any. You can see me reading them with a look of glee on my face; that is how I must have looked while reading Oliver's letters from Van Gogh or Edith's letters to Oliver. Habits are not easy to break. Fully formed, I am not changing my character. I nag the blind men until they play games with me using their braille card decks. Or I stare blankly at the man who is always asking me questions, pretending that I do not know what he is talking about. I am this way because of Oliver—what else was there for me to do in all those months when he never looked at me or touched me, in all those months when he was not there at all? Just invite me over and you will see. If you disappear for ten minutes, I will find your secret letters; I have an instinct about such things. I will know things about you that no one else does, find some hole or crack to peek through. I cannot help it. You must realize that it is something I am used to. But I won't steal anything. People find out about things that are missing. Oliver would have. I only memorize. You don't have to worry about any books or letters being stolen or mutilated. I don't do things like that. Everything is put back exactly the way it was before. Be very careful because I read upside down almost as well as I read the regular way. And I can watch you carefully while seeming to be absorbed in something else. Please invite me. I am pretty. Even though Oliver said I was ugly, you would think me pretty just as you would think Oliver loathsome. Of course my breasts are as flat as pancakes, just like an old woman's, but Oliver liked them. I am not worried about my breasts or about my character. All my traits come from my life with him and so they represent Oliver, the bad as well as the good. So don't think I am apologizing. The longer I live here, the more my original traits become magnified. For example, I lie. It was inevitable because of my sneaky quality, and also because no one believes the truth, I have found. Everyone encouraged me to lie. But I will never lie about Oliver. I will never change his name, soften his toenails, clean his ears, or keep his bottom lip from sticking out almost inside out very wet. I have never lied about Oliver. I have tried to be accurate. Maybe I couldn't always tell about his lovemaking with Edith. Maybe it wasn't going so well even with all that pumping and perspiring all day and night.

If Oliver neglected my character development, it was only because of Edith, because she mocked him for his impotence and for his odors. He had to think about her all the time. It is amazing that I have as good as character as I do. I don't steal, except a few clocks, and I have extraordinary patience and the ability to repeat the same things over and over again without ever being bored. That is a quality that makes me a good employee. It never tired me to type the same things every day; I have Oliver to thank for that. Nor do I find any conversation uninteresting. So don't worry about boring me if you come. Not listening, not being able to wait on line for buses, cutting into conversations are your traits. I am much better in that way. I don't know the meaning of boredom.

Yes, I am the type of person who kills roaches for pleasure. They certainly don't frighten me or even annoy me. It has to do with my mad giraffe. He tells me what to do. There is a certain pleasure in chasing a roach with an inverted tin can, giving him or her a certain leeway, making the whole thing a fair game, dragging it out and then finally quickly placing the tin can over the creature who probably does not realize what has happened, running round and round happily inside. I try to accomplish this without impairing the creature in any way. If an antenna is lost or a wing mutilated, then I am not satisfied. But if he is perfectly smothered I put him in a large plexiglass box and spray an acrylic emulsion over him. If the roach is marred in any way, he is dropped out of the window. In this I am like Oliver who I cannot imagine stamping upon anyone but who I can imagine locking someone in a room and letting her die slowly of neglect just because he forgot. Oliver taught me so many things without being aware of it. Whether or not a roach is beautiful is something I would need Oliver to teach me. As I must have explained before, he did give me some lessons in esthetics but a sense of beauty is a very difficult thing to attain. It is easier for blind people to decide about beauty since they can touch things and get a direct impression. So when I want to see if something is beautiful or ugly, I put on a blindfold and touch it. Naturally I cannot do this with gorillas and the sky. But in this manner I have decided that tomatoes, penises, thick flowers, hands and pebbles are beautiful while faces, paper, lettuce, tin cans and lamb chops are not. I have doubts about these conclusions because when I remove my blindfold I see that lettuce looks very much like flowers. How can I feel a roach since it is so small and each part moves in a different way and can easily be squashed or broken off? I would need Oliver to explain.

—

Oliver never sang. Experimenting when I was "young," I found sounds I liked by hitting things together, like glasses of water and spoons. But music, your music, is new to me. The blind men take me to concerts. I only like when one instrument is playing alone. The orchestra has too many instruments going at once so it is hard to hear anything except if someone plays alone all of a sudden. Those are the parts I wait for. It is nice when the count stays the same—one two three, one two three, one two three. But they get mixed up. They change it or forget to watch the man with the baton or else he gets tired of one two three and switches. I am saving money to buy a bass fiddle which I think has the nicest sound. Women don't play it in the orchestras we have gone to, so I hope I am not doing something against your rules. My favorite composer is Chopin. When I get my bass fiddle I will learn to play Chopin's waltzes. I have great patience because of living with Oliver and you can be sure that I will accomplish this unless I find out that I am doing something that you are not supposed to do here like being late for work or forgetting to brush your teeth. That is something I never forget—brushing my teeth. Oliver had a blue toothbrush with hairs falling out and a small green one for me. I suppose it was Edith's. Later, after my toilet training, when he realized how much I liked red, he got me a red one. Of course he went outside to buy things like that although I didn't notice for a long time. Perhaps he only went out when I was asleep. He wanted to fool me and didn't want me to know where the door was hidden. Sometimes I think that I generated myself spontaneously within Oliver's house or Edith's, if you want to be technical. Other times I think that Oliver may have created me by accident, not deliberately the way he created Edith. He made some terrible mistake in his calculations that he could not undo. No one knows that I think such things except you. I wouldn't dare tell anyone particularly after my studies of reproduction in animals. I am in fact quite a biologist since the beginnings of things obsess me. If I was smart enough to go to college and had the money or understood the scholarship system, I would study biology and learn how to create new animals and bugs that were never here before. I learned things about that in magazines, at lectures and in the movies. I think I could do that. Maybe I could make an Oliver just like Oliver, only with a few changes. This last thought shocks you since I love Oliver just as he is, but your world has changed me a little. I would make an Oliver who could only love me and who would never have heard of Edith. And my Oliver would be exactly the same except that he would spend more time playing with me and teaching me things and we would always live together somewhere without doors, not even hidden ones.

Although I do not understand about pity and guilt (I have no experience whatsoever), I do understand fear. I experienced it millions of times not knowing what to call it when Oliver disappeared, whether into his room or forever. But it had no name. It was more of a physical thing, my heart going faster and things happening in my stomach and feet. (Oliver taught me how the heart pumps blood around the body for food distribution and that it has four parts. He didn't use the words "nutrition" or "valves" at that time, being jealous of my growing vocabulary.) I don't like having this heart which changes rhythm suddenly all by itself or if I am frightened or run up the stairs. I don't like it at all. I prefer things that you can control yourself. Breathing isn't so bad because I can do it purposely or even stop breathing for a long time until I see all kinds of colored spots and fall down. But when Oliver disappeared, even for a short time, this heart all by itself would go faster and things squeezed in my stomach, and I felt my body shaking and my legs not being able to walk as well. And when he left and did not come back, it was worse. My left palm always sweating and the sudden trembling in my body even when I was lying down, my heart going too fast and then seeming to stop and then to jump up. I even had some throwing up which Oliver did sometimes but which I had never had before. Seeing Edith lying on his bed calmly without her heart pumping (because I put my hand there and felt nothing and no trembling) looking so pretty, I felt this sudden shock with my hand getting clenched like I was going to punch someone and the room going round and round. Edith was never frightened. I am surprised that Oliver forgot to give her a heart. In fact I am ashamed of him because the heart, as everyone knows, is so important. But I kept her pretty and did those chemical things, scoopings and oilings and other things with a white face, thin lips and shaking hands.

Full of hate and fear also because I was alone with her and I didn't know what I might do next if he didn't come back soon. I even spoke to Edith, accusing her of everything, but she just smiled and watched me. Oliver made her eyes so they watched. If you walk into the room Edith looks in your direction and follows every move until you shake even more, but she never says anything. It has to do with certain wires and magnets, I think, not yet knowing much about electricity or the magnetic field.

"I think you should get up and go find him," I said, as she watched me, seeming to know all about it. "After all it is your fault that he left. It couldn't be my fault since he never even looks at me any more and you made him so tired with all that pumping and sex." I turn something and Edith's breasts go up and down and breath comes from her mouth just like she is breathing. A thermostat can adjust the temperature of Edith and her breath. I would prefer to breathe like that and if I must have a heart I would like a dial to control it like Edith's dial.

"I might stop taking care of you," I threatened. "And when Oliver comes back you will smell terrible and not look so pretty any more, and he will see that I am better, particularly if I wash and put on one of your dresses."

I exchanged clothes and places with Edith one day, putting her into my room in my plaid skirt, messing up her hair which was the same roan color as mine. Then I made myself up as carefully as I could, dressing in one of the satin aqua gowns that Oliver had bought for her. Carefully I lay down on Edith's and Oliver's bed near the dials among the wires waiting for Oliver, breathing but not speaking. Then tzap tzap Oliver entered apologizing for some delay, his arms full of white gift boxes, beautiful stockings, shoes and lace panties for me. He didn't notice the change or that my heart was doing strange things. My eyes followed him and he said he loved me and was unable to leave me in spite of all the things that had happened in the past. He never even went to see if I, the other Edith, was in her room or had starved to death. I did not care. It served her right for being so ugly and having no name. I waited, thinking he would discover my disguise, but he never noticed any difference. All the chemical and pefumed smells were just right and I never said a word or lifted an arm or leg unless he adjusted the dials. He assumed that *she* had gone or else he had forgotten her entirely as she lay like someone dead in her small room with the print of Rédon flowers and the torn reproduction of Botticelli's "Primavera." Now Oliver putting his penis inside me I had to be very careful not to make sounds or even think anything and to act exactly like I was not real. But I had thoughts about Edith rotting in her room and a terrible fear that he would find out. Always this terrible fear but I knew it would go away and that I could get up and eat and go to the toilet when he was asleep. My Oliver sleeps very deeply for a long time and nothing awakens him. You can do anything you want. Or perhaps these human needs would vanish in time as I assumed Edith's identity.

My terrible curiosity was gone, my desire to learn words, to construct sentences in secret, to memorize Oliver's letters and utterances. All conscious or unconscious forms of rebellion against Oliver disappeared. An eternity of Oliver's devotion was certainly worth this transformation.

Once it began there was no stopping it. Eventually I behaved as the dials ordered, assimilated Oliver's chemicals, became inert and lost all autonomy. No heartbeat, hunger, desire—I became the creature that Oliver desired who could in no way disturb him. My partner in this deception gradually disintegrated in her room miles away, became extinct as though she had never arrived, a whining disheveled child. As though she had never existed.

—

Forever Oliver it will be like this: bound to you by wires and dials of your own creation, not thinking, still, waiting for any motion, smiling always. Dissatisfied with nothing asking no questions having no life apart from you, not daring to remember anything, total cessation of movement within and without. Finally not even knowing when you are there but behaving as you dictate. Forever, Oliver, you will remain changing me in discreet subtle ways when your passion recedes. Until you forget everything that she and I reminded you of until by force of will greater than ever I will lose my outside covering and become again what was inside you before. Dials will melt become embedded in your cortex with me, and I will have no existence outside you having gone through all these stages gradually. A corridor of silence, of motionless quilted tapestries through which you may wander alone.

We need no food or lost tree trunks, puzzled flies seeking refuge against hailstones hard or powder, rain real or false, people or games or languages.

I promise if you come back, we in a static orange light, no ocean tides throwing strange formations at our feet causing us to question the meaning of the stars; too vast these embryonic relics and malformations crusts and headbones of fish. The butterfly will never reach its final stage. Hurry because it is difficult with the heart and its valves pumping the blood up to the brain and the cells dreaming egg dreams from the textures I know already, from the sounds and colors and words and falling of sun snow rain and wild leaves. Hurry. Dry these braincell songs which disturb our peace which force us to think of beginnings endings and illogicalities. Yours is the form in which are all forms. It cannot be helped or changed any more. The shapes of shells stones insects furniture and sculpture are all only a disguise to me of your shape and form and walk, too strongly embedded in me to disappear.

This you know I dreamed and felt inside while waiting waiting for my Oliver to return.

—

That time, measured by you in months, waiting for Oliver, feverish unable to sleep, shaking from fear and hunger and his absence, constructing thoughts Oliver would not understand. Without pride then, without maliciousness, fearing that I would destroy Edith, not being able to administer to her any longer even when pretending to be her. Then I found the DOOR—that exterminating word—that took Oliver away. I went outside to find him. Hungry, sick, some agency here or there took care of me, fed me; it is of no importance having nothing to do with Oliver. Gradually my outer autonomy, rehabilitation, office work, blind friends, my cautious exploration of your world—the world that Oliver had presented to me in symbols. People always trying to find out about my origins, never leaving me entirely alone, never succeeding. Except the inspector or investigator assigned to my case by the Police Department. Oh, I knew him for what he was with his thin moustache, fleshy face and his blue and white striped shirt.

"And where did you first meet this man?" he asked, peering at me with a squint, looking inside but not knowing where to find it.

"I only remember being there with him, not meeting him," I said smiling as I have learned to smile, not the way Oliver does.

"Please try to cooperate," he repeated sighing and staring at his nails which had a coat of transparent lacquer.

Silence and then an abrupt dismissal with certain warnings about not going away and suggestions that I file complaints against Oliver before it was too late. Sly insinuations, scanning my body up and down.

Sometimes I doubt myself. These memories. How can I trust myself, particularly with all the things now going on inside my head? Endless the winding brain. Until I think I am a bird with frozen wings, my head bruised by silver iced needles of trees, wing cracked like a pale eggshell half paralyzed still fluttering in the wet gray sky. "Aaooow."

"Oliver, you've been away from our garden for many months."

I am sitting on the grass which is gray, next to the bush which has gray blossoms. "I wasn't invited," he says shivering. I am surrounded by a group of blind men, black-cloaked with white canes. They form a circle around me while an investigator walks slowly around the curlicued bench glancing at his broken wristwatch. Oliver looks at everyone. "Are they real?" he asks. "And if so, why have you brought them?" The blind men laugh together and tap their canes. The inspector is taking notes. "Do you want us to chase him away?" ask the blind men holding up their canes threateningly. "That won't be necessary," I answer too quietly for Oliver to hear. "I have allies now," I say loudly as Oliver falls on the grass looking dead. The investigator notices and halts his circular march to take Oliver's pulse. "Is he dead or alive?" I ask in a flat voice. "Dead for the moment," says the investigator writing a detailed report. I bend down near Oliver and take his hand. It is cold and stiff. "Are you alive or dead?" I ask him. "I am whatever you wish me to be," he answers. "Then you know how I have felt being at *your* mercy," I tell him trying to free my hand from his. It is ice cold. "You had something in mind, I realize," says Oliver barely breathing, patting my gray hair. A blackbird takes a bite out of my arm and Oliver looks away. "There is no blood, no life, nothing beating in your heart or mine," he says. "This is your last invitation, the garden is closed," I tell him. Oliver gets up slowly, kisses me with cold lips and goes away. The blind men have gone and I am alone.

It occurred to me to return to Edith's house—long after I had gone, after months of searching for Oliver, after our mutual desertion of Edith. An impulse I have not told you about. Not fierce, coming from nowhere one day finding my way tapping through the ruins of streets torn down houses half built ones ever changing round through the maze of men drilling below streets with lights attached to their heads. Past many walls with leaves growing from them pausing to pluck these with some curiosity, kicking rusted cans, hopping running weaving slowly, holding on to the sides of buildings, looking up at a forgotten sky with blackpink clouds racing together to hide the moon. Dark or light, I do not know, perhaps the star, one star or the sun blinking blinking in sudden patterns between trees across parks. Endless this journey. I remember skipping over waves falling and scraping my knee, sweating and then being cooled by a violent shower with winds that rocked the earth. I walked lazily thinking in my vague way but deciding something all of a sudden. It was a long time ago, this return. Did you think that I wouldn't try to go back? An empty space in my head like it used to be in the beginning without words, peaceful and still. Then all thoughts coming at once everything running together, not in those sentences with capitals and periods that I had never really learned to think with like other people think. Stopping to empty my green shoes which were full of pebbles or to put my yellow umbrella in the other hand. I never opened it when the showers came striking out. On a journey back to Oliver, not knowing if the house could be found or if there was a stairway or a door but knowing all the time that I could find it this way roundabout like blind men tapping and sensing space and distant vibrations that no one else can. A journey of days, nights not counting time or caring. It was before I learned to wear my wristwatch when I just began outside I think. Something calling to me, if you've ever been called like that without a sound to walk back to something and touch it again in a different time to see if it existed at all. Not thinking this just knowing like a loveliness you cannot ever imagine between where I started and when I found it. All things glowed like the skies of Van Gogh or El Greco and even more and differently, chiming softly so I felt I was doing what it was right to do. Not purposely studying anything to notice beauty but finding it there anyhow like starving saints or special people. So I could not say that this thing was beautiful and that thing was but everything, all blending together perfectly. It didn't matter which was which. Rubbing my back on the bark of trees or on the stony stars or bubbly weeds that popped kissing my eyes were the lights on the hats of the drilling men or the sunlight. The heart mine or someone else's not beating apart from the seatides or rain. It should have never ended but could have been death if there really are those angels and magic light. Growing nearer I knew exactly where I was going but not why I hadn't thought of it long before. I don't like the way it is usually with everything separated into categories even my thoughts which I now try to maintain in those categories having learned that it is saner to structure and separate things from each other like making lists of groceries to buy. Returning to the tapestried walls, on the way, all by myself, it was different. Even if someone stopped and said something it rang like a song. I felt as right as a tree or storm and my body as pretty as an eggshell whole before the egg is cracked on the edge of a pan.

It ended. Reaching someplace being so different from going there and everything changing upon arrival. Knowing exactly how many steps to take and what the address is things that spoil everything but exist anyhow.

Opening the door which was not locked I found them together—Edith and Oliver asleep.

Evil trick of Oliver's leaving tzap tzap waiting day day week week for me to go away. Peeking through cracks, holes, listening, planning to return. No need to search for Oliver. No need to wait. Leave. Return and find him happy without me, Oliver not having guilt either or caring about how I felt or what happened to me. Beginning gone. We carnival cracked. I knew. Guggle gugle hsssss pah pah. Gone the circular laughing dance. "Geeeeeeh." I searched the house quietly, tiptoed everywhere. Perfect order, plates scraped, put away. Nothing. Only the terrible sound of Oliver snoring. My hideous Oliver alive in our house without me. Not anywhere else.

ON THE WAY BACK TO OLIVER

Very slowly (for small electric organ)

Can you picture it? Me—finding Oliver sleeping there, after all that searching, after all that worrying, after all the time I waited for him with Edith? *You* feel it for me. I cannot feel it now or even remember what I felt or did. Do not ever think I would wake Oliver up from a sound sleep or let him know that I had discovered his secret plan to get rid of me. I am too considerate to do anything like that. I went away. What does the Police Department want with me? Why am I here? You tell me.

—

I realize that you do not believe me any more. You are disgusted with me and with my fantasies and cannot bear that I continue. Didn't you promise me? Remember when I told you that this world was not going to be like yours and that I am someone from a different star? I hoped you would realize that I couldn't possibly think the way you do or even experience things in the same way. I have been as honest as I know how to be. I even tried to speak your language. Give me credit for that. And I have fully confessed to my ignorance of pity and my absence of a conscience. Why then do you condemn me? Why now, when I have told you what I have told no one else, not even myself? If you doubt me you can check. You can always go to the proper departments and check. Then won't you be surprised? That I went back there is something I should have told you sooner but there are reasons. Nothing changed. I told no one, pretended I never went back at all and asked you to look for Oliver and to remember exactly what he is like. I have omitted some details but I will supply them if it will help you. Oliver has a gold jacket crown on the fourth tooth of the left side, counting the first of the two front teeth going leftward, as number one. Is that clear? When he smiles you will see it. His tongue has a rougher texture than most people's tongues. It is like the rough tongue of a cat and has a deep, deep crack down the center. Not the usual crack but a deeper uneven one. You know about his bottom lip and that he holds his mouth slightly open all the time and tends to breathe more through his mouth than through his nose. There is severe blockage in his nasal passages. His upper lip is very thin in contrast to the lower one. In fact it is hardly a lip at all and if his mouth is closed you will not see it, but since he holds his mouth open you probably will. But remember this: his beard goes around his mouth, not shaped like a moustache but growing wildly and coming with some hairs over his top lip, getting caught in his teeth. These teeth are his own and they are very small and grayish in color. The two front teeth from which you are to count to find the jacket crown are close together and tiny, not like the larger two front teeth of later generations. Then comes a space on either side. There is no jacket crown on the right side. I do not try to make Oliver repulsive to you. To me nothing about Oliver's physical being is distasteful. He has what you might call bad breath but it is a deeper chronic kind that does not go away when the teeth are brushed and which probably comes from something sick in his esophagus or elsewhere. It never bothered me. This will surprise you: When he is not talking, his bottom teeth are covered by his tongue which he habitually holds over them so that if you look inside you will easily see the huge crack in his tongue. I tell you these details now so you will understand that I am precise rather than hazy about important facts. I was going to spare you these details out of tact. For example, his nose which I told you is bulbous and full of purple crisscrossing veins is also pocked or pitted. But the rest of his face is not. It is soft white and fleshy. If Oliver were to go to the beach, he would get a terrible red burn. He is a fair complexioned man. His hair is a mixture or orange, gray and black. In the third year it turned mostly gray but his beard still has a lot of deep orange and black mixed into it. When he cuts it, he cuts it straight across and not in any style or pattern. Something like that can change so don't be so sure he hasn't had it styled somewhere, or even had the hairs tweezed from his nose and ears. You must differentiate the things that can be altered from those that are permanent such as his veined nose. His belly is fat, white and smooth, having only red hairs on it until you get lower down where they turn black. There is an important birthmark on his right side about an inch below the navel—it is a sloppily tied, complicated navel which would bulge outward if it weren't for the fleshy stomach. The birthmark is brown and not flat but standing up with six small sectional dots. You cannot miss this if you are observant and look with a candle or flashlight while he is asleep. You can even turn on the light and make noise because nothing wakes up Oliver when he is asleep. Have I helped you? Please memorize these facts. Oh yes, the bottom teeth are small and straight across as though some dentist filed them down and then smoothed them all evenly the same height—except for the incisors. They are small but usual as are the canines.

—

If I understood everything, could figure it out all by myself, why then would I have called upon you to help? Do not expect a logical working out of everything from me. It is not as though I am telling you a story for the fun of it.

—

When the sun comes up first blinding as red-orange geraniums and later cruelly white stabbing the tops of the pigeonwings silver as they flutter about above chimneys or roofs, pausing like immobile dead things and then ascending or descendng with some purpose in mind, suddenly smoke comes out like clouds making the distances harder to see and the sun even whiter coming through. It is the same in the city or country with puffs of smoke, some cool breezes early even in summer and then a persistent burning into the scalp, into the brain; then it is hard to think that Oliver is in the world but I know he is. Through the windows screens or iron bars. I would give anything for Oliver—to see his thick-stemmed neck bent forward with his large head thrusting out (not even looking at me), and his eyes which are every color but mostly greens, browns grays lit up with a yellow light in back. Not dark like the black part of night his eyes but dim multicolored light through thick fleshy pockets looking but not looking.

—

The beginning is always Oliver's hand, darker than the rest of him, spotted brown—these spots from too much sun sometime or age and things having to do with what he used to do before me and before Edith, very early when milk came clucking in horse-drawn carts when he watched the silver wings of birds maybe pigeons in the first sun.

I have thought Oliver might be Adam that first man half sleeping watching green things growing all day puzzled but not unhappy walking around a limited creation surrounded by huge waves howling then receding—smiling a long smile all through the time of the sun setting when the sky changed with drops of orange streaks of violet everywhere silver red through and then under the clouds dripping dripping pieces of untouchable rose fire and deeper purples taming the corals and hot orange as he watched until his eyes were all these colors too. Then Oliver made a woman Eve or Edith to witness these changes into dark purple bands purple orange purple orange brownish black orange across the sky until steady dusk. Both watching. She came from Oliver's finger and grew from that first joint of the third finger of his right hand excluding the thumb. Regretting it later as he looked at the bitten-off part wondering if it had been worth the sacrifice worth the intrusion bit by bit slowly she with her ceaseless questioning and curiosity plucked things ate everything changed the garden killed the sunset dulled the stars which used to be all as large as full moons and as bright. She turned it to ash. He didn't like her any more because she knew too much and touched too many things so it was not new any more. Her belly got larger and larger in the gray light so that he wished to be alone and when she left he pretended to go too but remained waiting for all to be like it was. But his sight was changed the skies were blind crying, having become used to her despite her horrible faults and her whining curious nature.

If I could paint I would paint Adam the first man huge Oliver in the sunset with his eyes closed creating a woman from the first joint of this third finger. I would not neglect a single detail. Each spot of pigmentation with a small brush, every hair on his head, the gold crown on his fourth tooth with gold leaf, hairs on his arms, in his beard, around his penis, with a thin brush. His penis large uncircumcised rosepale with huge blue veins erect, its scrotum crinkled pattern round half full and hanging down much lower than you would expect—I would paint with transparent glazes until life-red throbbed through the twisting veins.

—

I knew that Oliver was going away. When he was not in bed with his handmade Edith, he was staring at me thoughtfully from behind his opaque glasses. He never said, "Wash," "Eat," "Cook" or "Study." He had ceased to care if I slept or ate, did not notice that I was not annoying him any more. Oliver never went outside to get food like he used to, I noticed, noticing everything. Oliver. Food was melting, decreasing, flattening out. He did not write anything. And if I showed him what I had written, he turned away not even getting angry, not stamping his foot. I saw him look around at everything, slowly, and then saw him lock certain things inside drawers: history manuscripts, letters, a blue cross, red gloves, a transparent crystal box. The keys protruding from the breakfront drawers were turned and then hidden. Vanished. Edith's studio was checked and a double lock was put on it sometime, maybe when I was asleep. Nothing was said and I didn't dare to ask anything. But I knew. It was no big surprise when he didn't come back. What was he thinking when he looked at me like an unfamiliar object from behind his opaque glasses? Was he wondering if I would take care of Edith? Or did he intend to take me with him and drop me into an icy river, me—curled up inside a burlap sack, weighted with rocks; you've read about such things. No, I don't think he had such an intention; his thoughts were not clear enough to formulate such a plan. But then I might be underestimating Oliver. Oliver is trickier than you think. He knew that I had no money and could not get any more food than what remained. He could have disposed of it entirely so that I would have left sooner. But Oliver is smart. If he had done this, I would have remained and died of starvation. It was the slow hunger, the slow realization of what had happened that saved my life, that forced me to find the DOOR and go. He planned the whole thing knowing the importance of time. He preferred not to be implicated in my death; his life was difficult enough. Or else the whole thing was a subtle revenge; he knew waiting would be more painful than rapidly dying. He had a right to such revenge since I took away everything—his vocabulary, his fantasies, time, gestures—and I had surpassed him in verbal games and memorized his history book. Oliver is sneaky—he left as though he were going shopping. There was no suitcase, no bag of letters, no dismembered Edith in a plastic case. He left exactly the way he always left when he went to the store, wearing his opaque glasses and tapping his white-tipped cane, tzap tzap. Not noticing that I was not asleep, hoping that I was. Quickly. I watched silently.

Earlier, during the construction of Edith, he began destroying the word cards and diagrams he had made for me, slowly—thinking I was not noticing it. I did, but pretended that he was making new ones for me. Only something within me, something collapsing or crumbling somewhere deep inside. No tears, no whining, just some area of disease or emptiness that could be filled up with anything much later. Even hate. My kind Oliver, who had made the toilet red, changed it back to white. When? Little by little while I was still there, he destroyed all signs of me, all evidence of his creation—my oaktag cards, false clock, composition book, assignments; my pictures of elephants, dogs, monkeys. (Clever too, I hid a picture of a giraffe and the diagram of male and female anatomy and some compositions.) He threw away my box of crayons also. I had only a few pieces of paper and a pencil. Don't you think it was thoughtful of Oliver to leave me something? My Oliver is a brilliant man and not one to go to extremes that are brutal or completely terrifying. For example, he did not lock me in my room or cut out my tongue. I locked myself in my room at the time of his greatest need, when he was all alone, when he might have loved me. If you remember I would not come out. If only I had come out when Oliver scratched at my door, when he moaned the way I had done when he was locked up with the phantom Edith—then he would not have left, would not have destroyed all traces of me.

Perhaps he would have made the most of me, and continued my instruction. We would have been alone, resuming some sort of schedule. I had a chance, remember. Think of how many times he had forgiven the original selfish Edith, how many times *she* had wandered away. I should have come out immediately. What had I hoped to achieve by hurting Oliver. That was the lost moment. Oliver was tired. I doubt that he could ever do anything like that again—bang at someone's door, wanting her.

—

Foamworld of Oliver—porous sponge slowly squeezing green; liquid life swimming below beyond time in circles of secret words to Edith a shadow visible in the tangled folds of aging palpitating cerebrum. Dull white pain, no longer sharp-stemmed ice. A constant rolling foaming silence inseparable from the multiplying orange seagrowths in his brain.

If you are a woman and Oliver happens to be in your house, I have certain advice and warnings about Oliver's sexuality. Not that I want to dictate to you, but being a practical person in your world and assuming that you too are manipulating and practical, I will tell you what to expect and how to act. You may think that I am being strangely generous considering the depth of my feelings for Oliver. I am not. I don't really care about you; if you can you will return Oliver to me. In the meantime there is no point in making things any more difficult than they need be. I am a practical and realistic person. I get to work on time, make no typing errors and I am careful about budgeting my money. Never never do I forget to brush my teeth or to use a deodorant.

You must never make the first advances to Oliver. He will not like it, I assure you, and then you will feel offended and Oliver will not want to go into your bed at all. Wait until Oliver begins and then be as passive as possible. By that I mean do not try to please him in ways you imagine men like to be pleased according to what you have read about undersides of penises and what you have experienced with other men. Oliver is not like that. He will resent your expertise. Do not ever touch Oliver's penis without his permission, and don't try to be alluring or subtle or spectacular. He will hate you if you invent variations or unusual techniques. Don't stand on your head or do more than one thing at a time. Oliver doesn't like that. On the other hand you must never reject Oliver's advances even if they seem sudden or brusque. Have patience. It is true that Oliver is often not concerned with preliminaries. He will go thump thump thump eleven times evenly and quickly. (I have counted.) Or else he will go sloop sloop sloop sloop more slowly from six to fifteen times. This varies. Be appreciative but not active. Don't howl. Oliver will eventually satisfy you if you are patient and don't push his hand around. He is not ignorant about sex or about women. He knows how to touch breasts without squashing them or forgetting the nipples. And he knows about the clitoris and has no trouble finding it. Don't help him. However he may be preoccupied on occasion and leave abruptly. If you act angry or frustrated then he will not go into your bed for a long time. You must leave it up to Oliver. That is the main thing. If you can't do this or if it is against your principles (I've read about things like that) then don't consider sex with Oliver. And you will be missing something. Oliver is not the best lover in the world, not in reality—he is not subtle enough, doesn't take enough time at the beginning, only goes in from on top and he says nothing nice. But he understands female anatomy better than most men. As far as I am concerned he is the best lover in the entire world. I don't care what anyone says not even Edith. Who else would know? Who else would be nice enough to tell you the facts so that you won't make any mistakes. Don't tell him to take a bath. Of course I never even thought of it, but I think Edith did judging from her letters. I cannot be responsible for anything that would happen if you told Oliver to take a bath. Oliver will not care if you are menstruating or haven't taken a bath yourself. He likes imaginary things better than real ones if you have been listening to me. It won't really be you you know. If you are happy with Oliver write and tell me—I like to know everything about him. And if you are having troubles I will try to help you. I know that Oliver doesn't want to find me. I don't think he will like you either but certain things are unpredictable as you know. That is why I carry my yellow umbrella, even when the sun is out.

—

On my way back to Oliver stepping on starfish, being stung by thorns, bees and cactus, through that journey apart from everything I saw more things than ever before or since, swayed like trees sway silvergreen muted firgreens. Spinning stars, even red ones and sunsets, pale-green inside the pink I saw. I remember the cats poised like statues staring at me and then running. Everywhere bones crushed, squirrels dead and alive, accidents and festivities all at once it seemed, or stretching over all that time the last time. I changed, went forward to my old Oliver not expecting him at all. Chimes from dark churches, treeleaves falling on me, twigs cracking, butterflies white like big planets following. In all of it not knowing specifically or precisely the route or the best way or the quickest but knowing inside the same wounded place where he tore up my word cards, threw away my crayons and disappeared. Knowing in that same place where you may have sorrow or musical compositions or things you even you cannot explain in this language or any other language. That place with no location that led me that knew everything. I took a long time to get there stopping to flap around in oceans or synthetic chlorinated pools like it was the first and last time. The moon always left behind those black clouds still holding secret shades of red. It appeared again between gigantic trees. Owls moaned. It was summer but the snow tumbled crazily from the slanted roofs making my feet laugh with cold and crack crack crack over the ice into warm sand rolling over and over until my eyes looked at the sun and my face was everyone's face or the face of the whole earth and ocean and seasons all together not one after the other. Real or made up things joined together not caring or making distinctions. Water in the sun sun on the ocean sky down land up myself upside down every age at once, an old lady with a child's laugh, a child with gray hair garlanded like that. On and on. If the world could be like that for you and for me without a stop, without those beginnings and endings just a whirling thing with the branches down and the roots up so they can eat the rain as soon as it comes. And flowers growing in the snow and out of my eyes. GO THERE AND SEE IF IT IS REALLY LIKE THAT BEFORE IT ENDS.

How still those tapestries were, how familiar. It hurt me there at the pit of my belly. I remembered everything suddenly. All those years as if they were frozen. Blue envelopes fluttered on the wooden table. I stood very still and then it came—a fire from my own searing brain. Not waking anyone up, even Oliver. It was just a wad of cloth stuffed into his mouth way down and up his nose. No waking, no struggle. My Oliver sleeps deeply and nothing wakes him. I didn't plan it. Perhaps he was dead to begin with, even before I returned that day or night finding him there as though I had never happened. What would *you* have done? Important, important to me that there should be no Oliver in her house. He should have been wandering outside with his opaque glasses and white-tipped cane. He should have been looking for me.

In that quiet I re-read Edith's fresh letters. Then I took my bracelet with the initialed letter off her wrist and left. I walked slowly, not as before with the sky and water and all things unified. Blank, feeling nothing at all, walking evenly forward, forgetting this last time immediately. Not even remembering later. Not until recently, in fact, and then pretending I didn't. I must. Oliver is with you or walking the streets looking for the original Edith or for no one. Not for me. I looked for him everywhere and never, never took that long walk back again. That last visit—remembering it is like remembering a dream of dead tapestries. When did she come back to write those letters? I saw the other one he made lying silently on the other side of him as though she were melting into him. Then doing what I did very quietly without violence even though there were fires inside the pit of my belly. You can understand that he wasn't supposed to be there sleeping. He never understood me—not in all those years. No one lay dead in my unlocked room with the pastel of Rédon's flowers hanging next to Botticelli's "Primavera" (which looks like I looked once), and an old blue crucifix, blue paper scattered around, and a violet dress in the closet. No me, no Oliver. That's all there was to it that night with the bubbles of foam and the bright sting of the stars. No memory, no light and no crying.

—

It is up to you, *you*, the question of whether Oliver is dead or alive. If you look for him on every corner of every street, how can he be dead? I will not believe those stories of Oliver being found in bed with his mouth and nose stuffed neatly, expertly with white cloth. Who could have done such a thing? There has been no trial. I am being held on some suspicion—I forget things like that. Besides the arrest only happened yesterday or sometime recently. It is hard to keep track of such details. Everyone makes mistakes—I have heard this said over and over again in your world. Am I an exception to this? Haven't I the right to start all over again. You yourself have told me that it is only human to make mistakes, not the end of the world. And it wasn't even my fault. Am I an exception. Consider this carefully. Wasn't it all a vivid dream? What reason could I have had? I love Oliver no matter what he did. You must believe that. If I had known where Oliver was, I would have gone back before or waited until he awoke and then asked him why he left. I was an excellent employee and never made a typing error. I refuse to say he molested or kidnapped me because that would be a lie. It is in my best interests to say that he raped me but what do I have to compare his behavior with, Oliver being my whole life? It is all a trick played by Oliver or maybe by Edith who is so clever with her infidelities and letters still able to make Oliver love her. I can't do that. It is a trick and they will find out soon when they locate Edith. Then they will know who planned the whole thing. You are the only one who can understand my predicament—I don't know what I am doing here. Perhaps my assignment is to take care of Edith. I was doing so well in my office, typing perfectly, saving money, going to movies and to concerts. Wasn't I learning to live in your society? This building is new. The faucets and toilet work. The mattress is comfortable and the blankets are clean. The bars don't bother me with their vertical pattern always moving around the room. Edith must always have the newest and best. If it was *me,* I would be locked up alone in a sour smelling room with rats under the bed and gauze blankets. They would never let *me* have a pencil and lined paper to write letters to Oliver. She has everything. I am waiting here until they move her. Then I will be able to go about my business of reading, learing the customs and trying to understand why Oliver left. You will find me in the large toy stores looking through kaleidoscopes, turning them slowly to see all the patterns. I will be wearing a gray suit, blotched with irregular dark liver-colored patches separated by a network of broad white spacing. Under my yellow umbrella I will flutter my long dark eyelashes and tell you secrets. The psychiatrist who has a thin moustache and a striped shirt is always asking my name. What a nuisance. He won't believe that Oliver didn't give me one. Then he asks me if

I know why I am here. "To see that Edith does no harm, to keep her beautiful for Oliver," I answer. It seems they found some of Oliver's beard hairs in her engraved bracelet, and a transparent half chewed glove lying near his bed. I like to watch Edith's hand which is all scratched from the glass-cutting machine but is missing no fingers. I am beginning to suspect that she deliberately amputated Oliver's finger in a fit of rage. What do you think?

—

The letters were on the table. Table of my joy, of my first clear memory. It is important to me, *the beginning*. I remember it in detail with my eyes, with my tongue *then then*—fat fist clutching the handle of a large spoon, up in into my mouth hot colors—soft pale green leafwings, round orange flowers wet with yellow in the center, and those hard pieces of brown composed of thick threads lined down that had to be chewed. And ever always the taste to my teeth and tongue of Oliver's metallic, saltysweet finger. Freshly vibrating letters staining the table of my joy where my fingers had been born feeling the direction of every smooth and glorious grain.

Dear Oliver,

I have been away too long have nearly forgotten everything because there are so many things and faces and there seems no way to end it. Don't let the tapestries disintegrate or the dust gather too thickly over everything. I will find some solution. Please think of me.

Edith

Dear Oliver,

I think of you always, of glass birds in gardens, of gardens full of sweetsmelling things, blossoms that you show me, birdbaths, marble benches. It is always the same sunny garden except for sudden eruptions of snow hanging from the blossoms. You bring me things. If this dream were only real I would be very happy but it is a dream that I invent every day wondering where you are wandering down the streets hoping to see you before it is too late.

Edith

Dear Oliver,

What did you do with my glass birds? Did you break my green enameled plate with the sun radiating yellow light?

Love, Edith

Oliver, Oliver,

The past few years are like a dream. Were you dreaming too. I will not mention them again. Soon you will see me in my red dress and everything will begin again anew. I ask only to be with you. I don't care about anything else. I don't remember everything in the exact sequence. I hope that this doesn't upset you. Do you remember me? Nothing makes sense any more. Do you think they will not let me make any more birds?

Dear Oliver,

Did you scratch out the letter in my bracelet. I can't figure it out. It looks upside down. I can't remember lots of things. It is like something fluffy is inside my head. I am so tired.

Your Edith

Oliver,

Please don't go away. Wait a little longer and I will come back with bows in my hair. It is hard because my mind is full of things in the wrong order. Sometimes I can spell and sometimes I get mixed up and can't do anything. Then I sleep and have funny dreams with lots of colors. I swear I will find the way even if it takes a year or I get caught in the snow.

Forever, Edith

Strange letters, unlike the letters that I read secretly much earlier. I think Oliver wrote them himself wanting Edith to be contrite again. A different Edith I did not understand. Not caring, I tore up these letters after automatically memorizing them. I don't usually tear things up you know. I leave things just the way they are and just "steal" them in my head word for word. I don't care about Edith any longer. Before I left I painted the toilet red again—inside and outside except for the part with the water. I don't know how he did that before. What a shock for Oliver in the morning. How cruel. But I hate white toilets. Red is the color of Oliver's love for me short-lived. And I did another silly thing. Knowing that Oliver would not wake up, I cut off a piece of his beard straight across. I put it inside the heart of my initialed bracelet.

Are you going to kill Oliver? You know what such a thing would do to me, Oliver being all I have, and my hope of finding him and of living with him once again beneath dead tapestries. I will give up everything for him. You are too kind to do that. He was just asleep. I know, I am certain of that—never mind what was stuck into his mouth and nose, taking away the sweet breath of Oliver. No one must know because if it is proven to be a fact, I would vanish.

—

I do everything neatly and carefully, not leaving a mark, a fingerprint or a scrap. Oliver taught me to be meticulous when I was learning to cut out simple shapes called triangles, circles and squares. No shaking, no slipping or slashing inside the main form. Slowly, exactly crunch crunch around the sharp outline. All to please Oliver. "Very good," he said, orangesweet patting my head, playing with my breasts or giving me red paper to draw on. "Oom, oom." Later it annoyed him that I did everything so well, better than Oliver. Peeling the potato with a slow exactitude that made him stamp his foot and return to his room. I continued unaware of what had gone wrong. He preferred the way it was earlier when I used to cut myself with the knife, blood on the bluefoam potato; when I made errors, forgetting periods and capitals. I will be like that again, will bang my head on the wall or put a knife in my brain to mess it up—anything. Wait and see; I will wear a mask, opaque glasses, and stuff my mouth with cloth, forever unseeing, mute, while Oliver does what he wants. Maybe he will pat my head once in a while. He did not mean to ignore me, to abandon me or to become obsessed with Edith. I understand now.

If there is a trial, will you come and swear that you have seen Oliver walking down the street without his finger, his ears cupped forward full of hard brownish wax waving his cane white-tipped at passing cars? Look, you will see Oliver in a window in front of a greenish light, his hand waving, the outline of his stooped-over body moving as slow as calm night. I see him in all these windows and sunsets. It makes no difference if the sky has abandoned its stars or if the lit windows are golden suns or shooting comets in summer in winter. See him looking, his eyes every color, his bottom lip shining.

EPILOGUE OF THE MAD GIRAFFE

Now I will tell you the secret—a truth. But nothing to bring to a trial. You know him already, unseen by Oliver in my head a violet giraffe, bump a dump bump a dump with fluted horns twirling to the ceiling trotting up and down breaking eggs shiny stabbed in the center kuk splosh kuk splosh yellow mixed with cracked glass waiting for Oliver's feet to walk on. Remember me on the back of the bad giraffe smiling with an engraved bracelet on my head and green things growing from inside? The mad giraffe is real. He did the whole thing. And don't say giraffes are silent; my giraffe made whistling gurgling sounds with his thick vocal cords: "Geeeh, geeeh, guggle, gugle, pah pah tssss tsssss." I am the mad giraffe sweetly toothless innocently nibbling twigs and leaves of the acacia tree. With sharp cloven hoofs he jumped out of my head. "Aaooow." That day in the silence. It hurt like giving birth or being shot. I tried to get him back inside but he was too big, grew quickly and stuck out his long long tongue at me. "Go away," I said, as he looked at me fluttering his long eyelashes. "Count my horns." I climbed up up to the top. "One, two three, four, five." Soft with hairy skin. "Those are not horns. I want a giraffe with branched antlers or fluted horns," I complained. He laughed. Evil giraffe. It was all his fault—he told me what to do day by day, standing beside my typewriter, accompanying me to the movies with blind men, swaying and dancing like a saint with cloven feet. How could I have known about the pretty glottis, triangular slit between Oliver's vocal cords? Me—I am good at cutting cloth, folding it neatly perfectly into cylinders, the kind that fit right up there quietly blocking the air from Oliver's nose. As you may have guessed, Oliver has hypertrophied pharyngeal tonsils called adenoids; that is why he breathes mostly from his mouth with his deep wide open snore. Who do you think told me that but my pretty reticulated giraffe. Bad spectacular eyes that could see down down into the rosy darkness of Oliver's throat. Oliver sleeps soundly and nothing awakens him not even the stamping of cloven hoofs or gurgles or whistles. "Geeeeeeh." Wooden cylinders cloth-covered white inserted silently into his dry hairy hairy nostrils made little difference to him as breath came in and out of his wet mouth. How pretty my hands, tiny encased in transparent disposable gloves. I always carry packets of surgical gloves for dusting and changing typewriter ribbons. Oliver wouldn't like me to have dirty hands and smudge the white paper or white cloth. I hate the mad giraffe who knows everything up there chewing chewing acacia trees with his innocent smile and flirtatious eyes. Don't let him fool you. Examine his hooves, feel his heartbeat barumpth barumpth a bass drum pumping gigantic quantities of blood bright red up up through the rubber veins in his neck into his five-horned brain. Don't trust him or ride on his back or let him blink his black hypnotic eyes at you. Wider, opened Oliver's mouth with his nose holes locked—poor Oliver not dreaming of me or of a giraffe who found his trachea with the larynx perched on top divided into two parts by his sweet vocal cords. And in between the poor triangular glottis slit, a flower hole to suck breath for filling up his lungs. You must believe that I was never taught such things until the hooves came thrusting through my head. It is the secret—a truth. Because of Oliver and the perfect cracking of eggs kuk shwaaah kuk shwaaah against the pan, I have extraordinary manual dexterity. Who else could cut and fold plain white cloth into the exact shape of the glottis slit; a pure triangular cube my tiny crinklegloved hands inserted with impeccable elegance. Swiftly. "Glottis is the DOOR to the Trachea," said the wise giraffe, knowing how I hate the word DOOR. I smiled a long Oliver smile after closing the triangular DOOR. The mad giraffe chewed my gloves as though they were acacia leaves. Oliver lay undisturbed. I would never disturb Oliver or wake him up when he is asleep. That is when I cut his beard straight across and put the hairs into my engraved bracelet. My giraffe slept standing up, Oliver lying down while I painted the toilet red, color of Oliver's love, short-lived. Cruel to do that to Oliver who would wake up sometime not knowing how the white toilet became red. I like red. You should see me in my red dress riding across the fields clutching the mane of my bad giraffe.

I have told you the truth. Don't tell Edith. I don't want her to know that my head hurts all the time in the place where his heavy cloven hoofs jumped out.

I am the mad giraffe.

P.S. I have omitted some of the things that mean most to me, out of shyness, I suppose, or the fear that my sincerity was in question. I have not said too much about Oliver's voice. Perhaps you have noticed this omission. Such a beautiful voice is difficult to describe. It is very slow and halting, deep as a whisper—slightly hoarse because he didn't talk for a long time and used his mouth for all that inhalation and expiration. But sometimes when Oliver is reading he has a slight English accent, melodious rhythms vibrating from his chest. The hoarseness disappears and there is no stopping not even for a breath. Then it sounds like a bass fiddle and green stars. ("Chew.")

Please find him soon!

THE END

ACKNOWLEDGMENTS

I would like to express my gratitude to the Corporation of Yaddo, and to the Director and staff for maintaining an environment in which the creator can work with dignity.

My sincere thanks to Scott Kurtz for helping me with the editorial work and for re-copying my music.

ABOUT THE AUTHOR

ELAINE KRAF (1936–2013) was a writer and painter. She was the author of four published works of fiction: *I Am Clarence* (1969), *The House of Madelaine* (1971), *Find Him!* (1977), and *The Princess of 72nd Street* (1979)—as well as several unpublished novels, plays, and poetry collections. She was the recipient of two National Endowment for the Arts awards, a 1971 fellowship at the Broad Leaf Writers' Conference, and a 1977 residency at Yaddo. She was born and lived in New York City.